You & Me at the End of the World

BRIANNA BOURNE

SCHOLASTIC

Published in the UK by Scholastic, 2021
Euston House, 24 Eversholt Street, London, NW1 1DB
Scholastic Ireland, 89E Lagan Road, Dublin Industrial Estate, Glasnevin, Dublin, D11 HP5F

SCHOLASTIC and associated logos are trademarks and/or
registered trademarks of Scholastic Inc.

First published in the US by Scholastic Inc, 2021

ISBN 978 0702 31103 1

A CIP catalogue record for this book is available from the British Library.

Printed by CPI Group (UK) Ltd, Croydon, CR0 4YY
Paper made from wood grown in sustainable forests and other controlled sources.

3 5 7 9 10 8 6 4 2

www.scholastic.co.uk

FOR THE REAL HANNAH
1987–2003

Hannah

I should have stayed home.

I should have squashed down that want, that voice inside me that said, *Go on, Hannah. Go out and get more books.*

Bad things happen when I stray from the plan. When I don't do what I'm supposed to do. After all, I designed the plan so I wouldn't have to think about the empty.

Well.

I'm thinking about it now.

The street I'm parked on is as still as a painting.

Light filters down through the twisted branches of the oak trees lining the road, shielding me from the worst of the Houston sun. The temperature display on the dashboard reads ninety-nine degrees, but it's cool and safe inside my mom's big white SUV. I've parked here a hundred times before, half a block away from the used bookstore my best friend Astrid's family owns.

All those other times feel like another life.

I roll my window down a crack. The heat curls in immediately. It's only April—it shouldn't be this hot.

I turn the engine off so I can listen.

It's quiet. The kind of quiet that reminds me of long summer breaks and lazy mosquitos, of my grandma's house in the backwoods of East Texas. The highways should be droning like the white noise on a vintage vinyl record player—always there, but you only hear it between songs.

Right now, I don't hear a thing.

No cars. No people.

Only silence, empty and hot.

I keep my mom's car keys in my hand, squeezing as if the pointe shoe charm on her key chain will transfer some of her famous ballerina stoicism into me.

If I turn back now, all that's waiting is my echoing, empty house and a routine that's already starting to feel stale. Maybe having something to read will turn the volume down on the thoughts I haven't been able to silence.

I need to get out of the car. I don't know what I'm waiting for—maybe I'm clinging to a shred of hope that something normal might still happen. Maybe the front door of the house across the street will swing open, a woman in sunglasses will trot down the steps, keys jangling, and get in her car and zoom off.

It doesn't happen, of course. It's been five days, and I haven't seen another person. Nobody's out there, and sitting here frozen will just give my imagination a chance to rear its ugly head.

As if on cue, a shadow shifts outside the passenger window, right at the edge of my vision.

I whip my head around.

There's nothing there, except for one gnarled branch bending farther over the road than the others. The shadow must have been the flutter of its leaves.

There's nothing there, Hannah. It's just your imagination.

I've been saying that a lot lately. Dancing is the only thing that keeps my panic under control, but it's not like I can put on my pointe shoes and bust out a few sautés in the back seat. So I settle for the second-best thing. I close my eyes and run through the choreography for the "Danse des petits cygnes"—the little swans—from *Swan Lake*.

I use my hands as proxies for my feet, moving them with sharp, flicking precision. It's a rough sketch of what my legs and feet would be doing if I were dancing the complicated steps. It's a thing ballet dancers do to review choreography. Astrid says it looks like some kind of badass sign language. Hand up to the opposite elbow to show passés. The shushing slide of one hand in front of the other and then behind for échappés.

Entrechat passé, entrechat passé, pique passé.

Échappé, échappé, échappé, échappé.

Chassé relevé arabesque.

When I'm finished, I open my eyes and relax my shoulders.

No more shadows.

I pull my empty backpack over from the passenger seat and wrestle it on. I have to get out of the car before I chicken out again.

When I open the door, an oven blast of Texas heat hits me in the face. Instead of using the sidewalk, I walk right down the middle of the road. It's not like I'll get run over. There are cars parked along the curbs and in people's driveways, but none of them ever move. If there *had* been a mass evacuation, wouldn't all the cars be gone? It's almost as if . . .

No, Hannah.

I promised myself I wouldn't think about it. I'm allowed fifteen minutes after breakfast to sort through my theory board. It's not time for that right now.

As I walk, the black smell of asphalt rises up from the road. Small, tidy houses line both sides of the street, sitting like happy dumplings behind their iron fences. Like any city, Houston is a patchwork quilt, and this quaint row of houses leads to a street lined with battered strip malls. The bookstore is straight ahead, at the crossing of the T-shaped intersection.

A paper coffee cup stumbles down the street, tripping through town like an urban tumbleweed. I hitch my backpack up and walk faster. I don't know why I didn't park right outside the bookstore. Well, I do know why—there are No Parking signs all along that street. But it's not like there's anyone around to give me a ticket.

Something prickles at the back of my neck. Every time I leave my house, I get paranoid someone's following me.

Oh no.

I shouldn't have thought about it. Because now, after every soft thump of my Converse on the heat-cracked asphalt, I hear a softer echo.

Footsteps.

It's just your imagination. It's just your imagination.

I keep walking, resisting the screaming urge to run. The footsteps get louder. When I speed up, they accelerate to match.

They sound closer now.

And then they *feel* closer. Vibrations run through the ground. It feels like someone small. A kid?

No.

No one's there. Shut up, imagination. Shut up, Hannah.

At the end of the street, I slow down, squeezing my eyes shut, heart thudding and lungs aching.

When I stop, the footsteps stop too.

This time I say it out loud. "It's just my imagination."

I whirl around.

Wild-eyed, I scan the empty street. There's nothing there, but my heart twists anyway, sore with something worse than a haunted house fright.

I'm almost at the bookstore. *Keep going. There will be no footsteps, there will be no footsteps, there will be no footsteps.*

Despite the blood pounding against my eardrums, I still look both ways before crossing the street. Apparently not even an empty city can stop me from being a rule follower.

When I get to the shop, I cup my hands to the glass and peek inside. The lights are off, but everything looks normal. I test the door handle. Locked. It's a relief. Finally something is how it's supposed to be. The only other place I've been is the grocery store, and every time I walk up to the automatic doors, they whoosh open like nothing's wrong, greeting me with refrigerated air, fully stocked shelves, and empty aisles.

I still have my mom's keys in my hand. My palm is red and damp and marked with the imprint of the tiny pointe shoe ribbons. There's a spare key to the bookstore, in case of emergency. Somehow I don't think this is the emergency Astrid's parents were imagining when they gave it to us.

Taking one last glance back at the deserted street, I unlock the door and slip inside.

As soon as I'm in, I'm cocooned in *brown*. Everything is brown: the wood-paneled walls, the carpet, the crooked bookshelves made from scrap wood. Even the shop's name—Literary Devices—is stenciled on the front counter in brown.

All I want is to sink down against the wall until the tight fear in me loosens, but I force myself to stay standing. I came here to get books.

As I head down the aisles, I toss anything that looks decent into my bag. I want to get enough books so I don't have to make this trip again. Not that I'll be alone for much longer.

If today is Thursday, that means the biggest audition of my life is in less than forty-eight hours. The day after tomorrow. It's everything I've been working toward: a spot in a major ballet company's corps de ballet. And the audition isn't with just any company, it's my dream company. South Texas City Ballet is where my mom built her career. I already know the ballet masters and the guest choreographers and the layout of the building. I know exactly where I'll fit.

Everything *has* to be back to normal by Saturday. Any second now, I'll snap back into my regular life like none of this ever happened. I have to believe that. Because the alternative is . . . what?

I move to the next aisle, desperate not to think about it.

A book on a display stand catches my eye. A flower, a peony, bursting out of blackness, dusted with chalky pinks and pearlescent blues. I've been wanting to read this one for a while. Kept telling myself to wait until I had more time. As if a girl who dances for five hours a day and goes to school on top of that has any downtime.

I flip open the cover, powerless to resist the pull of the words. Before I turn the page, I glance out the window. I need to rehearse my audition piece again, but I've got the whole afternoon. I can afford to read a chapter or two.

I wind through the shelf maze to get to the woolly yellow armchair in the next alcove. It's my favorite place in the store to curl up and read. On Sunday afternoons, Astrid and I do our homework together here.

I drop my bag and push myself into the cushions, safe at last in my cove of books. The arm of the chair is speckled with drops of red hair dye. The last time Astrid and I were here, she had her head in a mop bucket, rinsing out the paste she'd used to touch up her roots, even though her mom forbids her from dyeing her hair at the store.

My stomach was sore from laughing. Astrid was telling me about her visit to a college in Massachusetts the week before, hamming up a tale of social incompetence when she got invited back to the dorms to hang out with some college sophomores.

Astrid's voice echoed from the mop bucket, thick with the Northern English accent I couldn't understand when our five-year-old selves met. Twelve years later, it's the most familiar voice in the world to me.

"You should have seen me, Hannah. I was so bloody uncool."

"I don't believe it." I can't imagine her being anything but cool, with her glossy red Doc Martens and her matching cherry-red 1940s-pinup-girl hair.

She pulled her head out of the bucket and reached for the towel I had ready. "Ah, well. You'll still love my face even if I can't figure out what I want to do with my life, right?"

"Of course. Love your face forever."

I can't remember now if the program she was looking at was for ethical hacking or puppetry. I don't understand how she has so many different ideas about what to do after high school. For me, it's always been ballet.

I rub my thumb over the spots of red dye. My throat tightens. When will I see my best friend again?

Now would be a great time for my brain to shut up. I crack open the book, devouring page after page. I let the words wrap around me and take me away from here.

This is going to work. Escaping into someone else's life can make me forget the same way dancing does—the way the exertion silences my thoughts, the way the movements take up all my breath and make it easy to ignore everything in my head that's screaming, *I'm all alone.*

As my mind buzzes with letters, I wriggle deeper into the chair and lean my head back.

That's when I hear the music.

Hannah

It's a single, tentative strum: the arc of a thumb over the strings of an acoustic guitar.

I snap my head to the left, straining toward the source of the sound. Everything in me goes still.

After the strum fades, a heavy thunk reverberates through the walls.

Cold panic drops through me. I didn't just hear that noise—I felt it. I sit, frozen, but everything goes quiet.

The silence stretches out like a slowing heartbeat. I squeeze my eyes shut and shake my head back and forth. *It was just your imagination, Hannah.*

I need to go home. Staying here to read was not a good idea. I lean over to grab my backpack. I'm about to sling it over my shoulder when another sound rips through the thin walls of the shop. It's the guitar again, screeching out a blazing, pumping fast riff. It's so loud I want to cover my ears, but my arms have quit working.

This is definitely *not* my imagination.

Apparently my fight-or-flight instinct is broken, because I'm the textbook model of the lesser-known third option: freak out so much you can't breathe or move. I just *sit*, holding my backpack in midair as the hollow parts of my chest vibrate.

By the time the screeching stops a minute later, my lungs are burning, begging for oxygen.

For another long minute, I'm motionless in the silence. I'm about to move, to make a break for the front door, when the music starts up again. It's not the same guitar—it's an acoustic this time, its volume soft and muffled through the wall. It's a real song now, melancholy chords in a minor key, haunting and mournful.

A hundred imaginings of what could be at the other end of this music flicker through my mind in rapidly escalating terror. An ax murderer. A freaky clown with sharpened teeth. The grim reaper, sporting lime-green spiked hair and a leather jacket instead of his usual hooded cape. Maybe he got bored of the scythe and carries a guitar around now, and this is the song he plays before he delivers the blow. A hard-rock harbinger of death.

No, no, no. Get it together, Hannah. Next door is a music store, so the obvious explanation is that someone in there is playing a guitar. It could be someone scary, but it could also be a regular person. A nice person.

I glance at the door. I could sneak away without them ever knowing I was here. But . . . my house is empty. My parents are gone. If this person is okay, I won't be alone anymore.

Maybe there's a way I can scope them out without giving myself away. It's something Astrid and I did when we were little, after she got a spy kit for her eighth birthday.

I unfold and creep across the shop on the balls of my feet. At the front counter, I grab the baseball bat from under the cash register. No sophisticated security system here, just a 2005 Houston Astros commemorative bat, carved of heavy shellacked maple.

I climb onto the counter, stepping between piles of books waiting to be reshelved. The music store is on the other side of this wall, and the two share the space above the ceiling tiles.

The tiles themselves are chalky with age and watermarked with yellow-brown halos. I cringe as I push one up and to the side, hoping it won't crumble into a shower of dust. I plant my left foot squarely on a stack of hardcovers. "Sorry," I mouth, wincing.

With the extra height from the books, I can climb up so the top half of my body is sticking into the crawl space above. My hands tremble as I reach over and lift the edge of a tile above the music store.

The song doesn't falter. The same sad notes play on, over and over. I hold my breath and move my arm slower than I would in even the most exquisite port de bras, easing the gap wider until I can look down into a slice of the music store.

All the lights are off. The single window is papered over with band posters, but a bank of electronic equipment casts a blue glow over the room.

There are guitars *everywhere*. They cover all four walls, mounted up with U-shaped hooks. Dozens more sit propped in stands on the floor. Some even hang from the ceiling, still and heavy.

In the middle of the forest of guitars, in a blue-lit glade next to a stack of amps, is the source of the music.

My heart stops.

It's a person. A living, breathing, human-shaped person.

They're sitting on a drum stool with their back to me, holding a guitar, swaying as they play.

It's the first person I've seen in five days. My mouth starts doing the downward turn thing it does when I'm trying not to cry. *I'm not alone.* I want to shout it out loud, because that means it's over. The awful, terrifying emptiness is over.

The fizzy joy of it almost makes me call out, but years of wary carefulness kicks in. I should get some more information first. The guitar player could still be an ax murderer.

I stare until my eyes adjust to the dark.

Okay. First thing: They're a he. He's white, and around my age, maybe. His hair is dark and messy, his fingers long and quick as they work over the frets.

He looks strong, but not in the same way as the boys I dance with. His shoulders are broad, and the muscles on his arms are full and warm, not sinewy like a dancer's. He looks like he could take a punch, not just spring around onstage like a gazelle on a sugar high.

And then . . . he starts to sing.

His voice is incredible. Low but clear, sliding over the notes with the gliding grace of an ice skater. He sings about trying to hold someone together who's falling apart. He pours sadness into every word, into every haunting minor chord. He sings with a conviction that makes me think it's something he wrote.

His fingers slide along the neck of the guitar, pressing and stretching in patterns. He shifts on the drum stool, swiveling enough so I can see the curve of his cheek. The next time he turns to check what his left hand is doing, suddenly this guy who could have been anybody—an ax murderer or a psycho or the grim reaper—is not just anybody . . . he's somebody.

He's somebody I know.

Leo

I shouldn't be playing this song.

It's making me feel like exploding out of my skin. My left foot keeps tapping ahead of the beat, trying to speed things up, and my knee bounces like an overcaffeinated rabbit's.

This is my life now. Leo Sterling, fighting the silence with a Fender. I've been running hot for days, bombing across Houston with my music blaring. I came here to get electric guitars and thumping subwoofers and massive speaker stacks—anything to fill the ringing emptiness.

Instead of grabbing what I needed and peeling out, my brilliant ass decided to sit down and play my slowest, saddest song. The one I keep all to myself.

Everyone in the Greater Houston area knows that Leo Sterling, lead singer of the eighties-style rock band Rat Skillet, does not *do* quiet music. I blame the acoustic guitar I'm playing. I stopped in my tracks when I saw it in the center of the shop, gleaming in the shadows. Dark mahogany wood coated with gloss nitrocellulose. Mother-of-pearl on the headstock, star inlays on the fretboard. The sound is deep and rich and resonant, and my song sounds better than it ever has before.

15

It sounds so good that it *almost* makes me want to let someone else hear it—but there's a reason I keep it all to myself.

I look longingly at the electric guitars that surround me. Every shred of me wants to stop and play something faster. Louder. I want to get the hell out of here so I can go back to blissfully ignoring the fact that I'm alone. But I have this weird thing—once I start a song, I can't stop right in the middle. I have to keep playing, letting it unspool until the end. It drives the other musicians in my band up the wall.

When I shift into the third verse, my leg jackhammers out of control and kicks the metal dog bowl by my foot, the one I filled up when I got here. There's an unholy screech and dog food goes skittering all over the floor, but somehow my fingers keep playing. They know the song too well to stop.

The punk-rock power couple who owns this shop, Sheena and Jett, have a dog named Muttley Crüe (named after Mötley Crüe, which happens to be number five on Leo Sterling's list of favorite eighties rock bands). I've known Muttley since I wandered into the shop at the tender age of twelve looking for a cheap starter guitar. When her little brown puppy body came barreling at me, it was love at first sight.

I've been coming to put food in Muttley's bowl every day, but there's still no sign of her. I don't know what I expected. I haven't seen anything moving in days. No people, no dogs, nothing.

But if Muttley comes looking for food, I don't want her to go hungry. Despite the rock-and-roll name, she's the least rock-and-roll of all dogs. She's a miniature dachshund with chronic back problems, and she wouldn't last five minutes out on the empty streets of Houston.

Hell, *I* can barely last five minutes out there.

I suck in a breath. It's so dark in here. I should have at least turned on the overhead lights. The guitars hanging above my head are freaking me out.

This is the first time I've sat still since I woke up alone. Images are starting to flash through my head. Empty highways. The abandoned halls of my school, echoing like a drained swimming pool. Waking up sprawled across the king-sized bed in the swankiest room at the swankiest hotel and hearing *nothing*.

My heart starts racing. I feel sick.

Shit. There's a reason I haven't stopped going like the Energizer Bunny. I feel it, creeping in at the edges: an empty black despair and all these questions, *What happened? Where is everyone?*

Now I know I can't ever slow down. Any shred of quiet, and all those thoughts are going to crash down on me. I've got to keep outrunning them.

Oh, screw it.

I'm going to have to finish this damn song early.

It takes a monumental effort to drop my picking hand, but I do it. The silence that follows sucks the life out of the whole room. I've got to move. I have to get the hell out of here. My hands shake as I slide the guitar strap off over my head.

And then, from somewhere behind me, I hear a voice. A girl's voice, and it's—

Saying my *name*?

I jolt. "Fantastic," I mutter. "I'm hearing voices now. Bound to happen sooner or later, I guess."

I bend down to open the guitar case on the floor. If I have to leave, I'm taking this gorgeous guitar with me.

I'm packed up and about to head for the door when something EXPLODES on the floor in front of me.

I yelp and scan the room wildly, holding the guitar case in front of me like a shield. I look where the thing exploded by my foot. The puff of white dust around it is just starting to settle. Wait—I think it's a piece of the *ceiling*.

I look up. There—one of the ceiling tiles is broken and tilted. Beyond, there's only blackness. See? There's no one here. Total coincidence that it happened at the same time I started hearing voices.

A pale white arm reaches through the gap, long fingers stretching toward me.

I stumble backward, panic bursting through me.

Shit. Hearing things is one thing—*seeing* them is another.

The fingers wiggle. "See? I'm real," the voice says, all urgent and muffled.

I start to laugh. Really laugh. "And why, exactly, are you up *there*?" I ask.

She sounds a little sheepish. "There's a bookstore over here. I was reading when I heard your music, and I wanted to see if you were . . . well, if you were real."

This just gets better and better. She thought *I* wasn't real?

"Okay, okay, Ms. Hand in the Ceiling, maybe you are real. Jump down here and prove you're not an eight-headed monster."

"I can't *jump*," she says. "I'll break my legs."

"If you have legs," I say, and then I laugh some more.

"I have legs," she snaps.

Now that my fear is fading, it strikes me that her voice is awesome. Raw and a little scratchy, hitting just the right pitch of husky. My ears perk up. I'm a collector of interesting sounds, anything I can hold a microphone to and record.

I'm going to need to hear this voice up close.

"If you're not going to jump down, I'm coming around to the bookstore," I say.

She starts to say something, but I'm already halfway to the door.

Inside, I'm an epic guitar solo. The shred to end all shreds. Like when my hard-rock heroes bust out face-melting, sweep-picked arpeggios, fingers flying at breakneck speed, *nee-nilly-nee-nilly-nee-nilly-nee*. Uli Jon Roth. Synyster Gates. Zakk Wylde. Slash. Eddie Van Halen. Buckethead. Fans erupting with cheers at their prowess. This is why my band plays covers of eighties hair metal—it's how I feel inside most of the time. Pumping power chords, raging distortion, blistering speed, excessive whammy bar usage. Dive bombs that make you feel like you're plummeting down to the center of the earth.

Okay, so I watch too many MTV rockumentaries. Guys with leopard-print spandex pants and teased-out manes. Sweatbands and glitter and roadies and drugs and hotel trashing. It's the most chaotic, happy feeling ever.

There's no other word for it: This is shredtastic. I've got a buddy, a pal, a sidekick, and now we can go on cool adventures and shit. I can't wait to meet this chick.

Even if she is an eight-headed monster.

I'm still laughing as I push through the door and spill out into the bright-hot street.

Hannah

Wait, what? He's coming over here?

Before I can protest, Leo *freaking* Sterling slings the guitar case on his back. Then he's gone, leaving the door banging and the old-fashioned shop bell ringing in the empty room.

I burst into action, pulling myself out of the ceiling and scrambling down off the counter.

While I wait for Leo to appear outside the bookstore, I chew my lip. I can't believe I threw a piece of ceiling tile at him. I didn't know what else to do to stop him from leaving. I didn't want to miss my chance to talk to him, but as soon as the tile left my fingers, my whole body flushed with mortification. I've never *vandalized* anything before. What's wrong with me today?

This can't be real. I can't believe the first person I've seen in days is *Leo Sterling*. How can that be possible? He goes to my school, and he's in my grade. What are the odds that the only other person in Houston is another senior at Grand Willows High?

I mean, it's not like I know him very well. I've never even spoken to him. There are 862 seniors at our school, and Leo's not on my tightly calculated locker-to-classroom circuit. We don't cross paths often, but whenever I do see him in the hallways I can never drag my eyes away from him. He's always laughing and smiling, looking swaggeringly confident—and undeniably *hot*.

I've never seen him without a black guitar case slung on his back, and he's usually with a guy named Asher, a huge hulking stoner with pretty, pale blue eyes. I had English with Asher sophomore year and he hardly ever spoke, but he radiated calm the way Leo radiates charisma. They're in some sort of rock band together—three weeks ago the whole school was abuzz after they were stripped of their Battle of the Bands win. Rumors were flying about a drug bust, but no one was suspended, so it was probably something boring like attendance records or a late entry fee.

I'm nervous. What will Leo think when he sees me? Every time I've seen him, he's been doing things he's borderline not supposed to be doing. Sipping leisurely from a can of Coke in the auditorium during assembly. Wearing headphones in the hallways. Emerging from a stairwell followed by an unfamiliar rubbery smell. Astrid laughed her head off when she had to tell me it was weed. Basically, he's like the opposite of me.

I only know his name because I asked Astrid about him. I asked quietly, late one night when I was sleeping over at her house, when I thought she was too tired to really pay attention to me. She bolted up from her makeshift pillow bed on the bedroom floor and howled with excitement, her fire-engine-red hair totally disheveled.

"Are you seriously telling me you've finally noticed the

deliciousness that is Leo Sterling? Absolute scoundrel, from what I hear. Could charm the knickers off a nun." She sighed dramatically. "Stunning hair, though."

She's right about the hair. It's thick and dark and a little bit wavy, and always looks freshly tousled. It curls down an inch below his ears, the perfect length for a bad boy rocker.

"Bet he's a seriously good shag," Astrid says. "Rumor has it he has a new bird on his arm every month. College birds, usually, because he's probably been through all the ones from Grand Willows that caught his eye." She stopped cold. "Erm, hold, please. Do you *fancy* him?!"

My face flamed. "You know I only date dancers."

"Mmm-hmm. And you know how much I hate that rubbish rule of yours." She grinned wickedly. "But you don't have to *date* him. Leo Sterling is more 'steamy fling' than 'devoted boyfriend,' anyway. You could just let him snog your socks off—as long as you're prepared to get ghosted after."

I bristled, suddenly annoyed at myself for even asking about Leo. Annoyed at being just another simpering girl caught in his spell.

Leo's the kind of guy parents hate. If they had their way, he'd have a warning label glued to his forehead: *BEWARE, ONE WINK WILL DESTROY THE REPUTABLE FUTURE YOU'VE BEEN WORKING TOWARD.*

Some people like boys like that, but not me. My rule about only dating dancers is in place for a reason. Other guys wouldn't understand—or tolerate—how much of my life ballet takes up. Leo Sterling would be a distraction at best, destruction at worst.

And he'll be at the bookstore any second now. I take a deep breath. Thankfully there's no danger of him being interested in me.

On the bright side, maybe he knows something about where everyone went.

Leo's knock on the glass door nearly makes me jump out of my skin, but I straighten my spine and draw myself up to full height.

So, even though Leo Sterling is not the kind of guy who fits in my world, there's currently no one else in my world. I unlock the door and push it open to let him in.

He looks the same as he did at school, right down to the guitar case always slung across his back. I look at him, this boy I would never have spoken to if he wasn't the only other person in Houston, and lift my chin.

His eyes widen with recognition. "Hey, wait, it's you! I know you!"

I falter. Not what I was expecting. "You—you do?"

"Yeah! Ballet Chick."

Ballet Chick. Of course. When my classmates look at me, that's all they see. Hair in a bun, scraped back and sprayed in place. Hard muscles instead of curves. A neck like a goose.

For some reason, *Ballet Chick* stings coming from him.

"It's Hannah, actually," I say. "Hannah Ashton."

"Hannah? Oh. I thought your name would be more . . . You know what, never mind. Hannah. Awesome."

24

We take a few awkward steps into the store to let the door close. We're Houstonians, after all. Trained from birth not to let a single gasp of air-conditioning outside.

The aisles between the display tables are narrow, and with two people in the space, it suddenly feels too tight. Leo sinks his weight into one hip. His energy takes up more space than his body, sunny and loud. He's wearing black jeans and a worn gray T-shirt that doesn't have a seam at the neck, just a ripped edge that dips down low over his sternum.

Shields, Hannah. The last thing I want to do is look like I'm fawning over him, blinking up at him like he's some god just for being able to play a guitar and having unfairly good hair and a very nice sternum.

I cross my arms over my chest, channeling my mom's unflappable ballerina attitude.

"Listen, maybe we should start over," Leo says. "What would we say in a normal world? 'Nice to meet you'?"

"I guess so."

"Okay, then. It's very nice to meet you, Hannah."

His smile is so wide and bright it's making the corners of my mouth lift in response. Ugh. He really is charming. I haul my shields up a little higher.

He sticks his hand out for me to shake, and that's when our eyes lock.

I'm stuck, frozen and staring. We're so close. Way closer than the times we've passed in the hallways. My thoughts trip over themselves.

Because up close, the sight of him is almost too much. I *have* to look, to drink up every detail.

He isn't movie star attractive, but he certainly isn't plain. Everything is a little . . . *too*. Mouth too full. Jaw too cut, but at the wrong angle, and too low. Eyes too large, lashes too thick. It's the kind of face that belongs in a photography exhibition. The kind that tells a story, the kind you can't take your eyes off of for whole long minutes.

Leo doesn't flinch or huff and look away. He just holds my gaze. It's rare to find someone who'll do that, who will let themselves be an open book. His eyes are the blue-gray shade of slate, but on him it's somehow warm.

I slide my hand into his, and in the touch of our palms, something changes. The way my hand fits into his . . . it feels *right*. Familiar.

God. I'm *that* desperate for human interaction.

"Nice to meet you, Leo," I croak out finally.

What does this little scene look like from the outside? The last boy and girl in the world shaking hands like businesspeople inside a dingy used bookstore.

"I'm seriously so glad you're here," he says. "I was starting to wonder if I'd gone around the bend. Unless you're not real, which is still a solid possibility."

"I'm pretty sure I'm real," I say. It comes out sounding more defensive than I'd meant it to, but Leo plows on.

"Hey, we should do a pinch test." He holds out his arm. "Go ahead. I can take it. Same time?"

I pinched myself a dozen times on my first day alone. Obviously I didn't magically wake up, but I'm willing to try again.

I hold out my arm. As Leo pinches the thin skin at my wrist, I pinch his.

"Holy shit, ow!" he yelps, snatching his arm away.

"Sorry," I say, clapping my hand over my mouth, but I think it's okay because he's laughing.

"Quite a pinch you have there, Ballet Chick." He gives his head a quick shake to get the hair out of his eyes. "So. Now that we've established our mutual existence, *please* tell me you know what's going on. Do you know where everyone else went?"

My heart plummets. For a moment, he made me forget the emptiness. He made me forget that I have no idea where my parents are, or the other two and a half million inhabitants of Houston.

I shake my head no. I hate how it makes his smile slip.

Leo

For a second, I feel like puking, but then I shake it off.

Who cares if we don't know what's going on? Because there's this:

I'M NOT ALONE ANYMORE!

I fidget with a stack of books on a table by my hip, pretending to be interested in *101 Advanced Crochet Patterns* when secretly I just want to get a good look at Ballet Chick.

We go to the same school, but I've never been this close to her before. I knew she was tall, but up close she's statuesque. Poised and gorgeous. She's this weird combination of willowy grace and hard muscle, and her face is really delicate, with a nose that reminds me of a red fox.

Now that we're only a few feet apart, I am not getting the impression that we're going to click. She doesn't look like the kind of girl who'd let her hair down. In fact, it's in this swept-up twist thing, coated with so much hairspray it looks like a hard shell.

I've been within conversation range a few times, but something always stopped me. Anyone looking at us could tell you why—we've got nothing in common. With her perfect ballerina posture, she's a pillar of cool, clean, has-her-shit-together marble and I'm . . . not. She probably listens exclusively to Tchaikovsky and never cusses. I bet she makes straight As and pays attention in every class, and I hang out with my best friend, Asher, nearly every night, jamming in someone's garage or slouched on couches smoking things we shouldn't smoke, and I stay up too late and fall asleep in homeroom. And first period. Okay, and whenever something bores me, which is often.

I put the crochet book down and shoot her an experimental smile. She stiffens, her spine going even straighter than before.

Shit. I'm starting to suspect Ballet Chick is going to be no fun at all.

"Have you seen anyone else besides me?" she asks.

I was right about her voice. The raspy, low timbre would sound incredible in a recording studio. It only adds to the unfairness of it all. Couldn't I have found someone *fun*?

"Uh . . . no," I answer.

"I haven't seen anyone either," she says. "Not in five days."

Five days. Is that how long it's been? Sounds about right. I haven't really been keeping track. It's all been kind of a blur. I'm not high right this *second*, but I have been smoking a lot of weed. Can she smell it on my clothes? It's our first conversation, and I don't want her to think I'm just an idiot stoner musician.

I take a half step back. I don't exactly have a reputation for being calm and composed, or having the best sense of balance, so it's basically a disaster.

First I bump into the table next to me, and a stack of books slides off onto the floor. When I bend down to pick them up, my guitar case snags on something behind me. Just when I think I can't get any more bull-in-a-china-shop, my foot slips on a bundle of pages that have fallen out of one of these crusty old books, and I start to go down.

Her hand shoots out to catch my elbow, and it stops me midfall, frozen in a scene like pressing pause on the remote.

Steadiness spreads into me where we're touching. The warm pressure of her hand keeps me upright. Girl has *serious* balance.

Her eyes lock on mine. Big, hypnotizing green pools of concern.

"I think I'm stuck on something," I say, and it sounds like I mean *her* but it's my guitar case—

I twist my head around. My case is stuck to a weird yarn tapestry thing on the wall that looks like it was made by a bunch of kindergarteners.

Ballet Chick reaches out before I can say anything.

"The zipper's stuck in the yarn," she says, and then she sets to work behind me to untangle it. A minute later, I'm free. I stand and realize the strap on my guitar case is twisted, digging painfully into my shoulder, but before I can fix it, Ballet Chick reaches out for me again. This time, I flinch.

"I'm just going to—"

Her hands flicker deftly at my shoulder as she straightens the strap.

It's such a . . . *nice* thing to do. It makes me uncomfortable.

She's so close. She smells really clean, like a just-ripe pear. She's wearing a tight cream-colored shirt thing that could possibly be a leotard, and right at the edge of her lacy sleeve is a constellation of four freckles.

Crap. Leave it to Leo Sterling to end up alone with a pretty girl. Recipe for disaster.

Ballet Chick—*Hannah*—gives my shoulder a little pat when she's done. The gesture is so foreign I can only swallow.

There's a long, awkward silence, and this time she's the one who breaks it, leaning down to pick up the books on the floor by my feet. I crouch to join her, and neither of us talk until they're all back on the table.

She avoids my eyes, looking instead out the window at the sun-drenched street.

"So . . . what do you think is going on?" she asks.

I bristle. That's one of the few questions I don't want to answer. I've been trying to ignore the whole situation.

"I think it's pretty obvious," I say. "We're dead."

I shrug my shoulders. Dead. Whatever. No big deal.

She takes a shaky breath but then gathers herself. "I thought so too, for a while. But I . . . I *feel* alive. Everything's the same, there's just nobody here."

"I guess I haven't really thought much about it. I've been a little busy. Spending a lot of time playing guitar."

"That song you were singing before—"

"Oh, that was nothing—" *No one was supposed to hear that.*

"It was beautiful," she finishes. "I probably would have kept hiding if I hadn't heard you singing."

"So singing equals trust, huh?"

"More like . . . it proved you were human and not a zombie."

"Is that what you're thinking? Zombies?"

"Not really."

That doesn't seem a hundred percent true, because as she says it, a little shiver runs through that straight spine of hers.

"I've kind of been hoping there was an evacuation we missed somehow," she says. "For a hurricane or a tornado or something."

"I guess those are possibilities. It'd be a lot cooler if we were in the Matrix, though."

Hannah considers it. "Some kind of virtual reality is on my list. Maybe we're pawns of a higher intelligence, and they're sitting on their hovering chaise longues light-years away, staring at holographic projections of us, clicking and dragging our bodies around. But maybe they didn't realize there's a glitch that made all the other characters invisible, or maybe they're kid aliens and they got grounded and aren't allowed to play with us."

I can't stop the laugh that burbles up out of me. What a fucking weird thing to imagine.

I like it.

I wonder what her aliens are doing now. Right-clicking on my head and telling me to take three steps to the left? Maybe they could do me a solid and have me stop staring at the way her wrist floats like a falling feather when she reaches out to straighten a stack of books.

I tap out a rhythm on the edge of the nearest bookshelf. I'm staring at that constellation of freckles on her arm again when the windows behind her go dark.

Like, for real dark. It looks like the middle of the night outside. One second ago, it was a scorching bright afternoon, and now it's . . . not.

We both freeze and look at each other. Her cheeks glow orange from the nighttime streetlights shining in through the windows. I can't see her freckles anymore, but I can see the WTF written all over her face.

I bolt for the window and press my hands against the glass. Outside, the street has been transformed into a strange, electric night.

This can't be happening. Suns don't just wink out, they go down slowly. Has a cloud passed over? But the sky was clear when I rolled up, and it'd have to be a really big-ass cloud to make it this dark.

I push open the door. Hannah yelps, "No, don't," but I blaze out onto the street anyway.

As soon as I'm outside, everything snaps back to normal. Fast as a hit on a snare drum. Beat one: dark as midnight. Beat two: bright as noon.

I close one eye against the glare of the sudden light, like I do when I'm hungover and forget to tape my blackout blind up.

Hannah steps out onto the sidewalk with the grace and suspicion of a cat.

"What the hell was that?" I ask.

Hannah's forehead creases with worry. "I've been seeing shadows, but I thought it was because I've been . . . on edge. But it's never been dark like that."

We both search the sky, but it's clear and blue. I imagine the sun with its hands tucked behind its back, whistling and pretending to be innocent. Like it didn't just massively screw up its one job.

"It must have been an eclipse," Hannah says. "Right? It must have been."

I walk out into the middle of the street and spin to look the other direction, over the roof of the store. The Houston skyline is cut out sharp against the blue. No sign of the moon anywhere.

Hannah sits down on the curb. She closes her eyes and starts doing this weird thing with her hands. Moving them really fast in swishing patterns.

I adjust the strap of my guitar case and clear my throat. "Hey, um, anything I should know about? Like . . . are you a witch or something?"

"What?" She blinks open her eyes and stops moving her hands. "Oh, no, this is just what I do to calm myself down. I go over my choreography."

Her voice—and her hands—are shaky. In fact, she looks like she's about to cry. Shit. *No, no, no, don't cry.*

"Hey, we're all right," I say, rushing to her side. "It was just a little shadow." I look around, panicked. There's nothing here that can cheer her up. No tasty food. No TV, no music. Maybe I can play her something?

My neck is getting all tense, and I don't like it. So much for my visions of popping champagne and having a party for finding each other in the first place.

Oh, wait! I twist around and pull an unopened can of Dr Pepper out of the front pocket of my guitar case.

I pass it to her. "Here, have some sugar. Just, uh, pretend that whole eclipse thing didn't happen."

Hannah eyes the can like it's arsenic, then finally reaches out for it. She takes the smallest sip and the ramrod stiffness of her neck softens.

"Carry drinks around in there all the time?" she asks, nodding at my case.

"Oh, totally. Emergency rations. I'm basically a Boy Scout."

And then . . . she smiles.

It's just a tiny strum of a smile, but it makes something inside me stumble.

It makes her look like a totally different person. A million times more gorgeous. But there's more to it than that.

For the first time in a long time, it makes me feel like I've done something right.

I sit down next to her on the curb, shoulder to shoulder. Her crisp pear scent is everywhere.

The corner of her mouth is still quirked from my joke. It hits me that I want to see another smile. And next time I want it to be more than a strum. I want it to be a full-on power chord of a smile.

"You know," I say, "whenever I'm upset, I do something fun. Something that feels good. I call it Leo's LifeHack. What would make you feel better right now?"

She thumbs the tab on the Dr Pepper can.

"Come on," I prod. "If you could go anywhere in the city, where would you want to go?"

The smile I was working so hard to coax out drops right to the ground.

"I want to go home."

Yeah . . . this is going to be harder than I thought.

Hannah

My words ring in the air between us. *I want to go home.*

"It's almost dinnertime anyway," I add, shrinking at how pathetic I sound.

Leo frowns. "Dinnertime," he repeats, voice flat.

I nod. "I eat dinner at five thirty."

He studies me warily, like I'm some kind of alien. "Let me get this straight. You can go anywhere in the city, literally anywhere, and you want to go back to your *house?*"

"Um . . . yes?"

Leo chews his lip. "Hannah?" He leans a little closer to me. I lean closer too, because it feels like he's about to tell me a secret.

"I'm not gonna let you hide out in your house!"

Before I can jerk away from his outburst of energy, he slings an arm over my shoulder. "The world is ours! Please tell me you've done something fun. Please tell me you've left your house."

"Just to get food. Why, what have you been doing?"

"Everything! Well, not everything. But I already raided my favorite record store, chilled out in my grumpy neighbor's hot tub, and went a couple of rounds on the Ferris wheel at the Aquarium. I went a little wild last night and broke into the Marriott Marquis. You know, that hotel with the pool on the roof?"

I blink at him. I would have never thought to do any of that.

"Hannah! Come on. What do you want to do? Oh—something ballet-related, right? Let me think. Do you want to dance on that really big stage down at the Wortham or something?"

"I already have." He knows I'm a dancer, but he has no idea how serious it is. I made my professional debut as Clara in *The Nutcracker* at the Wortham when I was fourteen.

"What, really? That's awesome, and I'm gonna need you to tell me more about that later. But what else do you want to do?"

I haven't thought about doing anything *fun*. I guess he's right, we can go anywhere we want. I drove all over town on the first day, but I was a little too busy freaking out to stop and relax.

Now that I think about it, maybe there are a few places I'd like to go. The ice skating rink. The planetarium. I could have gone to a movie theater and watched a dozen films. I could have come here and drowned myself in all my favorite books.

I look down at my feet. I've been such a wet blanket.

"So? Where do you want to go?" Leo prods.

"I don't know," I say.

He studies me. "Hmm. Well, you're in luck. I have big plans for today. Want to come with me?"

"What are your plans?"

"Well, before I died—sorry, before *we* died—my absolute favorite music festival was about to come to town. I know one of the bands, and the lead singer plays this extremely awesome guitar. I'm hoping the guitar is there already, locked up in their tour bus."

"And you're just going to . . . steal it?"

"Nobody's around to stop me," he says. "Wait, that sounds bad. Don't worry, Bruce wouldn't mind. He'd want me to have fun being dead. So are you in?"

I dig my fingers into my ankles. I need to get back home. Back to my barre and my pointe shoes. The number of hours I have left before the audition on Saturday is shrinking. My piece is in good shape, but I still need to run through it at least twice a day to stay at peak strength and flexibility. I have to keep training as if everything will be normal by then.

Leo nudges my shoulder with his, knocking me out of my thoughts. "Come on, live a little," he says. He's smiling, all bright and expectant.

He's . . . different than I thought he'd be. More complicated, more human. And he distracts me from the emptiness. My imagination is so close to slipping its reins, and dancing isn't going to cut it anymore.

I scrunch my nose up. "I feel like I'm going to regret this," I say. "But okay. Yeah. Let's go."

"Sweet!" The rings on Leo's thumbs click together as he claps. "Come on, my car's over here. This is going to be awesome!" He hops up from the curb and offers me a hand.

I eye it wearily. *Hannah. It's just a hand. He can't seduce you with a hand.*

I take it. The pressure of his fingers is warm and real as he pulls me to my feet.

Leo smiles down at me. He's still a few inches taller than me, even with his slouch and my perfect posture. We just stand there, holding hands.

It's the first time he's looked at me without a constant sparkle of amusement. I want to look away, but I physically can't. It must be that performer charisma again, or the magnetic good looks, and I'm bitter that I can't resist.

Leo cocks his head. "Hmm," he says. Like I'm a puzzle.

"Hmm what?" I ask.

"I think you're going to be trouble, Hannah Ashton."

I flush with heat. *I'm* going to be trouble? Ha.

This time Leo breaks the stare first, shaking his head to toss his hair out of his eyes again. He laughs, a quiet, surprised little thing.

I pull my hand away a little sharper than necessary. Leo reverts to his infuriatingly good-natured grin and points down the street. "Come on, then, Ballet Chick. Car's that way."

He takes off down the street, and I scramble to catch up. Once he's not looking, I press my hands to my cheeks to cool them down. He's just a charmer. I'm not special, and I'm *certainly* not trouble. That's probably the kind of stuff he says to all the girls.

Crap. I think my shields need some reinforcements.

I cross my arms and concentrate on walking. The quiet of the street closes in, threatening to erase even the sound of our shoes on the sidewalk. Leo is hard to keep up with. I should be tired and hungry, but all I can feel is the oppressive heat and a prickling annoyance that his legs are longer than mine. He plows down the sidewalk with a bouncing, carefree sense of purpose.

And then he stops—next to the most piece-of-crap car I've ever seen.

"Ta-da!" he announces.

I shade my eyes and look dubiously at the hunk of mustard-yellow metal. It's sitting right under a No Parking sign.

"Maybe we should take mine," I say. "How old is that thing?"

"Hey! Thunderchicken is completely reliable," he protests. "And she's not that old. I mean, fess up. It's not every day you get to see a 1986 Pontiac Firebird."

"I've never even heard of—whatever that is."

It's the kind of car that could go on display at vintage car shows, but it's in bad shape. On the hood there's a spray-painted outline of . . . a chicken's head.

"It used to be a phoenix with fire shooting out of its beak, but I made my own stencil and changed it to this majestic chicken," Leo says, trailing a finger over the chicken's red wattles.

"Um, very nice," I lie. It looks like a delivery car for KFC.

Leo smiles wider and gets in the driver's seat. With a horrible screech, the engine catches and sputters to life.

I reach for the door handle. It's gritty with rust and doesn't budge.

Leo cranks the passenger window down from inside. It gets stuck a few times, and eventually he has to pummel it with his fist to get it all the way down.

"You can climb in through the window if you want, or come around and slide over."

But . . . he's already in the car. Which means I'd have to climb *over him*. My cheeks flare with heat at the image.

I examine the open window. Rule-follower Hannah would go around and ask him to get out so she could scoot across. It's the easier, more dignified thing to do. But then Leo looks at me like that's exactly what he expects me to do.

Defiance flares in me.

"I'll come through here, on one condition," I say. "You have to look the other way."

He laughs and turns his head, and I grab the roof of the car. I do a deep plié, then jump. I press down on the roof of the car like I would on a pas de deux partner's shoulder, and with a half twist, I shoot my legs inside. Pretty graceful, except for the part where I knock my butt on the way in.

Leo laughs. "People usually do one leg at a time and look totally ridiculous. But I guess you can do cool jumps and stuff."

"You said you wouldn't watch!"

"Yeah . . . I lied. Are you okay, though? Didn't that hurt?"

"A little. Nothing compared to pointe shoes," I say, tucking a few strands of hair back under the bobby pins holding everything tight to my head. "Hold on, do you just leave your keys in your car, unlocked like that?"

"No one's stolen it so far. Who'd want such a piece of crap? But now there's not anyone around to steal it anyway." He nods his head at the empty street. Right, of course.

Even with the windows down, Leo's car is sweltering. My seat belt buckle is molten, but I manage to get it fastened.

"So how bad do pointe shoes really hurt?" Leo asks. "Is their reputation deserved or is it all hype?"

"Deserved. Even when everything is going well, I still have to take painkillers."

"Going well" means calluses and bunions, maybe a few corns. "Not going well" means bleeding, pothole-like ulcers, or awful-smelling infections. I cross my feet and tuck them under the seat, even though my toes are safely out of sight in my Converse.

"I thought maybe after you got used to them it would be like wearing fluffy bunny slippers," he says.

"Definitely not."

"Damn." He stares at me with something that looks suspiciously like admiration.

Then the moment breaks, and his hand lands with a thump on the seat right next to my ear. He cranes his head to look behind us, and the car lurches backward. I grab the panic handle on the roof. Instead of concentrating on my imminent death, I zero in on Leo's cheek, which is suddenly very close.

And just like that, all I can think about is how much I want to touch him.

Which I don't get. At all. I'm used to being physically close to boys. Ballet is a contact sport. When my leotard gets drenched through with sweat, it's a mix of mine and my partner's. During lifts, their thumbs dig in so hard they go up under my rib cage. I've become desensitized to their hands everywhere. I've never given it a second thought, never cared about them touching me or me touching them.

When Leo pivots to look out the front window, he catches me staring. I snap my face away, studying the suddenly very interesting door handle.

As he shifts from reverse to first gear with a clunk, I suddenly feel like I should know if he's with someone. If he has a girlfriend, it would make the thoughts I just shoved away a million times more embarrassing.

I could just ask him. But the thought of opening my mouth to say, *Uh, do you have a girlfriend?* seems so pathetic and obvious. Besides, I think I already know the answer. If he says yes, it's unlikely to be anything serious. Guys like Leo don't stay with one girl for very long. And if he says no—if he is single—he wouldn't want me. And I don't want him. I've just been alone too long.

I press my lips together. I won't ask. It doesn't matter what the answer is, either way, the plan is the same: Don't think about him like that.

Ugh. I'm annoyed with myself. I'm doing exactly what I vowed not to do. Stupid pretty boys.

As Leo navigates the one-way streets that lead to the highway, I don't know where to look or what to say. I just met this boy—I shouldn't be going somewhere alone with him.

But as we pass silent houses and deserted playgrounds, I remember that our circumstances are pretty unusual. It's going to have to be okay.

Leo taps his thumbs on his thighs, drumming out a song. His rings flash in the afternoon sunlight, and for the first time, I notice the tattoo on his arm. I can only see a sliver of it peeking out from the edge of his sleeve, sharply etched black lines hinting at more. I'm not usually into tattoos, but not being able to see the whole thing makes me want to know what he's inked onto his skin.

"Mind if I put on some music?" he asks.

"Go ahead."

I immediately regret my answer, because he takes his hands off the wheel and starts rummaging around under his seat. He's using his *thigh* to steer.

If there were any other cars on the road, I'd be hyperventilating. He doesn't have his seat belt on either, which sends another hiccup of wrongness through me, but I don't say anything. I don't want to sound like some killjoy helicopter parent.

Leo finally fishes out a battered zip-up CD case. I relax a little bit when Leo puts his hands back on the wheel.

"I know they're old school, but CDs still sound way better than the compressed files on my phone," he explains. After flipping through the pages and basically not looking at the road for many seconds at a time, he slides a CD in. The rest of the car may be a hundred years old and the air-conditioning doesn't work, but the sound system is full of pulsing lights and looks expensive.

I recognize the opening riff of Guns N' Roses' "Paradise City." It's old rock and roll, one of the tracks my dad plays on repeat when he spends Saturdays in our garage, motorcycle parts everywhere, hands covered in grime and oil.

I grew up listening to a discordant mix of my mom's classical music (Tchaikovsky and Prokofiev and Stravinsky) and my dad's classic rock (Van Halen and Aerosmith and Bon Jovi).

This exact song featured heavily in the rotation when I was in middle school. Every morning, my dad drove Astrid and me to school on his way to work. I'd be taming flyaways into a bun with bobby pins and hair gel, and Astrid would be air-drumming and headbanging next to me in the back seat, saying, *You have to burn this CD for me, Conrad.* My dad would laugh and turn the volume up. He's always had a soft spot for Astrid—I think he always felt like she was his weird little British second daughter.

I think of the three of us, stuck in traffic in a city of two million people, and smile.

Leo catches it. "Like the music?" he asks.

"Who doesn't like Guns N' Roses?" I say.

He does a double take. "I didn't expect you to know the band, Ballet Chick."

I bite down the urge to say something cliché and flirty, like, *There's a lot about me you don't know*, but it doesn't seem right coming from me.

Instead, I tell him that my dad listens to this kind of stuff all the time.

"My best friend and I were Axl Rose and Slash for Halloween two years ago," I add. I don't mention that it was Astrid's idea, because I like the awestruck look on his face. His eyes are sort of glazed over, like he's picturing it.

"Uh. Which one were you?" he asks.

"Axl. Bandanna and torn jean shorts and all."

"That's—" He clears his throat. "Sorry—I—just let me pick my jaw up off the floor. I'm used to girls *starting* to listen to eighties rock to get my attention, not finding out that they know about it already." He narrows his eyes. "Wait. Are you fucking with me?"

"I am most definitely not—um, messing with you."

Leo laughs, a whole-body, bright jolt of a thing, and then he's singing along to "Paradise City," wailing like a true rock star, giving Axl a run for his money.

I laugh too, feeling everything in me loosen. I let the rhythm settle into my body, into the tap of my foot on the floor mat, into the nod of my head. I'm not going to headbang like Astrid, but I wouldn't be my dad's daughter if I didn't know how to jam a little bit.

Leo smiles and shakes his head, like he doesn't believe I'm doing this. The sizzle of pride that jolts through me is new—I've caught him off guard.

This is kinda fun.

I pull my legs up onto the seat to sit cross-legged, sliding my hands under my thighs.

That's when my fingers encounter something hard and plasticky, melted into the seat's fibers.

I get a topsy-turvy feeling. Because somehow I know exactly what this hard plasticky thing is.

I know if I move my leg, I'll see a spot of blackened gum in the shape of Italy. But how could I possibly know that? I've never been in Leo's car.

Part of me doesn't want to look. But I have to see if I'm right.

When I shift my leg, sure enough, there's the gum.

I swallow hard. It's in the exact shape of Italy I knew it would be in.

Leo

I'm digging how loose Hannah is in the seat next to me. She's swaying, looking so fluid as she finds the subtleties in the rhythm most people wouldn't be able to find. I don't know why I didn't expect it from a ballerina, but it makes sense. She's trained to hear the undercurrents and to move with them.

The song finishes, and the next track starts. I reach out and turn down the volume. It's a sad, slow ballad, and I don't want us to come down from this high just yet.

I was wrong about her only listening to Tchaikovsky. If she can identify my favorite songs by their opening chords, maybe there's more to her than meets the eye.

"Okay, Ballet Chick," I say. "Give me some stats: What's your favorite album?"

"Um . . . have you heard any Orff? *Carmina Burana?* Or 'Dance of the Knights' from *Romeo and Juliet?*"

"Wait—is that the song that goes like this?" In my deepest voice, I start humming "Dance of the Knights." It's all dark and murderous, full of power and drama.

Hannah brings her hand up to her mouth to hide a smile. "Yeah, that's the one."

I ham it up, DUN-DUN-DUN-ing louder and louder until finally she breaks and laughs out loud. Success! See? I'll get that power chord smile eventually.

"I can't believe you know it," she says after I warble the last low note.

I grin. "Prokofiev, right? I heard it on a TV show."

I have kind of a freaky memory for music, and if I dig something, I google it. Still, it's pretty heavy for classical music. My eyes shift to her lacy cream leotard, her neat little twisty updo. It's not the kind of music I was expecting from her. Just like I wasn't expecting her to know who Axl Rose was.

When she told me she'd dressed up as him for Halloween, my brain went to all sorts of places it shouldn't have. Her leotard and yoga pants are tight enough that it's not a big leap to imagine what her long, sculpted legs would look like in short, frayed shorts. The way her stomach would look in a cutoff T-shirt.

I clear my throat, determined not to let my thoughts go any further down that road.

"Well, my favorite album is the Scorpions, *Love at First Sting*, 1984. Next question: If you were an animal, what would you be? And not the one you *want* to be—the one that's the most like you already."

"I'm not sure," she says. "Maybe an owl?"

"Hmm. I don't know." For all her composure, the outward things like her unbelievable posture and that maddeningly uptilted chin, there's something wound up under the surface that I didn't see in the school hallways. Owls are calm, right down to their bones.

Maybe I'm just getting the wound-tight vibe because we're the last boy and girl in the city. I don't know what she's like when there's a normal amount of people in the city.

"What's your animal?" she asks.

"Capuchin monkey. You know—one of those little black-and-white shrieky ones." It's specific, but I've given it a lot of thought. I'm always moving, I'm impulsive and loud and reckless AF.

I turn a corner too fast, and my guitar case tips over in the back seat. The headstock jabs into my elbow—the one I need to shift gears—but before I can deal with it, Hannah twists in her seat to move the case out of my way.

She takes a look at the angle of my arm with a little quizzical frown. Then she gently lifts my elbow, slides the lid of the center console forward, and sets my arm back down.

"Better?" she asks.

I look down.

I've been driving this car for two years, and I had no idea you could move the top of the console. It makes it ten times more comfortable to use the gearshift.

"Yeah, actually. Thank you."

I drum my fingers on the wheel. I'm not sure what to say next. Like when she fixed my guitar strap, I'm a little thrown by the way she so easily figured out what I needed before I even knew I needed it. When you have a mom like mine and a dad who's not really in the picture . . . let's just say I'm not used to being . . . taken care of like that. The only person I have who'd do something like this for me is Asher, but we'd make a bro joke about it afterward.

I hit eject on Guns N' Roses and fumble around for the Scorpions CD.

"This is the album with 'Rock You Like a Hurricane,' right?" she asks. "'Still Loving You' is my favorite on this one."

I grin. God, she's cute when she spouts track names.

"You," I say, taking my eyes off the road to give her a conspiratorial glance, "are full of surprises."

My voice comes out lower than I'd intended, and I'm leaning into her, my shoulder touching hers.

Shit. I'm flirting with her. With my track record, it's probably a pretty bad idea for me to start hitting on the only other person around.

Maybe there's no danger here. She's gorgeous, but there's no chance of her being into a guy like me. I can't help but wonder what kind of guy she'd be interested in.

I coast through the next intersection without stopping. Hannah pulls out her phone, and I get the feeling she's trying not to watch my driving. What's the point of stopping? There aren't any other cars on the road.

My own phone is in Thunderchicken's cup holder, silent as a tombstone. That first day, when I woke up downtown and heard a quiet so deep I thought I'd gone deaf, the first thing I did was call my best friend, Asher. Then my mom, then my older sister, Gem, even though neither of them are very reliable about answering my calls at the best of times. My fourteen-year-old brother is going through his grumpy-little-jerk phase, but I called him too, and the diner where my mom waitresses when she feels like going to work, and my dad's broke-down pawnshop. I ran down my list of contacts, calling every single person on it. My calls went straight to voice mail every time. My social media apps wouldn't refresh either. Last time I checked, they were still stuck, frozen on five days ago.

There's nothing fresh on the news websites either, no breaking headlines or military-issued crisis instructions. On the radio, there's nothing but music. No breaks between songs, no traffic reports, no weather updates. Normally that would be a dream come true, but now it's just creepy.

Just for shits and giggles, I press the button on the side of my phone. As expected, there are no new notifications. My stomach sours. I shouldn't have looked.

"Have you tried calling people?" Hannah asks quietly.

"Yeah. But no one ever answers."

"Same here. 911 never picks up either. I try them every few hours."

I tried them too—but only once, because it got so bone-shakingly terrifying that first night. I didn't know what I'd say when they answered. But no one did. It just rang and rang and rang.

"Leo? Should we be . . . I don't know, looking for people?"

I shrug. "I did, a little bit. The first day."

I could only take about an hour of searching before it started freaking me out. The slow crawls through downtown were the worst. In the suburbs, I could almost pretend it was normal, just a hot day where everyone was staying inside to keep cool, but the downtown sidewalks should have been jumping with life.

"I drove down to the coast to see if there was a storm gathering offshore," Hannah says. "I drove west too, thinking maybe it was just Houston that evacuated, but San Antonio was empty too."

Wow. She's really put some effort in.

"I just—don't you feel like we should be doing something?" she asks.

"Uh, we can if you want to."

The truth is, I really *don't* feel like I should be doing anything. What else are we supposed to try? We have zero clues about what happened to everyone else. We can't do anything if we don't have any leads.

God, we really need a change of subject. I guess I should have seen this conversation coming—find someone else in an empty city and you're bound to have a little meeting to compare notes. But I am seriously not interested in talking about being the last two people in Houston, because then I have to *think* about being the last two people in Houston. And any form of thinking makes me want to crawl out of my skin.

"I'll keep a lookout as we go," she says, like that's some kind of solid plan. "Maybe someone will be at the music festival place. We found each other, so maybe we can find some other people too."

She stares with laser focus out the window, scanning the edges of the road.

Okay. I'm going to have to take some drastic measures here. Time for some next-level distraction tactics.

I check my fuel gauge. It's nearly full.

Let's see if a little bit of speed-limit breaking can make her stop asking me about the emptiness.

Hannah

Leo maneuvers onto the feeder and picks up speed. Merging always makes me nervous, but with no other cars, it's easy. In front of us, the empty highway stretches west as far as I can see. There are herds of billboards on both sides of the road, blending into two long collages of logos. Personal injury lawyers, ads for new subdivisions, a giant foil-wrapped burrito. We're the only car on all twelve lanes of the highway.

I cross my arms over my chest. We shouldn't be out here. What if something awful is coming and everyone evacuated to outrun it? None of it adds up, though. The skies are still clear. And my mom and dad would never leave without me.

My fingers stray back to the hard patch of gum and acid rises in my throat again. How did I know what it would look like? What could that even mean?

Leo nudges my elbow, knocking me out of my thoughts.

"Hold on tight," he says, grinning.

The gas pedal thunks as it hits the floor of the car.

The sudden acceleration pastes me against the seat. Air rushes in, oscillating in the space of the car, whooshing and clapping at my ears. I try to roll up the window, but it won't budge.

Leo's fancy radio flashes like a rainbow disco. The music gets louder and louder as the needle on his speedometer goes higher and higher.

"Maybe we should slow down!" I shout over a screaming guitar solo.

"Why?" he yells back. "There's no one else on the road." He leans casually on the center console, driving with one hand draped over the top of the wheel. I grab his free hand and stick it back on the wheel.

"At least use both hands!"

He laughs. "All right, all right."

The needle pushes higher. The singer's wild falsetto is as shrieky as my heartbeat. Leo's car is *ancient*, and it feels like we're rolling down the road in a rusty birdcage. The buffeting wind blows some of my hair out of my twist, but this time I don't fix it. Partly because my hands are occupied in a life-or-death grip on the panic handle, and partly because a squirrelly, roller-coaster-drop feeling of chaos is blooming in my chest . . . and I'm . . . liking it?

The glove box pops open when we hit eighty. I let go for a milli-second to snatch a pair of neon pink heart-shaped sunglasses from inside. They squeeze my temples, but at least the ache distracts me from the fact that we're the only car pummeling down the road. Leo pulls his aviator glasses from his collar and puts them on, grinning at me.

I laugh.

Astrid would love this. She can't drive yet—she keeps failing her driving test because she's too busy chatting to the instructor to use her turn signal—and she always pretends to be embarrassed to be seen with me when we borrow my parents' SUV. She slinks down in the seat and puts on my mom's Audrey Hepburn sunglasses like she's a celebrity avoiding the paparazzi.

She would approve of Thunderchicken.

The wind rushes against my cheeks, over my bare arms, and a memory twists in me—another time when going fast had wind whipping around me. When I was little, my dad used to take me out on his motorcycle. I haven't been on it in years. I forgot how fun it was.

I lean my head back against the seat and close my eyes, losing myself in the speed. In the feel of the wind whipping my hair against my face. In the relentless tempo of his screeching rock-and-roll music. I feel *alive*.

I don't open my eyes until Leo slows the car down for our exit. I blink up at the tall buildings, trying to get my bearings.

Leo grins at me. "So . . ."

"Okay, okay. That was fun," I admit.

Leo pats the steering wheel lovingly. "Good girl, Thunderchicken. And that was only eighty-five. I got her up to ninety-one the other day. Want to try it on the way back?"

"Definitely," I say before my rational brain can kick back in. My heart is still beating wildly in my chest. Speeding isn't just against the rules; it's against the *law*. What else have I been missing?

As we drive through the deserted downtown streets, I run my fingers over the edge of the seat, where the rolled seam of burgundy velvet is worn thin. I get the most powerful feeling that it's a thing I've done before.

Leo pulls into a parking lot shaded by an overpass. We have free rein in choosing a space, but he ignores the handicapped spots beside the festival entrance and parks in a regular space.

There's an enormous arch over the entrance, a cosmic explosion of purple and teal and hot pink. The turnstiles look like giant Rubik's Cubes, and the festival's name is splashed everywhere.

SpandexFest: The '80s Rock Festival.

"No one parties harder than the rockers of the eighties," Leo says, flashing me another dazzling grin.

If you'd told me an hour ago this is what I would be doing, I would absolutely not have believed it. I don't want to go home anymore. I want to check out this festival and see this legendary guitar.

Leo puts the car into neutral and yanks up the parking brake, but there's something I want to say before we get out.

"Hey, Leo?"

"Yeah?"

"I think if I were an animal, I'd be a deer."

He smiles so brightly it stuns me for a second. The afternoon sun glazes everything with nostalgic light, and when he swallows, the way his throat bobs hypnotizes me. He really is fascinating to look at.

Leo turns off the engine, and I get out after him without stopping to think, because the cloudless blue sky is glowing and I'm wearing heart-shaped sunglasses and I just found out I like breaking speed limits.

Everything will be different now that Leo's around.

Leo

Hannah's glowing in the seat next to me. No power chord smile yet, but it's gotta be right around the corner. I'm pumped from the drive, and we're so stoked for this, grinning as we clamber out of Thunderchicken—

And then I remember the silence.

For a second, I can't move. All my excitement seeps down into the ground.

I spin around. There should be cars on the street, cars on the overpass. Cars crawling all over this parking lot. Cars, cars, cars. But there's nothing. No mosquitos droning, no birds chirping. Just the cooling-down clicks of Thunderchicken's engine and Hannah's soft footsteps on the pavement beside me.

"Kind of kills the high, doesn't it?" I say, frowning at the emptiness.

"Yeah." She crosses her arms and hugs herself like she's cold. She's not glowing anymore.

I fish my ancient wired earbuds out of my pocket and offer her one. "Want to listen?" I ask. "It helps. I wouldn't have made it this long without them."

She corks a bud in her ear, next to a prim little pearl earring. I wiggle the other bud into my own ear as I scroll through my phone, looking for something less high-octane than what we were listening to on the highway but still upbeat enough to cover up the empty. Power ballads it is.

We have to walk pretty close to each other to keep the earbuds from popping out. Hannah's arm brushes mine. I should walk a half step farther away, but touching her reminds me that she's not some hologram of my imagination. She's really here.

I've shared earphones like this with a few girls, and it always starts off clumsy and awkward. Feet out of time, hips bumping together, everything clashing with the rhythm of the song.

With Hannah, it's smooth right away. We lock into step, moving together like a well-oiled machine as we walk across the parking lot. I keep waiting for it to all go wrong, but it doesn't.

I put a lot of stock in rhythm, and it's not often you find someone whose beats per minute match yours. Hannah and me, though— ours match.

I sneak a sidelong glance at her, pleased to see that she already looks more relaxed. I offer her my arm with a cheesy flourish— strolling arm in arm is okay if I do it in a mock-gentleman way, right?

She laughs and shakes her head like I'm an idiot, but she obliges. Her fingertips rest in the crook of my arm, delicate as air. It tickles a little but in a good way.

The festival is supposed to start tonight, but for now a chain-link rent-a-fence still surrounds the grounds. After finding us a gap to squeeze through, I steer us to the main thoroughfare.

It's like a ghost town.

Before the gates opened last year, there were people already milling about between the food trucks and merch stands. Technicians in black T-shirts were sweating in the heat, laughing and swearing as they tested the equipment. But now it's just Hannah and me, walking right through the middle of it all like cowboys returning to their hometown to find it dusty and vacant.

It's so hot—weirdly hot for this time of year—and so still. The sun bakes down on my neck. I feel naked without a guitar case on my back.

We walk through the mini carnival area, passing booths where you toss rings and win dusty stuffed animals. The hot dog and funnel cake carts are shuttered up, but dozens of bags of cotton candy hang from their canopies, swaying just enough to totally creep me out.

I snag a bag and tear it open. When I offer some to Hannah, she plucks off the tiniest pink puff. I grab a whole handful and shove it into my mouth.

There's still no sign of anyone else. All the standard carnival rides are here, waiting to give you whiplash and part you from your last five-dollar bill. Teacups, bumper cars, Tilt-A-Whirl. Who set them up? Who hung out the cotton candy bags? It's like the festival is frozen in time, waiting for the clocks to lurch forward so everything can start again.

I turn our music volume up three clicks and walk a little faster.

Hannah's side-eyeing everything like she thinks something's going to jump out at us. I hip-check her to distract her, and she gives me another little strum of a smile.

The abandoned rides are freaking me out. The carnival lights should be flashing, and tacky carnival music should be playing. The bumper cars huddle together in the corner of their tent like the trash that collects at the edge of a pond.

I love SpandexFest. I've been six years in a row. But now all I can think is . . . why the hell did I think it would be fun without a crowd?

I can't turn back now. I've got to sell it. I promised Hannah we'd have a good time.

So we press on, past taco stands and beer tents until the sky opens out onto a huge field of dead grass. On the other side is the gargantuan main stage, built up on a ten-foot-high platform. Crisscrossing metal trusses shoot up tall, supporting a grid hung with a mind-blowing number of stage lights. Two line arrays—massive stacks of speakers—hang down from the grid like big black earrings. Last year, Asher said that it looked like a rad version of the Parthenon in Greece. I did a double take, because he always has his head on his desk in World History. He's either secretly a genius or absorbs knowledge in his sleep, because who's ever heard of a stoner who gets decent grades without trying?

"Where are the tour buses?" Hannah asks.

"In the back."

We cross the field and bank around the side of the stage. Behind the Parthenon, there's a whole village of vehicles, ranging from VW campers to glossy luxury tour buses.

"That's it," I say, pointing to the biggest one. *Slydekick* is airbrushed on the side in neon letters. I collect my earbuds and stuff them into my pocket.

We stare at the door.

"Should we knock?" Hannah asks.

"Why? The chance of finding someone else is pretty slim, don't you think? Besides, I haven't knocked on any of the other places I've busted into."

She frowns. "How exactly did you bust into them?"

"Well . . . there may have been rocks. And kicking."

The door of the tour bus is smooth and alien, and I don't see any big rocks nearby. "Uh, stand back, I guess," I say, preparing to karate-kick the handle.

"Wait, wait," Hannah says. "Don't you want to at least try it first? Maybe they left it unlocked."

I'm about to say there's no way they'd leave all their gear without locking the bus, but she's already trying the knob—and it gives.

It would have been more fun to kick it in, but I guess her way is okay too.

The inside of the tour bus is cool and dark. I mess around with the complicated bank of light switches next to the door and end up turning on black lights. Hannah's teeth and leotard glow like we're at a rave. I fiddle with some other switches until it looks more like a cozy living room, but I can't figure out how to turn off the purple LEDs running down the middle of the ceiling.

It's all leather and mirrors, expensive and sleek and awesome. Slydekick has everything: ice machine, fully stocked bar, huge fridge, fancy Italian coffee machine.

"Want coffee?" I ask, firing up the machine.

"Are you sure it's okay?"

"Hannah. We're dead. Have coffee."

I plop onto one of the leather bench seats as I wait for the coffee to brew. There's clearly nobody here. No dirty dishes, no socks or shoes strewn about. I don't know why, but some part of me was still hoping that Bruce and the band would be here. Hannah appeared today. Is it too much to ask that the rest of Houston would follow?

"So you know these guys? Slydekick?" Hannah asks, leafing through a stack of flyers with their logo on it.

"Yeah, I met them at last year's festival. I've been a fan since I was eleven, though."

I tell Hannah about how I met Bruce, the lead singer, and one of the last shred gods standing. Exactly one year ago, my band was playing on the smallest stage, the one between the empanada cart and the shitty penguin-themed fun house. By some crazy-awesome stroke of luck, Bruce watched our set. He wasn't wearing his performance outfit, so I didn't recognize him in the crowd. When he's onstage, he wears lace-up leather pants and goes shirtless to show off the planet tattoos on his chest, and he styles his bleach-blond hair to look like an electrocuted poodle. Turns out the hair was a wig.

After our modest (but devoted) audience cleared, Bruce came over and told me he'd never heard a better vocal cover of Whitesnake's "Crying in the Rain." I realized who it was then, from the star tattoos that start at his temples and blend up into his hairline. In my head I was shrieking, chasing my tail around the stage, but I kept my chill. I cocked my hip and kept on coiling the cable I was wrapping, chatting to him about music and amps. Just shooting the breeze with a rock icon. No big deal.

The next thing I knew, I was backstage during their set with a VIP pass roped around my neck, feeling the stage shake under my feet. I partied with Bruce's band all night, and he took me under his wing for the rest of the festival weekend. I even helped him finish the lyrics to a song he'd been stuck on, and he told me he owed me one, and that I could call in the favor if I ever wanted to give the music thing a real go.

On the last day, I met his producer, the legendary Salina Sakurai. I was playing one of my own songs, right here at the kitchen table of this exact tour bus, and I didn't realize she was upstairs. She heard me playing and came down. She let me finish the song—and then asked me if I'd written it.

I almost said yes. But if experience has taught me anything, it's that I'm going to fuck up any opportunity that comes my way that requires me to actually be on the ball about something. Sure, I can rock up to a bar at sort of the right time and play a few songs, but all the other stuff—the hard work part—that's not exactly my strong suit.

So I said no. Told her it was something I'd heard on the radio.

She gave me her business card and told me to call if I ever made anything fresh. She said I had good instincts, and that Bruce was impressed with my stage presence.

I kept the card in my guitar case for weeks. Obsessed over it. I thought about calling her and coming clean. But in the end, I shoved it to the bottom of a box of spare cables and tried to forget about it. It felt too much like my band's first-ever gig, when I convinced the guys we could handle playing in front of a huge audience. I got them so revved up about it, but I got the times messed up. We were stranded on a sidewalk in hundred-degree heat waiting for our ride while the show went on without us, and it was all my fault. That's how I lost my first drummer. We were twelve. There have been other, bigger screw-ups along the way, but that was the first.

I was so excited to hang out with Bruce again and get another taste of the life, but they're not here.

"Leo?"

Hannah's voice pulls me back from that extra-fun trip down memory lane. She slides a coffee cup across the table—she must have poured it while I was zoned out—and a packet of hotel cookies that she's already torn open for me. And then she's touching my arm, fingers soft and curled around my wrist. I go still, desperate not to move, to scare her off. I didn't know how badly I've been needing to just touch someone.

"Hey, Leo? Before today, were you . . . all right?"

I huff out a breath. "Do I look that bad?" She's so put together, and I'm in three-day-old jeans and haven't slept through the night once. I shift an inch away from her. Do I *smell*?

"No—sorry, that's not what I meant. Like . . . could you find food and stuff? Have you been eating? Have you been sleeping? I don't know, I guess I'm just asking if . . . are you okay?"

The question is so foreign to me that I almost laugh at the absurdity.

I can't remember the last time someone asked me if I was okay.

I take a sip of coffee before I realize that she's actually waiting for an answer.

"Oh—I'm fine," I say. "Shredtastic."

She doesn't move, doesn't say anything. Just waits.

Maybe I could tell her a little bit of the truth.

"I mean. Five days is a long time with no one," I say finally. "I like being around people. It wasn't the best time of my life."

She waits a little longer, just this open, relaxed silence between us, but that's all I can give her right now.

"Ready to find that guitar, then?" she asks after a while.

"Yes. Please."

I take a deep breath and shake off what feels like such a monumental moment. I didn't mean to tell her that, but it felt good.

I drain my coffee and stand up, and the hunt for Galaxe begins. I open up every cupboard, look under every seat. It's gotta be in here. Bruce is superstitious about it: He would never let it travel in the separate truck that hauls the band's equipment. I'm about ready to give up when I see something on the upstairs level of the bus. There are eight bunks with a narrow hallway down the middle, and each bed has a little privacy curtain. Through the gap in the last curtain, I can see something shiny and black on the pillow.

I pull back the drape. On the bed, laid out like a person, is the weirdest-shaped case I've ever seen.

"Hannah, come here," I call. "I think this is it."

She comes over and stands next to me. I flick open the case latches and raise the lid. If life were a movie, we'd hear singing angels.

Here she is, the legendary Galaxe, in all her savage glory.

Her neck is the only part of her that looks like other guitars. It's long and straight and has a standard set of six strings and twenty-four frets. But instead of the regular shape everyone thinks of when they think of a guitar, Galaxe splits into two fins like a jacked-up, razor-sharp mermaid tail. Every edge tapers into a knifelike thinness. If you swung this guitar into a tree, I reckon it would bite in just like an ax.

But the most amazing thing about Galaxe is her color. I don't know who painted it, but it's an airbrushed galaxy, all purples and teals, with swirling supernovas and twinkling stars. For a moment, I swear I see the stars shift and sparkle.

When Bruce told me it cost him ten thousand dollars, I nearly barfed. It took me three years to save up $599 for my Fender Strat.

"Wow," Hannah says.

"Right? Check this out." I ease Galaxe up and out of her case and loop the strap over my head. I flip the hidden switch that turns on the guitar's built-in LED backlighting. A fluorescent halo radiates out from the guitar, turning my arms and clothes blue. The stars painted on the guitar look like they're moving again.

"That's gorgeous," Hannah breathes.

It couldn't be more metal.

We head back out into the heat and traipse over to the stage. In the wing, Hannah watches as I dig through stacks of cables, shifting amps and pedals and fiddling with the soundboard.

And she watches as I fail.

I can't get this stupid sound system to work. The lights on the board are on and the tiny screens are lit up, but whenever I pluck a string, the metal sounds dead. The sound's not feeding to any of the speakers.

"Here," Hannah says, quiet at my side. "Let me see."

She studies the soundboard for a minute, then starts sliding things around, twisting knobs, unplugging and replugging the cables that feed out of the back of it. She goes onstage and checks behind a few pieces of equipment, and I'm just standing stock-still in the wing, watching.

She comes back to me a minute later with a heavy black cable draped over her arm.

"Don't think you needed this one. Now let's see." She reaches over to thumb a string on my guitar. I feel like she's touching *me*.

The sound booms out of every speaker on the truss, clear and clean.

"How do you know how to do that?" I ask, dumbfounded.

"I picked up a few things watching the theater technicians. It just makes . . . sense to me."

I suck at sound systems. Like, you should plug things in and they should just work, but when you have a real soundboard, it seems like there's always something going wrong. At least for me. Hannah clearly doesn't have that problem.

"You're badass, you know that?" I say.

She blushes.

I shouldn't have said that. Even if I think it's true.

She lets the cable on her arm drop to the floor with a loud slap-thunk, and then she's coiling it expertly into infinity loops—that's something I *do* know how to do, but she's fast and makes it look so easy, and it's . . . something else. Watching the lithe muscles in her arms flex under her freckled skin—it's making my head go light.

She lays the cable back on the pile and grabs a roll of black gaff tape. And she rips off a piece with her teeth.

Oh shit. That was hot.

Like. Really fucking hot.

I swallow. How am I supposed to play now, when my skin feels too tight and I'm so light-headed I feel drunk?

"You gonna play or not?" Hannah asks, that raw velvet voice of hers somehow even more alluring than usual. There's a flicker of mischievousness on her face, and for a second, I swear she knows exactly what she's doing to me, and that's so unexpected that I just blink.

"Yes. Sure. Yes."

I walk out into the middle of the stage, dazed. I can only hope that my wits come back when the backing track starts.

For the first time, I wonder if I'm in over my head.

Leo

A minute later, I'm strumming away on Galaxe, keeping up with Slydekick's biggest hit, and the main stage's speakers are amplifying me a million times louder than I've ever been amplified before. I feel like the whole city is throbbing with the notes I'm playing.

This stage is so different than the one in the bar where my band plays every Friday night. Shoelace is grungy and dim and it smells like beer and puke, but it's my favorite place in the world. When I'm there, Asher's always playing bass a few feet to my right, his white guitar covered in his signature skateboard-style doodles. Gage is on drums, in a sleeveless shirt that shows off the tattoos snaking up both arms. Oz is on rhythm guitar, slinging his man bun to the beat, and Rosalita's on my left in fishnet tights and a leopard-print skirt, shredding it on lead guitar. We've all dreamed of playing on a stage like this, and here I am, doing it.

I storm though the song, putting a little extra oomph into the last riff to impress Hannah. I grab the microphone and ham it up. "Rock on, H-town! Peace out and good night!"

Hannah pauses the backing track and comes out onto the stage.

"That was incredible," she says, the corner of her mouth quirked up, like she can't believe me.

"Thanks," I say with a bow.

She looks out over the empty field, rubbing her sneaker in a perfect arc across the floor. "You're really good. Is that Bruce guy your teacher?"

"Oh, no. He lives in LA. I don't have a teacher. Learned everything on YouTube. I'm not the best, but there aren't many people who are willing to get up on a stage wearing skintight pants and eyeliner and make a fool out of themselves, you know? Glam metal isn't exactly the biggest scene these days."

Musically, this is kind of as good as I'm going to get. It's not like I have money for guitar lessons or singing lessons. And I don't have the discipline for college.

"What's your band called?" Hannah asks.

"Rat Skillet."

She laughs. *Ooooh*, that smile was so close to being a power chord.

"Asher came up with it," I say, giving credit where it's due.

"Is Asher the really tall one? You're always with him in the hallways at school."

"Yeah. We've been best friends since third grade. He doesn't talk much, which works because I basically never shut up."

He was a big kid even back then, a gentle giant with sleepy eyes. He used to hang out at skate parks, doodling cartoony monsters on people's skateboard decks with fat permanent markers. Now he's in charge of making all our Rat Skillet flyers and album art, using the same whimsical, smiley monsters that he's drawn on his white bass guitar.

Thinking about him feels like a guitar string twang in my chest. Asher's such a good fucking guy. Everyone thinks he's just a dazed stoner, but his slowness is just him taking everything in stride, considering shit so he can drop the most insightful advice. He's talked me down from lots of panicked cliffs.

"So is this what you want to do?" Hannah asks. "Be a musician?"

Usually people ask me if I want to be a rock star, not a musician. And there's always a sneer hiding in there somewhere. But Hannah is completely genuine.

"Nah, Rat Skillet isn't going anywhere," I say. "My band members all have real jobs planned out, so we're just playing for fun." Which is fine with me. If I got serious about making it big, it would stop being fun.

I walk to the front of the stage, past the big fluorescent yellow strip of tape that you're not supposed to cross for safety reasons. It's a ten-foot drop down to the grass. I sweep one toe out over the edge experimentally, and because it's me, I lose my balance. Hannah's fingers are at my elbow, tugging me back before I teeter off the edge. I stutter at the softness of her fingertips on my bare skin.

"Sorry," I say sheepishly. "Am I allowed to cross the line if I'm sitting down?"

She nods, and her hand slides away.

I sit down and scoot across the yellow line until I'm perched on the edge of the stage and dangling my feet over the edge, Galaxe heavy on my lap. After a few seconds, Hannah comes and sits by me. She's close, but there's still a healthy few inches between our legs.

I shouldn't scoot over. I should definitely not wiggle around so I can pull a fresh guitar pick out of my back pocket, and I should definitely not let my leg settle back down right against hers.

But . . . I do.

Now we're touching, hip to knee. Her muscles are firm and warm. Her legs go on for *miles*, and I have to stop myself from imagining what I can do with that information.

All we're doing is sitting next to each other. Friends sit next to each other all the time. It's totally normal.

What's not normal is how aware of her I am. She's so willowy and graceful and the way she moves—

She's throwing me off balance. I feel like a skittish colt, like I'm new at this whole girl thing. Which I am definitely not. I've got to get my shit together.

I'm just excited I've got a friend now. That has to be it. Of course I like it when she touches me, because it felt nice and I like to be touched. The small things like her fingers on my arm, the brush of her shoulder against mine, it's a language I understand. It feels like she's saying *I'm here, don't fall off the edge, I'm glad you're here.*

I need some clear headspace to figure out a game plan, to get my feet back under me, because I'm a little bewildered by it all, but I don't want to be apart from her in this emptiness. Not even for a second.

We sit there in silence for a while, looking out over the field. I tap the guitar pick against Galaxe's body.

She breaks the silence first. "If your band was on board with it, would you want to make it big?" she asks.

I'm grateful for the conversation, even if it's not my favorite topic. "If it's going to happen, it'll happen."

She frowns. "I don't really think that's true. If you want something, you have to work to make it happen."

I shrug. "Maybe that's how ballet works, but rock star stuff is kind of subjective. It's more about luck."

"Really? I'm pretty sure rock stars have to put a lot of work in too. There's probably a ton of things you have to do to be successful."

She could have a point. But I tried putting in the hard work before and got burned. Life's a bitch. Bad shit happens to good people, and vice versa. Just take my mom, for example. She sucks at adulting, but bad stuff hardly ever happens to her. She once quit her job at the mall food court because she didn't like wearing ugly shoes, and the next day she won five hundred dollars in the lottery. Asher's parents, on the other hand, work their asses off, and I swear something horrible happens to them once a month like clockwork. Last month it was their car breaking down, and the month before that his mom got laid off. Just when they thought they'd saved up enough money for Asher to go to community college, Asher's dad had a fall at the construction site where he works. The company weaseled out of paying the medical bills, so Asher's college money went down the drain.

The one time that both of our moms came to a gig, I saw them standing together. It shook me. My mom was all chill and smiley and Zen, waving her Jack and Coke around to the beat, and Asher's mom was still in her work uniform, mouth drawn down from exhaustion. She looked so *gray*.

If working your ass off isn't guaranteed to bring success, and flying by the seat of your pants can actually work out, why take the harder path?

"What are you going to do after graduation?" she asks, and I automatically stiffen at the question, but she's not asking it like everyone else asks. There's no sharp edge, no sarcasm. She genuinely wants to know.

"I'm not sure yet," I lie. Right now, my plan is to just keep on gigging. I'm pretty sure my mom won't make me move out of the house. The only difference is that there won't be seven hours of school to suffer through every weekday.

"It seems like you want to do something with music," Hannah says. "Could you do something in the industry? Work for Bruce maybe?"

"Maybe."

If he hired me, I'd just disappoint him. I'm not really good at being dependable. But Hannah doesn't know that. It's interesting. I feel like I can say anything, because she didn't meet me when everyone was around. There's no one to tell her what they think about me.

There's a bigger problem, though. I look out over the streets of Houston, Texas, bustling metropolis. Population: two.

"Anyway, none of that matters anymore. We're dead." I try to keep it light, but Hannah goes pale.

"Everything might snap back to normal," she says quietly. "It's still possible."

I flick my hair out of the way so I can study her. She really believes it.

Maybe I can try believing that too. Maybe I can make a deal with this afterlife or evacuation or whatever it is. A bargain.

Here's the deal, Houston: If we get back to our normal lives, I promise I'll talk to Salina. I'll tell her I wrote that song. SpandexFest ends in less than forty-eight hours, so clock's ticking, world. If you don't fix yourself before that, my offer's off the table.

For a while, Hannah and I just sit there, watching the sun sink lower in the sky.

"It's cooled down a lot," Hannah says.

I grimace. "Mm-mm, no. You're not allowed to talk about the weather."

"What? Why not? Isn't that what people are supposed to talk about?"

"Exactly my point. Talk about something you're *not* supposed to talk about."

She's right, though. This morning, it was scorching. Way too hot for April. Now I'm starting to get goose bumps on my arms.

She's quiet for a moment.

"Okay . . . what's the last thing you remember?" she asks. "Before everyone was gone?"

"Next question," I say.

She shoves me with her shoulder.

"Okay, okay, fine," I say. "I don't remember anything. It all seems like it's really far in the past. Like how you can't remember what exactly you ate for lunch last Tuesday, you know?"

"Yeah. Same for me," she says.

What was my last clear memory? Stumbling out of bed and hauling myself to school? I really have no idea.

Beside me, Hannah stretches her legs out straight, then drops them with a sigh. Oh, Ballet Chick.

I sling my arm around her shoulder. It's supposed to be buddy-buddy, like a reassuring *hey, we're in this together*. But then she leans into me and all I can smell is fresh pear and all I can feel is the arch of her collarbone under my fingertips.

Somehow, for all her composed, perfect straightness, she fits against my side just right. I'm getting the strangest sense that we've sat like this before, her tucked up against me, warm and comfortable and in sync.

She looks down at our feet. "That song you played back at the store . . . did you write that?" she asks.

"Yes, indeed. Hey, maybe I should write a song about today."

When I say *today*, I really mean *her*. What notes would she be if she were a song? I unplug from the speakers and play raw, assembling a melody as I study her.

She hugs her arms around herself and looks out over the field, seemingly unaware of the way I'm staring at her. Her deer eyelashes dust against her cheeks with every blink.

That small thing—her blinking—makes me feel like I've been

stabbed in the gut with an electric fork. Desire climbs up my throat. Oh no. *Crap, crap, crap.* This is not how *just friends* think.

It's fine. She doesn't like me like that—I saw the way she first looked at me in the bookstore. So I'm safe. As long as she doesn't reciprocate, as long as she keeps thinking I'm a useless, washed-up stoner, I can keep myself under control.

But then she closes her eyes and tilts her head back to soak up the sun, and something about the long, pale stretch of her exposed neck and blissed-out look on her face puts a visual into my head that I can't shake. My mouth, on her neck.

What would she do? Would her breath catch? Would she lean back and let me?

Suddenly my whole body feels electric-hot. Dizzy and almost nauseous with *want.*

And then she's not looking up. She's looking right at me.

Her feet stop swinging, and mine do too.

Oh shit.

This is going to be a *much* bigger problem than I thought.

Hannah

A second ago, I was looking out across the field while Leo worked through a melody of stuttering, delicate notes, and now—

Now we're looking right at each other. The intensity of his stare has heat spreading across the whole right side of my body.

Something balloons up inside me. A swollen happiness. For a moment, I'm filled with one thought: *I'm so glad he's here.*

I want to lay my hand on his shoulder, to feel the heat under his soft, holey T-shirt. I want to feel the warmth of his pulse where I can see it jumping on his neck, just beside his Adam's apple. He smells of old cloth and incense and something else—like how it smells when you blow out a candle. It's rustic and warm and makes my head spin.

The corners of his eyes crinkle and his mouth curves in the smallest of smiles, but his stare is piercing.

Oh crap.

I've felt this warm rush of admiration before. I press my mouth and eyes shut for a second, trying not to think the actual words, but I fail.

I like him.

And that is the absolute last thing I need.

I'm only feeling this sappy fondness because we're the only two people left. The glow inside me is just a product of his stupid charisma and us being stuck together.

But . . . he's so different than how I thought he'd be. And the way he's looking at me has the stupidest of all stupid thoughts flickering through my head.

Maybe he likes me too.

God, how pathetic am I? I'm reading it all wrong. He's got a reputation for being an incorrigible flirt; this is probably just how he is with everyone. I really am just like all the other girls fawning over him because of his art-gallery beautiful face and his stupid messy hair and the guitar case that's always on his back. After Astrid told me his name, it seemed to pop up everywhere, in whispered rumors of girls crying in bathrooms or of exes throwing things at him in the cafeteria in fits of rage.

I want no part of that drama. I've got to get a grip. Get my shields back in place.

I finally dredge up the strength to tear my eyes away. I scoot sideways just to put some distance between us.

My cheeks are burning. I'm an idiot.

Leo looks down at the strings, and his notes peter out into silence. I pick at the hem of my shirt. I wish I could disappear.

He clears his throat. "You know what?" he says. "Let me start over. We need something more upbeat."

He starts picking out a cheesy little tune. He plays stiffly, without his usual confidence, but once he's got some notes down, he starts adding words.

I'm still reeling. I shiver and rub some warmth into my arms. The temperature is definitely dropping now. I scan the festival grounds. Sometimes it gets cooler before a storm, but the sky is clear.

Maybe my shivers are chills. Could I be getting sick? Maybe everyone cleared out of the city ahead of a nuclear disaster, and this is the beginning of the end for my irradiated body. I imagine my insides glowing and disintegrating.

I scan the buildings in the distance. One mirrored office complex glows blue for a fleeting moment, like the light on Galaxe. I squint, but it's already gone. Could it have been a radioactive halo?

Leo keeps playing, oblivious to my internal ridiculousness. Before I found him, I had to stomp down my imagination all by myself. Now I have something to distract me from thoughts of radiation and disaster. I force myself to concentrate on his hands.

I wonder if it hurts, sliding his fingertips along those metal strings. His fingers aren't as ugly as my toes, so it can't hurt as much as pointe shoes. His veins stand out blue green on his forearms, and there's a trail of holes in his T-shirt along the seam at his shoulders. Seeing his skin underneath, along with the edge of a dark mole, makes my face heat all over again.

The song he's playing is strange, disjointed and wrong somehow, but he's having fun. He stops to laugh at himself a few times. His sleeve shifts up a little as he plays, revealing more of his tattoo.

Another centimeter of sharp, inky angles for me to analyze. I still can't tell what's at the center, but it seems like whatever it is has a halo of geometric shapes around it.

He finishes the last verse with a little flourish.

"Ta-da!" he says.

"Very nice."

"Are you kidding? That sucked! Don't lie to me, I can take it."

"Okay, it was a little weird," I admit. I'm grateful for it, though—whatever he was playing when he was staring at me was too real.

I swing my legs against the edge of the stage. "How can you tell if a new song is good or bad?" I ask.

"Well, that one was obviously trash, but I get what you mean. It all depends on what people want, and that shit changes all the time."

I shake my head. Creative stuff like writing songs and writing words seems so hard to get right. No one's there to tell you that you're messing up, to bark orders at you and show you how to do it correctly. With ballet, there's a right way and a wrong way to do everything. At the Academy, we're trained to look for faults in ourselves. Hence the walls of mirrors. We know when we've done something wrong because there are rules, some of which are hundreds of years old.

Ballet is measurable. It's not nebulous and free like writing a song or writing a story.

"I have to write about ten crappy songs before a good one comes out," Leo adds. "I can tell if it's going to work right away—it's like a wheel slipping into a groove."

I think about the handful of times that I shared something I'd created from scratch. They stand out in my memory, achy as bruises. Little eruptions of my overactive imagination. The worst was in fifth grade, when we wrote our own adventure books and bound them with string. I was so excited to show mine to my mom after school. I created a whole world in that book, with heroines and villains and flower magic. That's what it was called—*Flower Magic*. A pretty unoriginal title, but I was only ten. When I got home, my mom was rushing around, herding me into the car to take me to a ballet recital. She gave the book one glance and made some over-the-top comment about it being wonderful like she does with all my schoolwork.

After the recital, she couldn't stop gushing about my performance.

At first I didn't understand. It was choreography someone else made up, and I was onstage with ten other girls doing identical movements like clones. *Flower Magic* was all me, words that no one had ever put in that exact order before. But my mom was more impressed by the recital, so it finally sunk in: *Flower Magic* was awful.

Leo's song was awful too, but here he is, tapping his rings on the edge of the stage, completely unconcerned. He brushed the failure off so easily. I'm having trouble wrapping my head around the concept. It never occurred to me that you could just discard something if it went wrong. With ballet we have to try again and again until it's perfect.

"Have you ever played something new and had . . . something bad happen?" I ask.

"Sure. One time I rolled out a new song that I thought was transcendent. I guess it was a little depressing, though. When I finished, the whole bar was silent. I made a joke about it and cranked up a crowd favorite. No one ever spoke of it again, not even my band. I have to let the songs out, you know? Even the bad ones. Because otherwise they'd get stuck inside me. You'll know about that—ballet's an art. It's creative."

"Maybe if you're the one choreographing."

"You get some input, though, right?"

"Nope. I'm basically a puppet. A highly trained, perfect little puppet."

Sure, ballet is an art, and the steps—temps levé, arabesque, pirouette—are the paint that the choreographer uses to create the painting. Our bodies are the tools—the paintbrushes. Some ballerinas would disagree with me, but that's always how I've felt about it.

For me, ballet is a sport, not an art. Dancers spend a lot of time outside the studio, cross-training to make sure we have the stamina and strength to dance. I'm constantly thinking about physical things: muscles, ligaments, bones. Stretching and perfecting and calibrating.

"But you're still training," Leo says. "Once you go pro, you'll get to express yourself, right?"

"Nope. Well, I *might* have a tiny bit of creative input in five or ten years, if I rise up through the ranks high enough that a choreographer would want to create new material on me. I'd have to be a soloist, at least. Probably principal."

Of course, none of that will ever happen if I miss the corps de ballet audition the day after tomorrow. If the rest of Houston doesn't come back by then, all my years of training will be for nothing.

Leo whistles. "Man, ballet is intense. Like, extreme effort and dedication. I would make the worst puppet ever." He studies me. "Just make sure you do stuff you want every now and then, okay?"

I look across the field to where the carnival rides are. The straight-drop ride towers above the rest, covered in plastic light bulbs that glint in the afternoon sunlight. I can't see the top of the swing carousel, but I know it's there. I did a double take when we passed it earlier, because it looked exactly like one I went on with my dad when I was little.

Swing carousels have always been my favorite. They're somehow calm and terrifying at the same time. When I was little, I'd close my eyes, stick my arms out, and pretend I was flying. I imagined all sorts of terrain passing under me. Fizzing purple lagoons, houses with white swan feathers for roofs, forests made of Twizzlers.

Leo leans over and bumps my shoulder with his. "You look like you have an idea," he says.

I nod. "Maybe we could go ride on that swing thing."

"You mean *you want* to go ride on that swing thing," he says.

"Are you correcting my grammar?"

"No. If you want something, it's okay to say it out loud. You don't have to beat around the bush."

"Okay. I want to go ride that swing carousel."

"Excellent. That just so happens to be my favorite ride here," he says, grinning.

I don't tell him it's mine too.

He offers me his hand to help me up, grabbing so tight it almost chases away the white-hot crackle that jumps from his palm to mine. An electric shock.

We must have built up some static electricity when we were swinging our legs against the scratchy black fabric covering the front of the stage. That has to be it.

So why can't I move? Our hands are fused together for the third time today, and I don't want to let go.

Leo breaks first, shaking his hair out of his eyes.

"Better get Galaxe tucked back in her bed," he says, letting go of my hand.

I nod, but I can't speak.

Hannah

After visiting the tour bus, we make our way back through the festival grounds. It feels less creepy now. I think I'm getting used to being outside.

Astrid would love this place. I can imagine her riding every single ride, even the ones that make her puke, and playing carnival games with the laser focus of a gambling addict. She'd twirl down the midway, leaving Doc Marten boot prints in the dirt.

She'd come up with a whole themed outfit to wear. Red-and-white-striped leggings and popcorn ball earrings, or a vintage A-line dress with Ferris wheels printed on it. Her hair would be in immaculate 1940s waves, but her gauges and industrial piercing would save the look from being too sweet.

Every year, Astrid drags me along for her back-to-school shopping trip, and every year it's the same. She pops out of the changing room in colorful combinations that verge on being costumes, not outfits. Sometimes I'd feel a flare of desire to join in, to use my allowance to buy flowing, paisley-print dresses so I could wear them with no shoes and ivy woven through my hair, but in the end, I never spent a penny on those shopping trips. Astrid filled the spot for zany dressing in our friendship. Instead of inspiring me to try different things, being her best friend had the opposite effect on me. I felt even more penned into my role as pristine ballet girl.

So all my clothes came from dance catalogs, pages dog-eared and items circled so my mom could order them, plus a couple of pairs of jeans and sweaters in solid pastel colors. Anytime I tried on Astrid's clothes, I felt like a fake. Like I was stealing her personality.

I cross my arms over my cream leotard as Leo and I stop at the low metal fence that surrounds the swing carousel.

"How do we get it going?" I ask.

"It can't be that hard. Let me take a look." Leo hops over the fence and jogs to the operator's hut. I look at the bouncy castle next door while I wait. The sign says Age 8 and Under Only, but I'm going to jump on it after this. I haven't been on a bouncy castle in forever.

The lights on the swing carousel blink on and start flashing in psychedelic patterns. After a few loud clicks, the swings jerk to life, chains jangling as the ride starts to revolve.

Leo runs out of the hut. "Quick, hop on!" he shouts.

I climb over the fence, and we jog alongside two of the chairs. I plop awkwardly into mine and pull the metal safety bar down just as my feet start dangling above the grass.

The ride takes us six feet off the ground and swirls us around. It's slower than I remember, tamer than my childhood memories.

Then the hydraulics hiss. The ride raises us up higher, and the spinning accelerates. We're looking down on the food trucks now.

The swings gravitate out, away from the trunk in the center hiding the mechanical parts. The carousel does the same thing to my blood that pirouettes do, flinging it into my fingertips and feet.

In front of us, twenty empty chairs sway, twisting peacefully without the weight of riders.

The air is even colder on my face now that we're going fast. Leo lets out a little whoop, and when I look over at him, our eyes catch. We laugh at the speed, at the thrill of the ride, and his face is a mirror of mine, lit with delight.

For a moment, I get the sense that even if there were a whole festival full of people milling around below us, it would still feel like only us.

The scenery passes in a whirl: stage, overpass, skyline, stage, overpass, skyline. Over and over, faster and faster. The ground below turns into a blur, and I'm glad, because now I can almost imagine there are people milling around down there.

"Close your eyes and hold your breath!" I shout to Leo.

He doesn't hesitate—he just does it. He's game for anything, and it makes something in me swell.

I close my eyes and let go of the chains.

Up here it's bliss. The g-forces pin me in place, but not being able to move makes me feel weirdly free.

Clank.

My eyes fly open at the sound. In front of me, two chairs judder like they've just collided. They're way off course, not swaying in formation like they're supposed to.

A sharp wind slices across my face.

I wait for it to die down, but instead it gets stronger and colder and louder. It's one long blast, like a giant with unbelievable lung capacity blowing out birthday candles.

Clank. The chairs ram into each other again.

That's not supposed to happen.

Down on the ground, bags of cotton candy roll across the grass like small animals scurrying for shelter. A whole stack of red Solo cups takes flight and smacks into the side of the hot dog stand.

And then . . . the wind stops. The swings settle back into formation like it never happened. The air we're zooming through is still and silent again.

"Uh, that was weird," Leo calls out into the calm.

The only time I've seen stuff fly around like that is in tornado videos. I try to recover the soaring feeling I had before, but I can't. I didn't know the chairs could hit other chairs, and now I just want to get down.

"Hannah? Do you think that—"

A second gust of wind rips Leo's voice past me and into nothingness.

The empty swings jump and twist, and then Leo's swing careens sideways and crashes into mine. My teeth knock together at the impact.

"Is this a tornado?" he shouts.

"I don't know!" I've heard of invisible tornadoes, but this time the air is all blowing in one direction, not swirling in a funnel. Another chair rams into the back of my seat.

Again, the wind blows for longer than wind is supposed to blow, and then, just like that, it stops abruptly.

"Are you okay?" Leo calls out.

"I think so." I swallow down a whimper.

"Oh shit," he says.

"What?"

"Uh . . . it's probably nothing."

I stop squeezing my eyes shut long enough to glare at him. "Leo! What's probably nothing?"

"It'll stop soon," Leo says.

"The wind?"

"No . . . the ride."

The *ride*?

My stomach drops.

"What do you mean?" I ask in a shaky voice. "Does someone have to be in the hut to turn this thing off?"

"I'm hoping not. It must be on a timer, right?"

The ground is fifteen feet below us. The panorama of Houston spins past as we go around and around and around. I'm not on the verge of panic anymore—I've gone over the edge to full-on freaking out.

"I'm gonna have to jump!" Leo shouts.

"What?! You are not jumping, Leo! No way."

"How else are we going to stop?" he asks.

"You'll break both your legs! Don't be an idiot!"

"If I can hang off the bottom of the swing, I can get at least six feet closer to the ground," Leo says.

I don't even know what he's talking about. But he's unclipping his safety bar and my stomach is flipping over. I bleat one last "Please, Leo, don't," but he's already out of his seat. He maneuvers down over the back of his chair, biceps straining. For two full carousel rotations, he just hangs there, legs dangling, his feet still a good nine feet from the ground.

I'm going to puke. I can't believe he's doing this.

Then he lets go. For a few heart-stopping seconds, it looks like he's going to be able to run it off, but he can't keep his balance. He trips and goes down face-first.

I twist in my seat.

"Leo!!"

The next time I glide past him, he's still on the ground, unmoving.

Oh my god, what was he thinking? There aren't any doctors or nurses or hospitals. I'm hyperventilating. What should I do?

But the next time I go around, he's moving. Picking himself up slowly, brushing off his clothes, rubbing his wrist.

"Are you okay?!" I shout, frantic.

"Uh, I'm good!" he shouts back.

I almost collapse in my chair as he disappears into the hut.

It takes forever for the ride to lower me. As soon as it stops, I bolt out of the chair and run over to him.

"That was so idiotic!" I yell, and then I'm touching him, checking his grass-stained arms for injuries, but he's in one piece. "I'm so sorry, Leo. I shouldn't have asked to go on this stupid carousel."

"What? Hey, no. We're fine. It was fun," he says.

Another gust of wind tackles us, blowing dirt into my eyes and up my nose. A metal menu board flies off a food truck, whizzing past my arm. I jump back—if that had been an inch closer the sharp edge would have sliced me.

"We need to get inside!" I say.

I grab his hand and we run to the nearest food truck, but the handle doesn't budge. *Think, Hannah.* The tour buses are too far away.

"Your car?" I shout. Leo nods.

We have to walk right into the wind. It's so strong, and I'm leaning so far forward that I can almost touch my fingertips to the ground. We fight through it in silence, and the moment the wind lets up, Leo stumbles at the sudden disappearance of resistance. I manage to stay up but only barely.

In the lull, everything is still again. Dead calm. We start flat-out running for the car.

When the next gust hits, there's a loud ripping noise. Behind Leo, something red and enormous looms.

"Holy crap!" he yelps.

It's the bouncy castle. The wind ripped it from its moorings, and now it's tumbling after us. The fabric swishes like some nylon monster, heavy and lethal. It's the size of a house. If we get trapped under it, we'll suffocate. It's so ridiculous I almost have to laugh. Death by bouncy castle.

"This is some messed-up Indiana Jones shit!" Leo shouts.

It's gaining on us. We dodge into an alley between two food trucks. My foot gets tangled in an orange extension cord, and I trip. For a moment, I'm falling, but then I land, still mostly upright, against something soft.

Oh. I've got Leo pinned up against the side of the food truck. His chest rises and falls quickly under mine, and we're both damp with sweat. And instead of focusing on my survival, my stupid brain can't think anything except: He doesn't feel anything like a dancer. He's warmer, broader, softer. When I'm dancing, my body feels like a tool or an instrument, and my partners' do too. Right now I just feel like Hannah. He just feels like Leo.

I'm about to push myself off him, mortified at being plastered against him from collarbone to knee, but his arms clutch protectively around me, pulling me farther into the gap between the food trucks.

Everything around us goes red. The sound of rubbing nylon gets loud as the bouncy castle presses up against the food trucks. It's freakish—like it knows where we are.

And then the wind nudges it along, and it billows past, down the main thoroughfare.

Once it's clear that we're safe, Leo loosens his arms.

I'm too stunned to move. Leo looks down at me and waggles his eyebrows. "As much as I'm enjoying this, maybe now's not the best time?"

How can he be cracking jokes at a time like this?

I peel myself off him, embarrassed.

We emerge from between the food trucks and watch as the bouncy castle, now a safe distance away, veers off course and snags on the corner of a Whac-A-Mole booth.

The wind dies as abruptly as it started.

In the lull, we make it to the car, fumbling with the handle on Leo's side before piling in. I slide across to my seat, and it feels like home base, like safety. Until I realize that the sun is too low.

It's almost at the horizon. Has time sped up?

At first I think I'm imagining it. I study the sky, and the darkness accelerates. It's not snap fast this time like the eclipse, but the quick fade is surreal and disorienting.

"Uh, Hannah? You know how I said I was okay after I jumped off the carousel? I'm . . . not totally sure I am."

I pull my eyes away from the sky and look at Leo. He twists in his seat and pulls his shirt up.

The skin on his stomach is so smooth it makes me gulp. His muscles flex as he lifts his arms, craning his neck to inspect the damage. There's so much skin, and just the right amount of hair, and oh god, he has a *happy trail*. The shadowy line starts at his navel and disappears under the four glinting silver buttons of his inappropriately low-riding jeans.

My cheeks burn. I should look away, or at least lift my gaze higher. When I do, I see the blood.

The scrape is a nasty red graze over his left rib cage, flecked with dirt and small bits of gravel.

Leo makes a strange noise. I flick my eyes up to his face. He's pale, his eyes squeezed shut.

"Uh, I'm not great with the sight of blood," he says. He doesn't look well at all.

I concentrate on the scrape, fighting the urge to let my eyes drift lower. What is it with him? I see half-naked dancer bodies all the time. The guys I dance with are always peeling off their sweat-soaked tops, and when they're in costume, that means their lower halves are usually only covered by a skintight layer of Lycra that leaves very little to the imagination. Leo's black jeans are positively proper in comparison.

Being hypnotized by a bit of exposed skin is another thing I don't need.

"Okay. I'll, um—take the gravel out." *Think, think. About bandages, not happy trails. NOT happy trails.* "Do you have a first aid kit in here?"

He shakes his head, eyes trained on the roof of the car. "Some napkins in the glove box, maybe."

I grab them. "I'm going to have to—" I make a weird helpless motion to warn him that I'm about to lean over his lap.

"It's okay, just get it over with."

I try not to breathe as I settle my elbow on his thigh. His candle-smoke smell is everywhere, earthy and alive and intoxicating.

I use my thumbnail to carefully pick out the pieces of gravel. One of them is large, embedded deep like an iceberg, and when it comes loose, a thin stream of blood trickles down his stomach. I press the napkins to it before I can think. My hand is so close to—

"What was that?" he asks. "Am I bleeding more?"

"You'll be fine. There's a cut underneath one of the pieces of gravel. Nothing a big Band-Aid can't fix." I'm lying a little. The cut is deep, maybe deep enough to need stitches, but we'll have to make do. I'm not a doctor.

Thankfully the bleeding doesn't last long.

"I can't keep pressing on this while you drive," I say.

"There might be some duct tape in the back seat," he says.

I rummage around and find a roll, taping a fresh wad of fast-food napkins over the wound. When I'm done, Leo blinks his eyes open and lets his shirt fall back over his stomach.

Outside, the wind strikes up again. It batters against the car, rocking it on its wheels. I'd almost forgotten about it. Happy trails will do that to you, apparently.

"I think we better go," Leo says, studying the skyline, the trees bending in the wind.

"Are you sure you're okay to drive?" I ask.

"Fit as a fiddle," he says. He's still a little gray.

"Stop if you need to and let me take over, okay?"

He nods.

It's still getting dark too fast. When we pull out of the parking lot, it looks like late evening, and by the time we get on the highway, it's full-on night.

We drive when there's no wind, in the silence between the gusts. When it blows, we stop, put Thunderchicken in neutral, and listen to it buffet at the roof and batter the windows and doors. We stay off the open highway, but down here in between buildings, things fly up and hit the windshield, leaving three spidering cracks.

My knuckles are white on the panic handle, and Leo holds the wheel at ten and two. I get the strongest urge to grab his hand, but he needs to focus on driving.

It took us twenty minutes to get to the festival, but it takes us an hour to get back to Grand Willows.

The intervals between the gusts have their own rhythms, and we can predict when we'll have to brake. I brace for the next one and Leo starts to slow down, but nothing comes.

We drive on through the stillness. A whole minute passes.

The sky is pitch-black now. The streetlights on the highway are bright and white, and we pass under them in stripes. Light, dark, light, dark. The clock on Thunderchicken's dashboard reads 5:24 p.m. Why is it so dark outside already?

"Do you think that's the last of the wind?" Leo asks.

"It seems like it."

There's a weird silence. We're both thinking the same thing: *What next?*

"Do you want me to take you to the bookstore?" he asks.

I swallow. "I guess. My car's still there."

What are we supposed to do when we get there? Do I climb into my mom's SUV and just drive away? Say *Hope to see you around sometime* and wave in the rearview mirror?

I can't say goodbye to Leo. It's not going to happen. Not after today.

We're the only two people in the city.

He starts to say, "Hannah—" at the same time that I blurt out, "Do you want to come to my house?"

I flush. "I have a spare bedroom," I add hastily, tripping all over my words. "I'm not— I've never asked a guy to come back to my place before. I don't want to—" *Shut up, Hannah.*

Leo pries one hand off the wheel and pats my leg.

"Hannah. Going to my house alone does not sound appealing. Your spare bedroom sounds awesome. Tell me where to go."

Leo

Hannah directs me to her house as I guide Thunderchicken through the neighborhood. I tap my fingers on the steering wheel, drumming out a nervous rhythm. The sky is black and the streets are deserted, full of a four a.m. kind of anticipation. That's the quietest time for a city—the partiers have gone to bed but the suits aren't up yet for rush hour.

But it's not four in the morning—it's six p.m.

Cars are parked on the side of the roads and most houses have their porch lights on, but nothing moves except for us. My spine is almost as straight as Hannah's as I keep my eyes trained on the shadows at the edges of the sidewalks. I'm checking my rearview mirror like someone on the run.

"Did anything like this happen to you before today?" she asks.

"No. You?"

"No."

I want to crank up some music, but that's not going to be enough to distract me now anyway.

"My street's the next one on the right," Hannah says.

I turn onto it and slow to a crawl. We go to the same school, so I should have realized we both lived in Grand Willows. How have we been orbiting each other our whole lives and only seen each other a handful of times at school? I don't remember her from middle school or elementary, but we go to huge Texas public schools and it's possible I missed her.

I know the streets. I've lived in Grand Willows my whole life. It's a nest of overgrown trees and disintegrating antique shops, a soft, rotten pit in the metallic sprawl of Houston. We have a termite problem, so half the houses in the neighborhood are about to fall apart and the other half already have. There's always a shiny new build going up somewhere, on the rubble of a razed termite house. I like the variety, though. Other parts of town are all divided up, but Grand Willows is a mix of broke-down and shiny.

"Which house is yours?" I ask.

"That one there," she says, pointing.

I pull up outside a termite house. It's short and squat, with an ivy-covered chimney and orange front steps. I bet the screen door screeches. It doesn't look like Hannah at all.

"Not this one. The next one," she says.

I take my foot off the brake and let Thunderchicken roll forward.

Okay . . . this is probably why we never met. Because this house is one of the sell-out new builds. And not just a reasonable, updated version of what was there before—it has *columns*. It's an ice palace, regal and white, looming against the darkness of the night sky.

"Wow," I say. "It's so . . . symmetrical."

She slides down in the seat a fraction of an inch. "I know. It's ridiculous."

"I mean . . . are those Greek columns?"

"Just wait till you see inside," she mumbles. "Last month my mom came home with *actual* marble busts for the alcoves in the hallway."

"No way, seriously? What do your parents do?"

"My dad works in finance," she says, skirting the question.

"Hey, so does mine! Well, if being a sleazy pawnshop owner counts as finance."

"Oh. Um. My dad is a little more corporate."

There's suddenly something between us that feels sharp and gritty. If we'd known about each other's dads' jobs sooner, would all our interactions so far have been different?

"You can park in the driveway if you want," Hannah adds.

"Oh, you mean this grandiose circular carriageway? I feel like I should have a team of horses and some footmen," I deadpan.

She elbows me. "All right, that's enough. It's not *that* big."

She's right—my house is about the same size. Only mine looks like a crumbling haunted house and hers is a brand-new McMansion.

I pull Thunderchicken up to the front door and give her steering wheel a little pat. *It's okay, T-Chick, you're beautiful. You deserve to be here.*

It's pretty clear that Hannah and I come from different backgrounds. I mean, I knew she wasn't poor, her clothes and stuff were proof of that, but this is . . . more than I expected.

I shake off the annoyance rising in me. Money doesn't matter when you're dead, right? Maybe her parents are crappy too. Having money doesn't automatically mean you have nice parents, just like being poor doesn't automatically mean you have crappy ones. Too bad I got the short end of the stick with both.

Hannah slides out across the seat after me. I grab the acoustic I stole from the guitar shop, and we walk to her front door in silence. The uplights on the Greek columns cast sinister shadows. Hannah punches a code into an electronic keypad, and then we're inside.

The foyer is a pristine icebox with stupidly high ceilings. I think of my termite-ridden house with its missing shingles and shitty air-conditioning, about the broken gate that I have to climb over to get into the yard. I feel a little sick. Even if my mom had the desire to keep it in good shape, where would the money come from?

Being indoors makes me feel penned-in and jittery, like a hundred squirrels are running around inside my body. I've been out every day, driving around and breaking into places, because holing up in a house means I might have to actually think about what's going on. Maybe Hannah has some good movies or at least a piano to mess around on. Or—ooh—maybe her corporate dad has some off-limits alcohol locked in a cupboard somewhere.

I spin around in the foyer but stop dead when I see her face. She looks shaky, like she's about to fall apart.

My first instinct is to look for the nearest exit.

But she asked me before if I was okay, so I think . . . it's my turn.

"Do you . . . need anything?" I ask. The words are hard to get out and feel strange in my mouth. Hopefully she'll just say no.

"I think—I might just need some tea," she says.

Tea? Not exactly whiskey, but it's easier than whatever request I was bracing myself for.

"I usually have chamomile before bed," she says. Tiredness has scratched her voice low and raw, and it's gorgeous to listen to. "When I was little, I had a serious nightmare problem—like every night for years—and tea helped a little. Well, that and dancing until I dropped. Do you want some too?"

"Uh, sure," I say, and it feels like another offering, another small comfort to help me get through this.

She's . . . *caring* for me. It makes my throat feel lumpy and thick.

I follow her to the kitchen in an awkward daze.

It's spotless, all marble counters, but by the light of one low lamp, it's kind of cozy. I lean onto the island and try to pluck a grape from a bowl overloaded with fruit, but it's fake. All of it's fake. God, rich people are weird.

Watching Hannah as she moves purposefully around the kitchen helps my jitters a little. She heats some water in a kettle that actually whistles and sets two teabags into flower-patterned mugs.

She pours my cup first and hands it to me. My fingers cover hers for a moment, and I can't help but think of the drinks we've passed between each other today. The Dr Pepper, the coffee, the tea. Small comforts that seem to come at the exact right time.

I take a sip of tea, and somehow, it's better than whiskey. It's exactly what I needed. It doesn't seem like anybody ever gets what I need—including me.

The tea tastes like flowers and laundry detergent, but I kind of like it. It warms me up from the inside. The jittering stops, and I suddenly feel really chill and grounded.

The last time I felt like this was when I accidentally moved into Asher's house for three weeks when we were fifteen. It started out as a sleepover, or whatever you call it when you pass out in your best friend's bathtub after an epic concert, but I stayed the whole next day. And the next. Asher's mom made us breakfast every morning when she got home from her night shift, and his dad made us dinner when he got home from his nine-to-five. We ate at the same time every day, and we had to be home by nine on school nights, eleven on weekends. I thought I'd hate it, all that structure, but I didn't.

Of course I went and screwed it up, but while it lasted, it was great. I kept waiting for Mrs. Rosenberg to tell me it was time to go home. She finally did, one night when Asher and I got stuck at a venue on the other side of town without a ride home. When we snuck into the house at midnight, his mom gave me A Talk. I didn't catch all of it, but it went something like this:

> *We can't support another child*
> *bad influence   very fond of you*
> *another mouth to feed*
> *especially if they're making bad decisions.*

She said I could stay until morning, but I left right away. I took my pile of clean, folded laundry home to a kitchen full of dirty dishes. Joe—my little brother who was twelve at the time—was home alone, playing video games and eating ice cream. My mom came home an hour later, her smudged lipstick hiding an impish grin, and my sister, Gemini, who was seventeen then, stumbled in an hour after that. My mom didn't say anything about curfews, because we didn't have any. Still don't.

I lean a hip against Hannah's marble countertop as we sip our teas in silence. Usually I can't handle not talking. It's why I like to be in big groups most of the time. But this silence isn't tense or weird. I feel . . . okay. I don't need to turn on the giant TV in the corner or fire up my playlists. It's so calm and quiet that I almost feel like humming, "I'm easy like Sunday morning."

Maybe this is why she's been hiding at her house. Maybe there's a better way to cope with this stupid emptiness than wheeling around the city like a maniac.

After a while, I meander over to a shelf with a bunch of framed pictures. I grab a frame studded with red and green jewels. "Oh. My. God. Is that you?"

She sighs and comes to stand beside me. "Yep."

In the photo, she's on a wide stage framed by an ornate red curtain. She's wearing a flouncy lavender dress with about a hundred layers of frilly lace. Her hair is a mass of glossy ringlets, a lighter shade of brown than her hair is now.

The photographer caught her midleap, holding a weird doll high in the air. Her legs are perfectly level like she's doing a split—only she's hovering four feet off the ground.

"I knew you were a ballet chick, but this is badass! What show is this?"

"*The Nutcracker.* I played Clara for the South Texas City Ballet."

Hannah picks up another photo, and I move behind her to get a better view. Oops. Big mistake. Her body is just millimeters away from mine, and my chin is so close to her neck I want to lean down and . . .

I close my eyes, gathering the strength to step to the side, but she moves at the same time and I end up bumping against her. For a split second, her whole back is pressed against my whole front. Electricity surges through me.

I set her aside gently, but my palms burn where I've touched her. I'm buzzing.

If I'm not careful, I'm going to get hooked on this feeling. Like I always do when there's something new and beautiful to touch.

Maybe it wouldn't do any harm if we became the sort of end-of-the-world companions who make out every now and then.

Nope.

Nope, nope, nope. I clearly need to be reminded that it would be a very, very, very bad idea.

Every hookup I've ever had has ended in flames. There's always a lot of tears from them, and total confused bewilderment from me.

110

I still can't tell you what I did wrong. I just always seem to fall short of the mark.

So no matter how good it would feel to give in and turn my charm onto full beam and take this from friends to friends who maybe *kiss*, I CANNOT go there.

I take another step away, putting lots of cold air between our bodies. I focus on the next frame. In this photo, the girl next to Hannah has bright red hair tied up with a black bandanna.

"That's Astrid," Hannah says. "My best friend."

I recognize her from school. "The English chick, right? She seems cool. She's not a dancer, though, is she?"

"God no. She kind of doesn't know what she wants to do with her life."

"Well, who does, really?"

Hannah shrugs, but I can tell she doesn't agree with me. She's the kind of girl who has a plan.

"Astrid's amazing. And loud. You'd like her."

I raise an eyebrow. "Hannah, are you implying that I'm *loud*?"

She flushes with embarrassment, so I let her off the hook with a wink—*Oh, for fuck's sake, stop winking at her*—and pick up another picture.

This photo is of her and her parents. She must be about ten. Her mom is all haughty and angular-looking. Her hair is slicked up into a bun just like little ten-year-old Hannah's, even though they're on a beach. Now I know where Hannah gets her long neck.

Her dad looks cool. His dark hair is wavy and chin-length, and he's one of those guys who has a perpetual five-o'clock shadow. Sadly, I'm not one of those guys. His nose is exactly the same as Hannah's, and his smile is huge and warm.

"What's that thing you're holding?" I squint at the photo. It looks like a big matted ball of hair, almost as big as Hannah's head.

"Um. It's a stuffed sloth. He's named David Lee Sloth."

"Come again?"

"It's my stuffed animal," she says, blushing ferociously.

"Wait . . . is he seriously named after David Lee Roth? As in the lead singer of epic eighties hair band Van Halen and one of my top-five rock-god idols?"

"Like I said. My dad loves classic rock."

"Your dad and I would so get along."

Not sure about her mom, though. She looks a little snobby. I'm not the kind of guy moms want their daughters running around with. Yet another reason why I've got to shake off this urge to get closer to Hannah. We'd never work. Humans want to think we've come a long way since the Victorians raised their noses at the lower classes, but we haven't. People like Hannah's mom don't understand that some people will be poor no matter how hard they work—like Asher's parents.

Hannah takes the family photo and puts it facedown. "No more photos tonight, please."

Oh, right. She's probably missing them. I wonder how I'd feel looking at pictures like this. Not that there are any in our house. My mom's not the type to have kitschy scrapbooks of our baby years. I'm lucky to have a few grainy cell phone pics of my first steps or my first day of kindergarten, and Joe has even less. The only thing on our walls is peeling wallpaper.

Hannah pads over to the kitchen table and takes an oversized cardigan off the back of a chair. It's the definition of cozy, fluffy with stripes of rose and cream, but there's a sense of familiarity when she slides it on.

I'm sure I've seen her wearing it before.

I cock my head. "Were you wearing that earlier? At the bookstore?"

She shakes her head no. I don't know why I asked. I know she wasn't. She's been in her leotard thing all day.

"Why?" she asks.

"It looks familiar. I must have seen you wearing it at school or something."

"I got it for my birthday a few weeks ago. I haven't worn it to school yet."

I'm more disturbed by this fact than I should be. I can't pinpoint why. I just know that I've seen it, and I don't understand how.

I take another hot gulp of tea to wash away the weird feeling.

Suddenly I realize that I'm *starving*. "Do you have any snacks?" I ask.

"Oh, sorry! We should eat something. Yes." She beckons for me to follow her. "Help yourself, there's stuff in the pantry—"

Her words cut off as soon as she realizes she shouldn't have opened the pantry door. She tries to hastily close it, but I grab her hand in a silent *wait—I want to see.*

The door is covered with neatly arranged Post-it Notes. At first I think it's a crazy wall, but there aren't any crisscrossing red strings or creepy newspaper articles. Each one has a single idea written on it:

Evacuation. Ghost. Zombies. Nuclear fallout. Hurricane. Dreaming. Virtual reality. Aliens. Rapture.

We just stand there, frozen, staring at the words. I'd almost forgotten the emptiness outside her house. The seriousness of the situation looms up every now and then, hollowing me out, dropping dread through me.

"Are these your theories about what's going on?"

Hannah nods.

I study the Post-its. There's one at the very top, above all the rest, four letters written in neat block capitals.

DEAD.

I dredge up a smile. "You said we weren't dead."

She shrugs. "I don't *feel* like we are, but maybe it makes the most sense. Actually, after the wind . . ." She steps forward and takes *Evacuation* and *Hurricane* and moves them up to the top. "Maybe we really did get left behind. Someone will figure it out soon and come back for us."

It's been five days, so that seems unlikely, but I don't want to be a bummer and say that out loud.

She chews on her thumbnail. "I get a little messed up if I think too much about what's happening, so I only let myself look at this for fifteen minutes right after breakfast. I guess I felt like I should do something. Like I should be thinking about it all the time and trying to figure it out. But it's stupid, I shouldn't have made it. It gets me worked up every time I look at it. My thoughts start spiraling."

This creepy little collection of Post-it Notes means she's more shaken than she's letting on. I could sense it, sort of, the tight coil of something under the surface, hidden beneath all her ballet poise and her perfect hair.

"Okay," I say.

"Okay?"

"We'll think about it after breakfast tomorrow, right?"

"Right." She gives me a tiny twang of a smile, just a high faint note on the E string.

"I think I'm done with my tea," I say, helplessly, all trace of hunger gone. The word *dead* fills up my stomach better than food ever could.

We start walking toward the sink at the same time. My hip bumps against hers, and her cardigan slips off her shoulder. Before I can stop myself, I'm pulling it up for her, and my fingertips glide along the perfect curve of her shoulder. She shivers, and we both freeze.

The corner of her mouth quirks up, soft and sad. Everything about her looks soft.

"You know, you're different than I thought you'd be," she says.

Now that it's late, her voice is like smoke, velvety and low. I'm not going to lie, it's doing something to me.

"Right back atcha, Ballet Chick," I say quietly.

And then she looks up at me with misty, grateful eyes, and I know I'm in trouble.

I stiffen. This is bad.

She's getting attached to me. This has happened before. Those other times, those other girls, I thought things were casual, just FeelGood fun, and no matter how hard I tried, I couldn't dredge up anything more for them. They accused me of leading them on, of treating them like emotionless hookups, all sorts of things.

I've got to shut this down.

"Hey, don't get attached to me, okay?" I mean for it to sound jokey, but it comes out harsher than I wanted it to.

She takes the smallest step back.

"I'm like a pathological flirt," I continue, "so don't read into anything, okay? My friends say I'll flirt with anything with a pulse."

She inhales sharply, hurt flashing across her face. She takes my mug and goes to the sink, keeping her back to me.

"I think everything's already set up in the spare room," she says briskly. "My mom likes to be prepared. I'll get you some bandages for your cut."

Oh. Right. I slide a hand over my ribs and the duct tape tugs on my skin. I'm going to have to deal with it before I get some sort of infection.

I groan. Asking Hannah to help me with that now is impossible.

We trudge upstairs in a cloud of awkwardness, and she opens the first door in a whole hallway of them.

The guest room is like something out of a catalog, all cream and ivory, expensive headboard and textured wallpaper. I'm going to get it dirty just by being in it.

"There are towels in the bathroom," Hannah says crisply. "I think the remote for the TV is in the bedside table drawer. Hope you sleep okay."

She won't meet my eyes, and it's making me ache. I've screwed everything up. She turns to go.

"Wait, Hannah—what time do you usually get up?"

"I've been setting my alarm for six thirty."

"Riiiight . . . why?"

"That's what time I usually get up for school."

This girl is a piece of work.

"Hannah. There's no school in the afterlife."

"I know, I know. But I need to do barre and stuff, so . . ."

"Well, I'm not going to set my alarm, but wake me up if you need me, okay?"

"Okay. Good night," she says.

"Night."

Everything in me is gasping to say, *I'm sorry, I didn't mean it*, but she's gone.

I close the door. My jaw is tense and burning with prickly heat. I feel weird inside, like something's squirming around in me. What the hell's wrong with me?

I flop onto the enormous and very clean-smelling bed. It has about fifty decorative pillows on it. The cool air conditioner hums, and the lamps glow. There's a boring but pretty painting of a lake on the opposite wall, and my throat is still warm from the tea.

I rub shaky hands over my face. I wish I hadn't shut her down. Everything was so . . . I had to do it, though, right? If I'd let her carry on looking at me like that, like I was some sort of person worth getting attached to, we wouldn't be in separate rooms right now.

The chemistry is intense. There's no denying it. But we can't act on it. We can't let these looks and touches become more, because I've never hooked up with someone and had it not turn into a giant mess.

There's a Leo Sterling formula to dating. Here's what will happen: It will be amazing in the beginning. Like can't-keep-my-hands-off-her amazing. Maybe even better with Hannah than it's ever been before, based on how every time she touches me it's like getting drunk.

But eventually I'll fall short of her expectations. With the other girls, it always started with a small sadness. They'd want to slap a label on us, which I sometimes reluctantly agreed to, or a declaration I couldn't give them. It would turn into a crack that ruined their self-esteem, and before long, it'd be an outright disaster, them sobbing, *You led me on* and *Why can't you give a shit about anyone but yourself?*

I've been with a lot of girls, but I've never told anyone I loved them.

118

Because I haven't. It never seems to go deeper than the FeelGood for me. Makes it kind of hard to write love songs.

Hannah's the only other person in the city. If that happens with us, Hannah will leave, and I'll be alone again.

I can't lose her.

Being alone—it's like death to me. Before Hannah found me . . . I was barely here. I need other people around me or I start going nuts.

So no matter how enticing she looks or smells or moves, I can't act on it. I just can't. It will bring whatever this fragile thing is between us tumbling down over our heads.

I grab a pillow and shove it over my face to stifle my groan.

Starting tomorrow, I've got to start doing a better job of not thinking about touching her. No flirting. No seducing.

We have to be Just Friends.

It's a new tactic for me, but I've got to try it.

I peel my shirt off and miserably start to pick at the edge of the duct tape.

Hannah

I'm such an idiot. Such a pathetic, stupid idiot. Leo's shutdown stings in my throat like the worst kind of heartburn. *Don't get attached to me.*

Why does he have to be so charming and smiley and UGH.

I throw myself down on my bed. The worst part is that I knew this would happen. I was prepared, I had my shields up, and he battered through them so easily.

I can't believe I thought he might like me too.

I'm suddenly exhausted. I need to get up and brush my teeth.

It feels weird being in my bedroom knowing that Leo's the only other person in the house. I know he can't see through the walls, but I try to brush without getting a toothpaste mustache, and I change into my pajamas with my closet door closed. He's a whole room away, and I'm still aware of him.

I pull one of my mom's old warm-up tops over my head, and for a second, it feels like she's here.

When I climb onto the white four-poster bed I've had since I was three, I start to feel a little better. My room is the only place I let my imagination peek out. Everyone assumes it will be all neat and pink, with cartoony ballet shoes everywhere. Instead, it's a den of fairy-forest magic, strung with fake ivy garlands and Christmas lights. A gauzy mosquito net curtain makes my bed feel like an elven bower.

Once I'm snuggled under the covers, I plug my phone in and start an email to my dad. I've written him one every day. He'd love to hear about SpandexFest and the tour bus and Galaxe. Maybe I won't tell him about almost getting killed by objects flying in the wind.

I hit send and click my phone off. I try to shift into the mood for sleep, but my mind refuses to settle. I grab David Lee Sloth and pull him tight to my chest.

Even though I know better, I can't stop thinking about how it felt when Leo pulled my cardigan up on my shoulder in the kitchen.

I'm trained to be exquisitely aware of my body. I know how every muscle links with the next and how to move them, like my body is one long bowstring that can pluck itself. When he touched my shoulder, though, everything was all over the place. The bunch-and-release feeling under my ribs had to be a muscle contraction, but it made no sense—I didn't tell anything to flex. Words and looks shouldn't be able to make things in another person *move*.

It's surreal that it's been less than twelve hours since I saw Leo in the music store. My body is humming, the way it does when I nail a double pirouette, and it's been like this all afternoon. For a little while, Leo distracted me from the weirdness of this world with no people. I should be focusing on where everyone went, not thinking about his smile when we topped eighty in Thunderchicken. The warm brush of his arm when we were sitting on the edge of the stage downtown. How animated he got when he was talking about writing music.

That reminds me—that book I wrote in fifth grade. *Flower Magic*. Before today, I hadn't thought about it in years. Now I'm desperate to see if it's as ridiculous as I remember it.

After *Flower Magic*, I didn't stop writing altogether—but I did stop showing people what I'd written. There are other stories, hidden in summer notebooks at my grandma's house.

And then I did stop writing altogether. Freshman year. When I started training at the Academy.

I slip out of bed, shivering in the air-conditioned cold, and cross over to my bookshelf. I reach behind the alphabetized paperbacks, my fingertips stretching for the book I threw behind them seven years ago in a fit of ashamed anger.

There—I feel an edge. I fish it out.

The corner is bent from when my mom shoved it into her glove box, and there's an oily stain on the cover. The glue in the binding is crispy now, crackling in a dozen places when I open it.

I lean back against the wall and start reading.

It doesn't take long. When I'm done, there's a tiny kernel of pride glowing inside me. It's actually not bad for a ten-year-old.

The thought makes me brave. Strings of words have been hovering around me all day. Simple descriptions of the things I saw at the abandoned carnival, echoes of the words Leo and I spoke out loud, things his songs made me think about. They've been circling all afternoon, nudging into my thoughts.

I reach over to my desk for a spiral notebook.

In the moonlight, I pull the words out of the air and write them down.

With Leo in the house, I sleep hard enough to dream.

In my dream, I'm riding in Thunderchicken, but in that vague way that dreams have, sometimes I'm gliding like a ghost with no car around me. The streets of downtown Houston slide under my feet in stripes of gray and orange.

I pass under the same set of traffic lights again and again. Each time I go through the intersection, the lights change from green to yellow to red. Green, yellow, red. Green, yellow, red.

Normally my dreams are a reel of unrelated scenes that wheel around drunkenly in my head, but every now and then something comes into sharp focus. A bleed-through from the real world. Most of the time it's pain, like if my arm goes numb in bed, in the dream I'll be dipping it in a shimmering fairy pool of acid. This time, it's the soft, slow stroke of a finger from the middle of my forehead down to the tip of my nose. Over and over.

Right now, I'm convinced that someone's stroking my nose *outside* of the dream.

Could it be my mom? She used to do that. The first time I was aware of it was after I fell during an Academy performance of *Giselle*. I landed wrong coming down from a grand jeté. It was a showstopper—the stage manager had to scramble her crew and fly in the grand drape and everything. She made an announcement on the god mic to the audience that we'd be resuming in ten minutes due to "unforeseen circumstances." As if two thousand people hadn't seen me crumple into a heap on the floor.

Someone else's mom might have had to wait in the audience, wringing their hands, but Eliza Ashton tore through the pass door and into the darkness of backstage. Through the fog of pain, I heard her shoes clattering toward me, and then she was settling my head on her lap. The company manager and the stage manager were huddled over me, and the physio guy was down by my feet, cutting the ribbons off my pointe shoe and carefully testing my ankle.

The pain was awful, and I was so scared. Ballet was all I knew how to do. I would have fallen apart if my mom hadn't been there, asking the questions that needed asking, barking for more ice.

They moved me to a dressing room, and Gabriella changed into her copy of the Giselle costume and finished the show. While we waited for my dad to get the car and take us to the hospital for X-rays, Mom never let go. As my sniffles morphed into hiccups, she started running her finger down my nose, over and over. I closed my eyes at last and fought for breath.

"I used to do this when you were a baby," she whispered. "It was the only way I could get you to sleep in your crib." I saw a photo once, of her long fingers curved around my tiny ear, her thumb on the tip of my nose.

"You're going to be just fine," she said.

She must have been terrified. Her own career ended when she went down in the middle of a run of *Madame Butterfly*. She ripped her Achilles like a sheet of paper, and she never recovered. But she just kept on stroking my nose.

My ankle turned out to be fine, and I was dancing again two weeks later. My fall wasn't a career ender like hers.

No one else has ever stroked my nose like this. My mom must be here. I'm sure of it. I just need to wake up. I climb out from under the rubble of the dream, but when I open my eyes, my room is blue with moonlight. It's silent. Even the air-conditioning has clicked off.

"Mama?" I whisper.

My room is empty, and my clock reads 4:53 a.m. I rub my nose. There's no one here, but there's an ache in my chest that has me worrying my lungs are collapsing.

Could it have been Leo? I ease out of bed and sneak out into the hallway. I need to make sure he's still here, that the whole afternoon wasn't a dream.

The guest room door is ajar. I start to push it open, but then I notice that I can't feel the handle. My skin isn't registering the handle's smoothness, or its metallic coldness. Maybe I haven't fully woken up yet.

I nudge the door open anyway. Leo is facing away, twisted up in the sheets. He's not wearing a shirt, and his back is smooth and pale in the moonlight. He's breathing evenly, shoulders rising and falling. There's a single dark mole on his shoulder blade. It's almost unbearably intimate, seeing that, seeing him like this. A mix of embarrassment and fascination buzzes through me, flooding into my cheeks.

His tattoo is a spidery blur in the shadows. It's about the size of my palm. If I took a couple of steps forward—if I let the glow from the night-light in the hall spill in—I might finally find out exactly what it is.

Instead, I take a quiet step back. I close the door quickly, embarrassed that I've seen him in that private, sleep-warm state.

I need to focus. Leo's still here, so at least I know yesterday wasn't a dream.

But that means it wasn't my mom stroking my nose. She and my dad are still gone.

I retreat, zombie-walking back to my room. I close my door and start to shake.

This isn't normal.

Being the only two people in the city isn't normal.

After yesterday, I can't pretend the emptiness is just going to magically end. Finding Leo almost eclipsed the weirdness of being in a world with no people, but I can't ignore an *actual* eclipse. We saw the sky go black in the middle of the day, and the sun went down long before it was supposed to, and we almost got killed by a freak windstorm.

My thoughts swarm on me, and I almost crumple to the floor.

No. Get up, Hannah.

I fling my bedroom door open. I make a break for it and run through the dark house, into the kitchen and down the flight of stairs to the ballet studio in my basement.

I need to shut my brain up. I need to dance.

Hannah

My heart thuds and my legs scream, but I force myself to do another set of sautés. I have to keep jumping. The effort of holding my arms in first position makes my teeth grind together, but I keep my fingers curved low by my hips. Entrechat, entrechat, entrechat. With each landing, I change the front foot: right, left, right, left. Every time my feet hit the floor, another thought shakes down out of my head. If I keep going, if I can just do a few more jumps, I'll shake the last of the thoughts out and my mind will be completely empty. I won't have to think about the dream, or the wind, or the eclipse, or the dark. I'll be too focused on the physical to think about the emptiness outside my front door.

I've been in my basement studio for four hours now. I knew Leo and I should have come back here yesterday instead of gallivanting across the city. It doesn't get dark at the wrong times when I'm here. The sun rose right on schedule this morning. There's a reason people do the things they're "supposed" to do. If you go around only doing things you want, you'll end up living in a cardboard box. Or get killed by high-speed winds while riding on an unsupervised swing carousel.

I push myself to do another set. *Jump, jump, jump.*

I wasted a whole day yesterday. I missed my afternoon barre routine, my evening yoga session, and my workout on the stationary bike.

My calves spasm and turn into spaghetti as I hit my physical limit. I double over and stumble to the barre for support. I think I'm going to throw up. The edges of my vision go dark.

Breathe. Breathe. Breathe.

I did more jumps than I normally do, but I shouldn't be on the verge of collapse. Missing those sessions must have thrown me off more than I realized.

The speakers keep pounding out a brisk, peppy beat. I drag myself over to the other side of the room and slide the fader down on the basement's built-in sound system until there's silence. I slide down against the mirrored wall. As the cold from the glass seeps into my spine, I let my shoulders slump and catch my breath.

I look around the converted basement that is now my professional-grade ballet studio. My mom had it installed after I got accepted into South Texas City Ballet's Upper School, when dance went from taking up about twelve hours a week to thirty. The room is stage-bright, flooded with a dozen inset spotlights. The floor is sprung, which means there's a layer of curved wooden strips underneath. When I land a jump, the whole floor moves with me to save my bones some shock. On one side of the studio, there's the requisite expanse of mirrors; on the other there's a smooth wooden barre bolted to the wall.

I thump my head against the mirror. Having a studio like this means there's even more riding on my corps de ballet audition tomorrow.

Tomorrow. The thought sends a sizzle of anxiety through me.

I need to push on. If by some miracle I get out of this mess in time for the audition, I have to nail it. When I come out of that studio sweating and nerve-wrung, I want to be able to tell my mom that I blew the competition out of the water. I want to see her beaming elation when I get a phone call from the artistic director and see her giddy scramble for a camera when the papers come in the mail and I sign the contract to join the corps de ballet.

If I'm not ready, if I'm out of shape—if all I get is an email with words like *regret* and *next year's audition* and *thank you for your interest in South Texas City Ballet* . . . I don't even want to imagine how she'll react to that.

I lurch up from the floor and flick through the songs on my phone to find the one for my audition piece. I'll cool down for a few minutes and then work through it. I also need to change my shoes—I did this session in flats. I peel off the floppy canvas shoes and wiggle my toes.

I freeze when I hear the faint, ghostly sound of someone calling my name.

For a moment, it's the music store all over again, but then I remember that Leo's upstairs.

"Hannah?" His voice is muffled by the walls, but it's definitely Leo.

I go over to the base of the stairs and shout, "Down here!"

I steel myself. I head back to the stereo as he comes down. He stops in the doorway, shaking his hair out of his eyes. He gives me a lopsided smile. Attraction slices through me. He's wearing the same black jeans from yesterday, but now they're paired with a black Aerosmith T-shirt. He must have had it in his car. Like everything else he owns, the cloth is worn and soft and makes me want to snuggle him.

The fizzy, on-edge feeling I had all day yesterday comes rushing back. Suddenly I feel like I could do a million more pirouettes, like food and sleep are things I'll never need again. When he's around, I'm a live wire, a constant pulsing drip of adrenaline in human form.

I reinforce my shields. I don't need a repeat of *Don't get attached to me*.

"I got a little freaked out when I couldn't find you," Leo says, scrubbing his hand through his hair. I'm a little annoyed at how good it looks after a night of sleeping on it. Leo with bedhead is the kind of look pop stars pay their hairdressers ridiculous money for.

He comes into the room and spins in a circle. "Wow. I was not expecting this. I think most people have dingy horror basements full of cinder blocks and spiders."

His eyes are puffy from sleep, but his smile is already full-power.

"How long have you been up?" he asks.

"A while. I had a bad dream, so I came down here. I'm almost done, I just want to run through my audition piece."

"Neat. Do you mind if I watch?"

I hide my bare feet. "I guess not. I just need to put on some shoes first."

Leo heads for the five pairs of pointe shoes hanging from hooks on the far wall, spaced wide like a gallery installation.

"Cool, cool," he says. "Which ones do you want?"

"I don't dance in those. They're my mom's."

"Oh. Your mom's a ballerina too?"

"Ha. Much more of one than I am."

In the corner, I dig around in my duffel bag for my current favorite pair of pointe shoes. I have about five pairs in the rotation. I don't want Leo to see my feet, but he's not paying attention to me. He's enchanted by the shoes on the wall. I hastily wedge my toe spacers in and bind my two smallest toes together with medical tape.

"Am I allowed to ask why your mom's shoes are on the wall? Is that a thing dancers do?" he asks.

"No, it's not a thing. She doesn't dance anymore, so I guess they're like a shrine to her old life." I recite the significance of each pair for him. "The smallest ones were her first pair. She was five when she started, ten when she went on pointe. Then there's the pair from her first standing ovation, the first time onstage at the Kennedy Center, the first time she guested in Europe, and the night my dad proposed." They met after he got promoted at work and joined South Texas City Ballet's board of directors.

"So she's a big deal, huh? Have I heard of her?" Leo asks.

"Probably not, unless you're into ballet. Her name is Eliza Ashton."

"Nope."

"Who *have* you heard of? Baryshnikov?"

"Yeah, and um, Olga someone? Or Natalya? No, that's a Bond girl. Yeah, never mind."

I finish winding the silk ribbon around my ankle, tying a serious double knot and tucking it into the hollow near my anklebone. I smack my other shoe on the floor, whacking the toe end on the wood.

"What are you doing?" Leo asks over the ruckus.

"Tenderizing," I call back. Brand-new pointe shoes are shiny and beautiful, but they're undanceable. This pair has gone through hell—I used a heavy-duty wire cutter to split the shank, poured hard-drying shellac in them when they were too soft, hammered them when they were too stiff, and used a Zippo lighter to burn anything that frayed. Hours in the studio have rubbed all the shiny pink satin off the end of the shoe, so when I'm on the box, I'm dancing on dingy gray canvas.

Finally my shoes are on and ready, fitting like high-end bionic limbs. I rise up and shake each foot out in turn, making sure there aren't any gaps that my foot can slide around in. Leo can't take his eyes off my feet. I'm used to being watched now, but I can still remember being the one watching. My mom would take me to rehearsals to meet her friends. When they weren't dancing, the women would randomly rise up onto pointe. They stilted around like egrets in a marsh, poking the floor in a lazy rhythm as they hovered in front of my mom and me. They peered down at us with horribly slouched shoulders, their chicken-bone arms akimbo. But once they were dancing, their backs were straight and their form was perfect.

Up on my toes, my eyes are level with Leo's. At the barre, I do a quick series of tendus, dégagés, and rond de jambes. The muscle memory is so deep I can do them in my sleep. With a hush, the worn tip of my slipper slides in an arc across the polished wood floor. After that, I do a quick pirouette in the middle of the studio to test my center of gravity.

Leo leans against the mirror and crosses his arms. Dancing for him here feels way more intimate than that cardigan moment in the kitchen last night. There's something tight and humming in the room, all his attention focused so intensely on me. We're yards apart, but I feel like we're touching.

"So what will you be gracing your audience with today?" he asks.

"It's a variation from this thing called the grand pas classique."

"Sounds kind of . . . classic."

"Yeah. It's a standard audition piece. It's not the most exciting thing in the world."

"What's the most exciting thing?" he asks.

I think for a moment. "There's this random solo from STCB's production of *Madame Butterfly* that I really like."

Ironically it's the same dance my mom was doing right before she fell. We learned it at the Academy last year, and whenever I rehearsed with my mom, she cringed every time the song reached its crescendo.

"Can you show me that instead?" Leo asks.

I should really rehearse my audition piece. But the *Madame Butterfly* solo *is* more interesting. I scan through the music on my phone to find *P* for *Puccini*.

Leo comes over to check out the six-channel mixer that my phone's connected to. This time I preempt him. "Yes, I know, I'm spoiled."

But he surprises me. "It's only spoiled if it's more than you need. You've obviously worked up to needing this kind of stuff."

I hand the remote to Leo and take up position kneeling downstage right. All I see is the image of my mother's face in the YouTube video of her final performance. She stared out longingly over the audience, not knowing her career would end two minutes later. I nod at Leo, and he presses play.

There's a lead-in and then the boom of a sound-effect cannon. I'm not going to lay on all of the acting, but ballet isn't just about body movement and a good dancer never ignores the emotions behind the choreography. It suddenly strikes me that maybe I like this piece more because there's a story to tell. The grand pas classique, on the other hand, is just technical artistry.

I rise onto my toes, closing my mind to everything but the dance. The work. The noise. I love the sound of ballet up close. The clop of shoe meeting wood when my toes tap the floor, the shushing slap of a cabriole as the calf of my left leg brushes the shin of my right. The hard puffs of breath and the fast, sucking inhales right before the harder moves. I'm a better dancer because of my mom. Without her guidance, I'd be breathing at all the wrong times, leaving my muscles weak with lack of oxygen.

The music builds, strings layered on strings as the violins swell. At the end of the piece, I bourrée en pointe in a zigzag. It's my favorite part, even though it's hard to do. Your feet have to move so quickly, microscopic shifts that give the illusion of hovering. I waver to the far end of the room, then toward the door, back and forth, like a leaf floating to the ground.

It never fails to give me chills.

The dance finishes, and I drop down to my heels. Before I can ask, Leo fades the music down slowly. I wonder if pressing pause is a pet peeve of his as well. I've never liked shifting too abruptly back into the real world.

Sometimes he's so much like Astrid, but in this he isn't. She's seen me rehearse in this basement hundreds of times, and when she presses pause, the music cuts dead before the last note can ring through. Then she's up and cheering like I'm on a TV talent show.

I glance at the corner where she usually likes to spread out, and my chest goes tight. I miss her. I'm so used to seeing her there with a pile of chopped-up magazines and bright kid scissors and glue sticks, or homework strewn everywhere and her fire-engine-red hair pinned in perfect victory rolls.

Other than the heavy sound of my breathing, Leo and I are silent for a long time.

"Holy shit. You're really good," he says finally.

I shrug. I'm used to non-dancers being impressed with what I can do, but it feels different this time. The awe written all over Leo's face . . . does he only like me because I'm a ballerina? The thought makes me irritated and prickly.

Everyone thinks ballet is incredible. They romanticize it. I get it. And I get that I'm spoiled and ungrateful for not shouting about how much I love it from the rooftops.

"You're not smiling, though," Leo observes.

"Dancers don't really smile a whole lot," I say.

That's not strictly true. I see the professional company members smiling in rehearsals. Laughing, even. And the other dancers my age at the Academy smile—when they're not in the building.

"Really?" Leo asks. "That's depressing. But are you, like, smiling on the inside? Because that was amazing."

"I didn't mess anything up, so I feel okay, I guess. Why, how do you feel after you've performed?"

"Oh my god, so alive. Like I'm going to blast off into outer space. I also generally feel like puking up my guts. In a happy way. JoyPuke." He tilts his head thoughtfully. "I should trademark that."

Maybe I don't get that feeling because ballet is more physical. At the end of a piece, I'm exhausted and huffing and puffing. Closer to actual puke than JoyPuke. I think I've seen it on my classmates' faces, though. They don't smile in the studio because they can't let the ballet masters see if they're smugly pleased with their performance. We're all supposed to immediately berate ourselves for what we could have done better, but I see the brightness in their eyes. I think they were smiling on the inside. And my mom definitely was, in all the other YouTube videos where she didn't fall.

Once I join a company, I'll probably be smiling on the inside.

JoyPuking. Life is like a tricky pas de deux—if you do all the steps right, turn more fouettés, extend your leg a little higher, the audience will clap at the end. Even though I don't feel fulfilled right now, it'll happen, after I join a company. If not then, when I make soloist. It's what's supposed to happen, if I do everything right.

A thought strikes me.

Was it JoyPuke last night when I was crouched on the floor in my bedroom writing in my notebook?

Leo folds himself down to sit cross-legged on the floor next to me while I stretch out my muscles. I drape in half to touch my toes, folding so far over that I can rest my cheek on my shins. I always think of Astrid when I do this; she squeals at me until I stop, saying my stretchiness freaks her out.

When I come back up, Leo's ready with another question.

"So if you're not JoyPuking, what is it, then? Why do you dance?"

"I don't know. It's just what I do," I say. "Ballet Chick, remember?"

Leo rasies an eyebrow.

"It's like, mine and my mom's thing," I add.

She was there for every lesson, every rehearsal. My teachers let her come because most of them shared a stage with her twenty years ago.

My mom always stood on the other side of the studio windows, watching me with this . . . light. After class, she'd hold my hand on our way out to the car and gush about all the things I'd done right. I snuggled into her side, rooting out the smell of home that clung to her. Someone at school once asked me if ballerinas smell like French perfume and clouds. My mom smelled like oatmeal and leather and hairspray.

Something twists in my chest at the memory. I can see her face so clearly. When she smiles, the skin at the sides of her mouth pulls back like a stage curtain, a grand drape. When I was little, my fingers would always reach out to trace the lines. She served up demure ballerina smiles to everyone else, but my dad and I got the real ones, the ones that revealed her single twisted tooth, the one that got knocked in her childhood and will forever be a shade yellower than the others.

It's been six days now. Will I start to forget little details about her?

Leo leans his head back against the mirror and closes his eyes, and then he starts to hum.

It'd be rude to interrupt, so I sit awkwardly and listen to the melody he's working out. Sometimes he tweaks the repeating set of notes. Riffing. Composing. It's incredible to watch. His thumbs tap softly on his thighs, drumming, and his rings flash under the studio lights. The way his neck is tilted back makes his already obvious Adam's apple look more pronounced.

Suddenly he opens his eyes. They're crystal clear under the bright lights. More blue than gray. I feel caught.

"I need my guitar," he says, voice crackling like a fire that's about to die out. "Wait here a sec. I want to try something."

He disappears up the stairs. I pry myself off the floor and hike a leg onto the barre, dipping my supporting knee to stretch my hamstring while I wait. When Leo comes back, he's holding his guitar. He sits against the mirror again and starts playing the song he was humming.

"Try dancing to this," he says.

"What?"

"I just want to see what happens."

"I'm not a choreographer," I say.

"Just feel it. Do what you want. Loosen up."

He plays the same intro pattern over and over, staring at me expectantly. Well, goal of the day achieved, because my mind is totally blank now. Like a deer caught in headlights. I poke a foot out and grind the box of my shoe on the floor.

After a while, I do a little adage combination, copying from the center work routine I do every day. It kind of fits. As I add movement to movement, linking steps, something magical happens. I start to add things that aren't in my classical ballet rep. Stuff from when I learned about modern dance masters like Martha Graham and Alvin Ailey. Some stuff that I'm sure I made up.

As I dance, Leo's music grows and shifts, evolving with me until it's soaring like the string section of an orchestra. I do a fierce run of chaînés, spinning, spinning, spinning from one end of the room to the other, and I hear a few bobby pins fly out of my hair and smack the wall. I start laughing and come out of the turns ungracefully. I bend over, my hands on my knees. It's not that funny, but I'm laughing like it's the funniest thing in the world.

Leo finishes playing with a flourish.

"Your *Madame Butterfly* thing was cool, but that was out of this world," he says, laughing too. "I especially liked the flying hair-thingies at the end there. Lethal."

I collapse next to him, still snickering. He beams at me, and then we're both cracking up. The emptiness has finally gotten to us. We're not laughing about the bobby pins anymore, it just feels like a release.

"That was fun," I admit, wiping tears from the corners of my eyes.

"It was fun watching you, Ballet Chick." Leo pushes himself up from the floor and walks over to the sound system. "All right, time for your classic grand thing."

I look at my bag in the corner. My audition is in twenty-four hours. I really should get back to work.

Should.

But I was working all morning and I was still thinking about the empty. Maybe dancing myself to death isn't the best idea.

"Actually . . . let's go upstairs," I say.

"What? Don't you need to practice more?"

"I can do it tonight."

If he's right—if we are dead—there might not even be an audition to attend. I can't let my thoughts snag on that, though, or it'll bring me plummeting down.

"You know what I kind of feel like?" I say.

"Hmm?"

"Eating one of the enormous stuffed-crust frozen pizzas from my freezer."

They're my dad's Friday night tradition. Sometimes I sidle up next to him and steal slices while he watches his rock documentaries.

Leo grins. "Pizza sounds awesome."

He fiddles around with the sound system while I take my pointe shoes off. On our way to the door, he bumps my shoulder again. This time I bump back, making him veer off course. We smile at each other, and it would feel comical and cheesy except I'm getting that bunch-release thing again.

And then, out of nowhere, Leo stops walking, puts an arm around me, and pulls me into a hug.

He crushes my ribs in the loop of his arms, and my face smashes against the cotton of his T-shirt. What little air I can breathe smells of him so intensely that it makes my head swirl, like I've just swum a whole lap underwater.

He's so warm. I let my arms tighten around his waist. He lowers his face into my neck. I hold very still, marveling at heat gathering there as he breathes, at the heaviness of the arms tight around me. Why is he doing this? Yesterday he was recoiling from me, and now he's playing songs for me, looking at me like I'm all the light in the world, *hugging* me.

"Hey, are we okay?" he asks.

I'm glad he can't see my face. "Yeah, of course."

"So . . . friends?"

"Sure. Friends."

Maybe he thinks this is how friends hug?

I'm about to faint. Because he's shattered through my shields, *again*. This is the first time touching someone has met my expectations. Exceeded them. I think of the books on my shelf upstairs, the ones *Flower Magic* was stuffed behind. The ones with hearts in the margins, the ones with dog-eared corners and highlighted passages. The sentences and scenes that shaped my idea of relationships are all gathered there. An accidental first kiss when danger gave the characters courage. The slightest touch that had the power to shut down or wake up a whole body. I was starting to worry that this feeling was fiction. That nothing would live up to the daydream.

Finally Leo steps away. He blinks. I blink back.

He clears his throat. "Right. Pizza."

"Pizza," I repeat.

I wave at the stairs in a silent *after you*. My fingers fumble as I try to find the light switch. The ballet studio plunges into darkness, and I climb up after him.

Leo

Okay, so I am SUCKING at the whole "just friends" thing.

I could kick myself. What the hell was that hug?

I shake my head. This girl, seriously. What is it about her? She was just so . . . ethereal when she was dancing. And after her butterfly dance, when she was sitting next to me against the mirror, flushed and loose, she suddenly leaned forward into some contortionist circus act of a cool-down stretch. I wanted to brush my fingers along the ridged path of her spine, every vertebra so delicate and perfectly aligned. I couldn't breathe.

The back of her neck was so soft-looking, dewy from the exercise, and a few wisps of hair had escaped from her crispy hairdo thing. What would she look like with her hair down? I'm aching to see it, spread out over a pillow, twined through my fingers.

Restraint, Leo. Just friends. No flirting.

AKA STOP FUCKING THINKING LIKE THIS.

Okay. It's pretty clear my plan is not working. Whatever's making me *insane* about her didn't magically disappear overnight.

I try to get myself back under control as we climb the stairs to the kitchen, suddenly very glad she's behind me so she can't see the blood rushing to my face—or to other, way-less-appropriate parts of me.

Hannah's halfway to the refrigerator when she suddenly stops, blinking like someone's shining something bright in her eyes.

"Leo, did you see that?" she asks, eyes locked on the window.

I turn to where she's looking. "See what?"

Her eyes are trained on her living room window. It's not raining, but the sky is freakishly dark, the sun obliterated by low, heavy clouds. One of Houston's torrential summer storms might be on the way. She strains forward, not breathing, not blinking.

Suddenly the grayness is broken by a blur of light, high up in the sky.

"There!" She rushes to the window. I follow her, and we cup our hands on the glass to get a better look.

The light is on the other side of the city, maybe farther. And it's moving. It's slow, but it's definitely moving, sweeping over the underbellies of the clouds. My eyes adjust to the dark, and I realize it's not a single patch of light—there's a whole beam. At first, it looks like it's coming straight down from the sky, but it tilts and moves constantly. Every few seconds, it turns straight toward us, flaring bright white and making my eyes burn.

It makes me supremely uncomfortable.

"What do you think it is?" Hannah whispers, as if the light can hear us.

"I have no idea."

We keep our hands curled on the glass, watching as the beam

skims over the tops of trees and weaves through the dark silhouettes of the buildings downtown.

"Leo? Is it . . . a searchlight? Like on a helicopter?"

Something in Hannah's voice makes me turn to look at her. Her eyes are open wide, her face clear and hopeful. "Do you think someone's looking for us?"

I study the light. It's too wild, too quick to be a helicopter.

Everything in me is screaming to ignore this. To turn her around and plop her down on the couch and somehow convince her that going out there is the worst idea she's ever had. To tell her that, no, no one's looking for us, because we're dead. But then I look at her face, all upturned with the first glimmer of *hope* that I've seen from her and . . .

I can't do it. She thinks this is our ticket out. Our salvation. She still believes this is all going to magically end with some heroic rescue.

"I don't know what it is, Hannah," I say softly. "But there's only one way to find out. Let me get my keys."

The way she brightens is breathtaking. Look at me, being all unselfish. Putting someone else's wants before my own. All my exes would be ecstatic, but I'm pretty sure they wanted me to put *their* wants first, not Hannah's.

She shifts into gear and flits around the living room to find her phone and her shoes. She's jittery and less graceful than I've ever seen her. I grab my keys from the kitchen counter and follow her out the front. She fumbles with the keypad on her door, punching in the wrong numbers, and then the right ones, and then we're clambering into Thunderchicken and zooming down the street. I set a course for downtown, heading toward where we saw the light.

The stores and houses and buildings of Houston watch in imposing silence as we race through the city like two little rats in a maze. The beam keeps moving, dancing away, luring us on. We zigzag in its wake.

What's at the top of the beam? I can't tell yet. Whatever it is, it must be hiding behind the thick layer of clouds.

When the streets morph into the one-way system in the heart of downtown, something inside me stalls. I lift my foot off the accelerator. Maybe we should turn back.

But then I look over at the bundle of hope in the seat next to me. She's straining forward, searching the sky, desperate to find this thing. She clocks me watching her and turns to me with an eager smile.

"We might be with our families again soon," she says.

She really thinks this is the end of all the mystery and the emptiness. For her sake I hope it is.

She turns back to the sky, the smile still on her face. My chest feels weird and swollen at the sight of her happiness, and I wonder if that's something I'm going to have to figure out later.

The column of light is only a few blocks away from us now. I still can't see what's up at the top of it.

"Turn here," Hannah says. Thunderchicken's brakes screech, and we swing around a corner. A wide street stretches out in front of us, block after block of traffic lights that get smaller as they fade into the distance. The traffic lights shift through their cycles, green-yellow-red, green-yellow-red.

The beam of light is so close now. I can see it through the gaps between the buildings. We're closing in.

I turn another corner and slow down, and then there it is. A wide pool of light beaming down.

I put the car in neutral and we tumble out, slamming doors in our haste to look up at the sky.

And that's when the light swivels, shining directly into our faces again. I flinch, staggering in the interrogation-level light. I have to fight to keep my eyes from rolling back in my head.

I can feel my pupils constricting to pinpricks, and I get the freaky impression that the light is scanning, looking for something.

And then the light snaps off.

My eyes burn, and there are starry pops of phantom purple lights everywhere. The street is so dark. Not a single beam of sunlight is getting through the ceiling of heavy clouds above us.

I reach blindly for Hannah's hand. She's frozen beside me.

"It's gone," she whispers. "I don't get it."

We scan the sky, turning in circles, but the light is gone.

It was never a helicopter.

It was never a rescue.

Hannah is glazed over beside me, staring at nothing.

"I'm so sorry, Hannah," I say, but it doesn't feel like enough. It feels like my insides have fallen out, or maybe hers have, and I'm trying to scoop them up off the ground and push them back inside her.

We shouldn't have come out here. This is why I don't do hard shit. Because nothing's ever guaranteed to end happily anyway.

"Come here," I say. I wrap an arm around her, and she crumples into me. "It's no big deal. Nothing's changed. We've still got each other, right?"

She nods.

My eye catches on something moving in the street a few yards away from us. I startle, but it's just a plastic bag in the gutter, swirling in a little whirlpool of wind.

Wait—wind?

Shit. Not this again.

The wind kicks up, carrying a heavy moisture with it. The air *tastes* like rain. Maybe she was right about the hurricane. Maybe there's one coming in from the Gulf. That would explain these sinister clouds.

When she cranes her neck to look behind me, her body goes rigid. "Oh my god, Leo—"

I turn, and everything goes slow motion.

Hurtling toward us is a fucking *enormous* wall of wind, blasting past traffic lights to bear down on us like some horrible end-of-the-world movie.

There's no time to hide.

"Holy shit!" I yell.

We grab on to each other as it hits.

I get soaked through in about one-tenth of a second. The first drops of water hurt when they smack us, but then we're swallowed up by the gale and it's like being under a powerful sideways shower. But it's not only water—the wind has swept up all sorts of crap. Something hits my arm with a flat smack of pain, and wet leaves stick to my face. Beside me, Hannah yelps. Has something hurt her?

We have to get inside.

"Hannah! Over there!" I shout, getting a mouthful of rain. Our hands slip as we try to cling to each other. We link arms instead, desperate not to get separated.

The rain forces us down the street, away from Thunderchicken. I can barely see the outline of the next smooth, windowless building, but I remember it's some sleek private museum.

We fight our way up the slick steps. Hannah tugs on my hand and pulls me behind a marble column, but the rain is relentless, swirling and pounding at us.

"We have to get inside!" she shouts.

I dash out from behind the marble column, pulling her with me. Instead of kicking the glass in, I'll try this Hannah's way. The rain pushes me sideways, but I lurch to the door and grab the handle.

It opens.

Hannah

Leo and I explode into the museum lobby. The rain pelts in after us, making me slip on the slick tiles, and I crumple forward to catch myself.

With my hands flat on the floor, I finally suck in a breath that's not half water. Leo pulls the door shut, and we're safe from the pummeling rain at last. It sprays against the windows, just a swishing wall of white noise now.

Inside the museum, the air is still. Ominous. It's dark too—hardly any light is filtering in through the storm. In one corner, a single exit sign glows a ghostly red.

In the silence, my thoughts catch up with me.

The beam of light wasn't a helicopter. No one's coming to rescue us.

My breath catches, but I manage to swallow a ragged cry. I'm on the verge of a total breakdown.

Leo shakes his hair out like a dog after a bath. "Whoa! That was a trip!"

I press my fingers against my eyes to keep them from filling up with tears, but Leo's too busy pacing by the windows to notice I'm still down here on the floor.

"It's like we're in a car wash," he says, peering out. He's trying to keep his voice light, like he's not shaken by the storm, but I know him better now. He's not much more than a dark shape in the gray dimness, but I can tell he's bouncing on the balls of his feet and twisting his thumb ring.

Leo turns and scans the lobby. Finally he notices me on the floor.

"Oh shit. Hannah, are you okay?"

I nod yes, or shake my head no, I don't know. My vision blurs with peppery tears.

He takes a step toward me, then shuffles back. "Um, uh, hold on," he says. "I'm gonna go turn some lights on."

I close my eyes. *Breathe, Hannah. Get it together.*

I'm okay. I'm out of the rain, and Leo's here, and we're alive.

Probably.

I focus on my breathing, counting the seconds of each inhale and exhale, over and over until I'm ready to open my eyes.

I shiver. The museum is cold. Asleep. The air-conditioning hums quietly. My clothes are soaked through, but there's not really anything I can do about it.

Leo's at the ticket desk, riffling through some papers. "Hang tight," he calls. He finds a switch, and a light over the desk turns on. It's so tightly focused it looks like he's about to be beamed up by a spaceship.

He rustles around some more. "Ooh, found some instructions," he says. "Good thing Robbie the Intern needed to learn how to turn on the lights." He sits down in the swivel chair and peers at a built-in panel under the countertop. "There. Think I got it."

Electricity whirs as hundreds of lights throughout the building turn on. The hallway branching off to my right begins to glow. Leo taps some more buttons on the screen, and the lobby blazes with light. I instinctively raise my hand to shield my eyes.

"Ouch, too bright," he says, punching at the screen. The lobby lights go off, except for a strip of lights around the bottom of the desk, and the shadows wrap around us again.

It shouldn't be like this. It *should* be brightly lit. There should be someone sitting at the desk, frowning at Leo for making so much noise. There should be visitors milling around, enraptured or bored or trying to impress a date. Instead the lobby is empty and echoing.

Leo comes out from behind the desk and crouches down by me. "Did that help? What can I do?" he asks.

"I'm okay. I don't need anything," I say. Except my parents and Astrid and for this to all be over, but that's not going to happen.

He helps me to stand and offers me his arm. I'm trembling all over, but the softness of the inside of his elbow is warm and absorbs my shivers.

His shirt is so wet that it's sticking to him like Saran Wrap. His hair isn't a carefully arranged mess anymore—it's just a mess.

He walks me over to the desk. Now that I'm coming down from

the shock, I'm suddenly aware of a dull, thudding pain on my cheekbone.

"Ow," I say, covering the swollen ache with my hand.

"What's wrong?" Leo asks, his voice tinged with worry.

"Something must have hit my face," I say. "Everything was so chaotic out there I didn't even notice." Whatever it was, it missed my eye by half an inch.

"Are you—bleeding?"

I pull my fingers away and check them, but even in the low light, I can see there's no blood.

"No. I think it's just a bruise."

"Let me have a look. If you're sure there isn't any blood," he says, smiling a little sheepish smile in the dark. He advances on me, crowding me up against the counter.

My back digs into the marble edge. Like every time we're this close, my body starts thrumming. I'm pretty sure I'm about to lose control and accidentally kiss him.

To save me the temptation, I hike myself up to sit on the counter. There. Even if he stands right in front of my knees, our faces will be at least a foot apart.

My genius idea to sit on the counter works for exactly two seconds, because when he shifts forward to get close enough to examine my face, his other hand snags my knee and pulls it out to the side.

I stop breathing.

He's standing *between my legs.*

Don't breathe, don't breathe. If I just keep still, I'll be able to make it through this without doing what my body desperately wants to do, which is to pull him to me and—

He lays his hand on the side of my face, tenderly, but his thumb presses against the bruise. I flinch, but I'm grateful for the pain. It keeps me focused. Keeps me from getting too lost in this.

"Sorry," he says. "It's bad, Hannah. It's already turning purple. You look like you've been in a bar fight. Maybe we should try to find an ice pack or something."

"It's fine. I don't care."

Ballet doesn't give me bruises on my face, but this is nothing I can't handle.

Even though there's no blood, Leo's cheeks are a little pale, and his eyebrows are scrunched with worry. He keeps his hand on my face as he tilts it this way and that. He's concentrating so hard and being so gentle with me. The fact that he's helping me, that he's doing something just to make sure I'm okay—it has my heart clenching inside me.

Against my will, my eyes close.

God, I wish I didn't like him. I wish I could snuff out my feelings like a candle, because he obviously doesn't share them.

And then I feel his hand on my knee.

I open my eyes to find him looking down at my leg. His touch is cautious, like I'm a wild animal that might bolt.

"Your muscles are insane," he says softly, tracing a fingertip down to my ankle.

I'm not even flexing. I point my foot to make my calf even harder, and Leo swallows. His hand glides back up to my knee, slowly, so slowly, marveling at the place where my calf curves with hard muscle.

He's touching me.

I had no idea that touches like this were a thing I would crave. That they could convey so much. It feels like they're saying, *I like you, I care about you, I* want *you.*

I want to believe them, but I know better.

My eyes shutter closed again as I imagine Leo's head tipping forward, his palm sliding just a little higher up on my thigh. I'm so warm, all over.

I've got to stop thinking about this.

When I open my eyes, his are on me. Vacuuming up all the oxygen in the room.

"You okay?" he says. There's a new roughness in his voice. Something about him reminds me of a prowling, rumbling lion, power checked and held at bay.

I can't find my voice, and the moment draws out too long.

His hand slides away, and he steps back.

I want his warmth again. I want his hips wide between my knees.

I can't feel the ache on my cheek anymore—the thrill of him touching me made everything else scatter.

Leo offers me his hand to help me down off the counter. For a moment, I almost think I catch a glimpse of something on his face. A mirror image of the *want* that I'm feeling.

"I think we might be stuck in here for a while," he says, dropping my hand as soon as I'm on my feet and putting cold distance between us. "Might as well make the most of it and check this place out."

I take a deep breath to gather up the swirling, unbound pieces of myself.

Breathe. Forget what just happened.

I walk in a slow circle around the lobby. The museum is entirely ours to explore.

Something in me shifts. It's just a little twinge, but it changes everything. I've read books about people alone in museums, and it always seemed like such a magical privilege. I even daydreamed about it on school trips. While my classmates colored in pictures of dinosaurs, I stood off to the side, imagining myself alone in the exhibit. Climbing inside a rib cage of bones. Lying under the twinkling planetarium sky all by myself. Not having to rush through the VR exhibit so the next person could try it.

"Shall we?" Leo asks.

I nod. If anything can make me forget about the storm, it's this. Maybe instead of trying to squash my imagination, I can use it for good.

We follow a glowing hallway to the first gallery. It's smaller than the foyer, and the ceiling is made of glass. The rain beats down, dropping straight from the darkness of the sky beyond.

When my eyes slide to the walls, my stomach sinks. Of all the artists throughout history, did it have to be this one on exhibit right now?

"Hey, check it out! Ballerinas!" Leo says.

He tears off across the room to look at the paintings. I trudge after him. Of course it had to be Degas—the French guy who was obsessed with ballerinas.

"This dude is a big deal, right?" Leo asks. He climbs over the velvet rope to get a closer look.

That prickle of annoyance is back. Leo probably thinks I'm an updated version of the girls in these paintings. A porcelain statue to be admired.

He's studying a scene of a ballet rehearsal in an airy room. One dancer is posed in croisé, turned toward the ballet master for inspection. Others stand at the barre, stretching or chatting or being judgy. I see the same body language at the Academy every day, on girls born a hundred years after this was painted.

"Is this what it's like at your ballet school?" Leo asks.

"Well, we don't wear dresses like that, but yeah, kind of."

Their soft white skirts flow down to their knees, contrasting their black ribbon chokers.

"You wear sticky-out tutus now, right?" Leo asks.

"Not for rehearsals, unless it's for a pas de deux and you know the costume is going to be a classic tutu."

At my school, we have to wear plain black leotards and ballerina-pink tights, no exceptions. That's one good thing about going pro, I guess. The dancers in the main company get to wear whatever color leotards they want.

"This guy looks intense," Leo says, squinting at the mustachioed ballet master. "Are your teachers more or less strict than they were back then?"

I shrug. How am I supposed to know? These were painted in the 1800s. I'm not a freaking ballet historian.

Shoes squelching, I cross over to the next painting before he can ask me anything else.

Everywhere I turn it's ballet, ballet, ballet. My skin feels itchy.

I stare blankly at the painting. It's another rehearsal scene. This time the dancers have their legs extended in développé.

Leo's hand appears between me and the painting, holding an earbud out. I bristle, expecting another question about ballet, but when I push the earbud in, an explosion of reggaeton fills my head. When the song reaches its chorus, I snort a little bit. Very un-balletic of me. The chorus is an endless repeat of "Lift up your leg, lift up your leg, come on, girl, lift up your leg." Perfect for this développé painting. I imagine the uptight accompanist clicking into the rehearsal hall with his cane and his top hat, opening up his violin case to lift out a boom box blasting this song. Degas's dancers would be bewildered. I have to cover my mouth to keep from laughing out loud.

Leo takes his earbud back and smiles at me.

We walk together to the next painting. In it, a lone dancer looks down at the floor, lost in thought. She's miles away from ballet. She reminds me of . . . me. In the background, another dancer ties up her hair, probably thinking something normal, like worrying if she'll be able to hold her arabesque without wobbling, or if the ballet master will rap her with his cane again for sickling her feet. But the miles-away girl is thinking something else. I spin some possibilities out, and her life becomes a vivid reel in my head.

I've always done this—tried to figure out what's going on in other people's heads. I'd scribble it down in the margins of my school note-books. Astrid used to love reading the backstories I made up for people, but my imagination got out of control as we got older. History classes were the worst—I'd make up whole families in my head, giving them names and faces and happy pasts, and then I had to watch as they suffered through wars and famines. I could see their lives so clearly. My nightmares came back—until I made it into the ballet academy's Upper School. After that, I was too tired for bad dreams.

Astrid tried to make up backstories a few times, but they sucked. She had to force it, but for me it just happens. Now I'm even doing it for people in paintings.

"Whatcha thinking about?" Leo asks.

I startle. I was so absorbed in Lonely Dancer's life that everything else faded away.

"Oh. Nothing, really," I say.

"Aw, come on. You were totally captivated. Is there something about this girl?"

I cross my arms. "I don't know. I like that she's not thinking about ballet."

"She's not?"

160

"Obviously I don't know for sure, but see her eyes? She's not looking right down at her shoe, like she would be if she was thinking about a painful blister or the steps she's about to dance. She's looking farther off, staring into space. Maybe something's wrong at home. Like . . . maybe her older sister is really sick? The sister's usually at the next barre, but now her spot is empty. Lonely Girl is worrying about the rattling cough in her sister's chest, because that kind of thing could be the beginning of the end back in those days. Or maybe it's something else totally. Maybe she's thinking about the book she was reading before she fell asleep last night, how the world in it felt bigger than this one she's in now. She's tired of wearing the same things, doing the same things as all these other girls."

Leo stares at me. "That's incredible," he says. "Did you just come up with that?"

I nod. "It's kind of a thing I used to do. I haven't done it with a painting before, though."

He turns to the painting. "Hey, Lonely Girl," he says softly. "You have a story now."

I feel like JoyPuking all over him.

We make the rounds, stopping at each painting. Half of Degas's paintings are ballerinas, and the other half are the backs of women bathing, as if we're spying through a crack in the bathroom door. Seeing them side by side . . . I'm used to my body being stared at and studied, but something about this doesn't feel like a respectful nod to the dancers' athletic ability or grace. It feels . . . creepy.

"Can we go to the next area?" I ask.

Leo looks puzzled. "Of course. Yeah, sure."

The next room is tiny, more like an antechamber. The walls are black, and there's no art. Only the framed bio of an artist and a notice explaining that her exhibit has to be dark, because she uses ultraviolet and radioluminescent paints. One time she even used bioluminescent ink collected from sea organisms.

Black curtains hang over the door leading onward. Maybe it's not the best idea in the world to go into some dark room when you're hiding from a storm and you're the only two people in the world, but Leo peeks behind them anyway.

His face lights up. "Hannah, you've got to see this."

I follow him through the curtain and descend into a magical world.

The walls are matte black to soak up any light leaking in from the Degas room, and each piece of art has its own black light. The paintings pop with UV purples, searing salmon reds, and ghostly glowing greens. From the bio, I thought it would be like Laser Quest in here, garish and basic, but the work is delicate and detailed. There are a thousand shades of color, sunsets and sunrises and night skies that look more real than any painting I've ever seen before, because the light is coming from within them.

Leo whistles. "Psychedelic."

We marvel at each piece in silence, moving around the room. I think I can actually feel things shifting around in my brain as I try to make sense of up and down. Is that a person, or an animal? Or nothing at all?

At the far end of the room, there's another partition. I venture behind it. On the wall dead ahead of me is a painting that's obviously the pinnacle of the exhibit, on a canvas bigger than the rest, as wide as my arm span.

It's a woman floating in midair, bursting with momentum like she's been caught in the middle of a jump. She's turned to the side, and her back is arched. Chin tilted up, head thrown back, eyes closed. Her hair flies out around her, then turns into multicolored swirls of fluorescent chaos. Black stars fleck her arms, sharp cutouts where there's no paint, only darkness. She doesn't have feet; her legs just blend into a swoosh of blue. The silhouette of her body pops out against a surreal galactic sky that reminds me of Galaxe.

At the bottom of the painting, far beneath the woman's feet, is a field of tiny stacks of cubes. A geometric landscape. Laying on top of the blocks are her two discarded feet.

I read the plaque on the wall below the painting: *The Day She, the Starburst, Shook Loose.*

I stay there for a long time, staring. Losing myself in the swirls of color, in the arch of Starburst's back, in the tiny voids of the stars on her arms, the way her chin tilts up. Free and wild.

I feel Leo beside me before I see him.

"Oh. That's . . ." He shakes his head, unable to find the words.

"I know," I say.

His arm brushes against mine, and he clears his throat. "Hey, um. Sorry I kept asking about ballet stuff back there," he says. "I thought you'd want to keep talking about it, to distract you from things."

"I'm sorry I was grumpy," I say. "I'm just a little tired of always thinking about ballet."

As soon as the words are out of my mouth, I realize how true they are. I haven't had five minutes to myself in the last year. Ballet has consumed my life.

Before the empty, every day was the same. I struggled out of bed every morning, feeling like I'd had eight minutes of sleep instead of eight hours. I floated between classes at school, my head blank. My body ached all the time. Ballet is hard. But the thought of not doing it is even harder. At least in my case.

Sometimes I wish I didn't care so much about what I'm supposed to do. To be brave enough to make my own choices, like Leo does.

The Starburst woman certainly doesn't care about what she's supposed to do. I wish I had her hanging in my bedroom.

"I wonder if there's a gift shop in here," I say. "Maybe I can get a print of this."

Leo shrugs. "Just take this one."

"What? I can't do that. That's stealing."

"Who's here to catch you?"

He has a point. And the artist would probably want her painting to go to a good home, loved by one of the last two people in the world, instead of being sealed up alone in this museum.

I step forward, angling for a good grip on the frame. Once I find one, I lift the painting off the wall, but something clicks.

The room starts pulsing red, then the wail of an alarm pierces my ears.

I freeze and look at Leo.

"Seriously?!" he shouts up at the video camera in the corner of the room. "Let her have it—there's no one here!" He turns back to me. "Don't worry about the alarm. Let's just get out of here." I start to put the painting back, but he stops me. "Bring it with you. May as well now."

We retrace our steps to the Degas room. The flashing lights are less noticeable in here, but the shrill alarm makes my ears ring. I clutch the painting to my chest.

At the far end of the Degas room, a thick metal panel is lowering over the exit.

"Oh, you've got to be kidding me," Leo mutters. He sprints for the door. Under the weight of Starburst, I trot awkwardly, but I can tell we're not going to make it. Leo drops down to a crouch but jerks his fingers back to safety when it's clear there's no way he's going to stop a solid slab of metal. We spin, about to turn back, but the door to the ultraviolet room is blocked by a metal panel too. At least the alarms have stopped shrieking.

"Um. This seems a little excessive," Leo says.

We stand there for a long moment. Trapped. The rain pounds down on the skylight overhead.

Leo stomps petulantly over to one of the velvet benches and sits. I lower Starburst to the floor and drop down next to him.

I'm so stunned by the whole day that I don't know what to do. I lean my head back against the wall and watch the rain swish against the glass above us. It really does look like a car wash.

My toes are going numb with cold. I roll my ankles to get the blood pumping again, but when I look down to stretch my toes, what I see makes me jerk my feet up.

There's water on the floor. It's already an inch deep, across the whole room. And it's rapidly rising. How did it even get in? I look at the metal doors, at the skylight. Nothing's dripping down.

"Leo!" I slap at his arm and point to the floor.

"What the—" He pulls his feet out of the water. "Could this day get any more ridiculous?"

I scrabble to lift the painting onto the bench with us. The bottom edge is wet, but the paint's not running. The whole surface is hard and smooth, protected by what looks like a layer of clear varnish.

The water is rising fast. We huddle and watch, stupefied, as it climbs. Four inches. Six. It's not slowing down. I knew we shouldn't have come out again. The rain is going to fill up this whole room, and we're going to drown.

In the flash of a second, I can see it all. How we're going to frantically tread water as we rise up to the ceiling. We'll press our hands against the smooth glass of the skylight, trying to break it with our car keys. We'll press our noses into the last bubble of air. Exchange sad glances when we realize we can't save ourselves. We'll hang on to each other as we drown.

Oh, cut it out, Hannah. Think, think, think.

Maybe instead of imagining doom, I can imagine a way out. Wait—what if there's a secret passage? Like a hallway that the janitors use. I start searching for a gap in the crown molding, or a camouflaged handle. Something. Anything.

I don't know what to do with Starburst. "Hold this," I say, shoving her into Leo's arms. The water is knee-deep now, almost covering the benches.

"What are you looking for?" Leo wades behind me, splashing through the murky water. He's balancing the painting on his head.

"A door, or something—here!"

It was a ridiculous idea. A desperate, grasping-at-straws kind of hope, but . . . I think I just found a door. There's a crack in the wall running up, over, down. A panel. I run my hands along the crack, but there's no handle. I bend down and plunge my arms under the water. At the bottom of the door, there's a pin that shoots into the floor. I lift it up, and the door is free. I pull it open, fighting against the force of the water. Leo grabs the edge of the door, helping me pull.

And then we're through. The water rushes into the next room, spreading across the floor like a spilled vat.

"Go!" Leo shouts.

We sprint through the next room, and the next, following the glowing red exit signs. Leo pushes a fire door open, and more alarms blare. We tumble out into an alley between the buildings, and the rain sideswipes us. The storm is still raging, and for a second, I think about turning around and running right back into the museum, but Leo shouts, "Thunderchicken!" and then we're shoving back against the rain, using Starburst as a shield. As long as the untreated back of the canvas doesn't get soaked, I don't think the rain will damage the painting. The flying shrapnel is another story.

When we break out of the alley and onto the street, the wind swats at us, but it doesn't knock us off course like before, and we press our way toward Thunderchicken. Leo wrangles Starburst into the back seat, and then we're piling in through the driver's side door.

"Shit, we left the windows rolled down!" Leo yells. We both work on cranking them back up, and then, finally, we're safe again from the storm raging around us.

The seats are sopping wet, and my arms are shiny with rain. I twist to arrange Starburst more carefully on the back seat, pinning her in place with Leo's guitar case so she doesn't slide around.

I squint out the window, trying to figure out where the storm is coming from or what direction the wind is blowing, but it seems to shift every second. Out the back window, I'm sure the clouds are denser, darker. They're coming our way.

"Leo?" My voice wobbles.

"Hey, hey, hey, we're safe."

"No—I think we need to leave. I really think this is a hurricane."

I'm starting to shiver again. "We need to get out of the city. We need to evacuate."

Leo says something, but I'm envisioning us swimming under overpasses and getting electrocuted or eaten by alligators.

He shakes my knee. "Hannah? I said we'll go."

"How are we going to drive through this?"

"I can do it. Hannah. Hannah, look at me. I can drive in this. I've driven in worse," he says.

I cover my mouth. I don't know if I'm going to cry or throw up. Maybe both at the same time. It's a thousand times worse than my almost breakdown in the lobby, and I can't stop it.

Leo throws one wet arm around me, squeezing, holding me until the worst of the shaking passes.

"I can drive in this," he says again, firmly. "Where are we going? Just away from the Gulf?" he says.

I nod. And then, somehow, through the panic and chaos and the death scenarios flying around my head, I remember. "My grandparents."

"What about your grandparents?" he asks.

"They live out that way."

"Do you know how to get to their house?"

I nod.

"How far?"

"I don't know. An hour? Maybe a little more?"

"Okay. We're doing this. Put your seat belt on," he says.

169

"Do we have enough gas?"

"Tank's at three-quarters, so it should get us there. I filled up yesterday before I went to the guitar store."

"Was the gas station—"

He nods. "Just like the grocery stores. All the lights on, no one home."

Leo pulls Thunderchicken away from the curb. Her headlights refract off a million raindrops. It's like driving into a wall of light, so he switches the headlights off.

We crawl along, using the green-yellow-red blurs of the traffic lights to navigate. Every now and then, Leo pats Thunderchicken's dash like she's a horse that might get spooked. My cheek starts throbbing again.

When we finally hit the highway, there's an LED sign on the overpass.

HURRICANE SEASON IS HERE.
BE PREPARED.

"That's so great of them to give us a heads-up," I say, and I swear I see the corner of his mouth lift.

Thunderchicken plows through the darkness and the rain as we leave Houston behind us.

Leo

This is awful. It's the furthest thing from comfortable in the entire history of Leo Sterling, and that's including the time my PE teacher made me run two miles without walking.

Thunderchicken's windshield wipers slash back and forth like a psychotic metronome, but they can't keep up with the rain. It just keeps coming, lashing at us from every angle. Hannah and I have been driving for three hours, and now we're on an unlit farm road. I'm straddling the lanes, making sure the yellow stripes disappear under the exact middle of Thunderchicken's hood because I'm terrified we're going to hydroplane and end up in a ditch.

I adjust my white-knuckled grip on the wheel. This is the road trip from hell. No tunes, no enormous gas-station drink sweating in the cup holder, no giant bag of M&M'S on my lap. My back hurts from leaning forward, my legs itch from wearing wet clothes for so long, and my stomach hurts because I'm worrying about Hannah. Even my eyeballs hurt from squinting through the wall of rain.

I can't remember the last time I was this stressed out. I'm

starting to suspect that something is going on with me. Why am I doing all this for her? I don't think I can use the same excuse I've been using. It's not just because she's the only person here anymore.

I glance over at Hannah. She's an ultra-tense, rigid column beside me. She's watching the road, helping me keep away from the edges. Her shoulders are shaking, but it's not cold in here. She's either in shock or in her own head again. When I take my hand off the wheel to give hers a squeeze, our fingers intertwine like they've got minds of their own. My rings clack against the plain silver band she wears on her middle finger—the only finger I don't have a ring on.

I shouldn't be holding her hand. But it fits. Like it belongs in mine. A fresh wave of adrenaline hits as I think about whatever happened in the museum lobby. What was she thinking when she had her eyes closed? I wish I had time to soak in the memory of how warm her skin was under my hand, how my eyelids felt heavy with want, but we've got bigger shit to deal with right now.

A gust of wind knocks into Thunderchicken's side, and we veer off course. I can't drive with one hand, not in this storm. She realizes it too, and we untangle.

Why are we doing this again? If it had been up to me, we would have stayed downtown. We could have broken into the outrageously expensive hotel next to the museum. We'd be wrapped in silky sheets, drinking champagne, living up our last hours before being obliterated by the hurricane or whatever this is.

But Hannah wanted to come out here, and I can't turn back now. I have to get us to her grandparents' house.

Hannah's ballerina spine gets even straighter as she peers out the windshield.

"Slow down," she says. "I think it might be the next turn. Yes—yes! After that green mailbox."

I pull off onto a narrow, unpaved road. Crooked trees reach their branches out at us like fingers.

"This looks like a horror movie," I say. "Are you sure this is the right road? Where's the house?"

"I'm sure. Keep going—their driveway's a mile long."

Who has a mile-long driveway? But I follow orders. Finally the trees thin out and the dark shape of her grandparents' house looms up through the curtain of rain. Gravel crunches under Thunderchicken's tires as we roll up.

I twist the keys out of the ignition and leave Thunderchicken's headlights trained on the front steps like searchlight beams.

I slump back against the seat. "Oh my god. We made it."

Beside me, Hannah slumps too.

"Told you I could drive in it," I say, even though I was only about six percent sure that I could. Now that we're stopped, the rain sounds like handfuls of tiny rocks being chucked at us.

I stretch my cramped hands. They feel like arthritic claws, curled around the steering wheel for so long—and suddenly Hannah's taking them in between her own hands, rubbing away the soreness. I'm afraid to talk. I don't want her to stop.

Whatever it is between us, it's sweet right now. Completely separate from the moments that burn me up.

She puts my hands down a few minutes later, warm and limp in my lap.

"Thank you for driving," Hannah says softly. Then she pats the glove box. "And you were brilliant, Thunderchicken."

She smiles at me for the first time in hours, a grateful strum of a thing, but I have to manually restart my breathing.

I like the way that one small *thank you* feels, the same as when she smiled outside the bookstore after the eclipse. Like I've done something right.

I lean forward and study the house. I'm not sure what I expected—another shiny white Parthenon? Instead it's a small farmhouse with a wraparound porch, all dusty blue siding and white shutters.

"If the door's locked, which window do you want me to break?" I ask.

"None of them," Hannah says. She dips her hand into the cup holder and brings up her key chain. "I've got a key."

"Excellent. Ready to go?" I brace myself—we're going to get soaked again between here and the door.

"I guess," Hannah says, but she doesn't move.

"What's up?"

"I knew there wouldn't be anyone here. I didn't expect there to be, but it's still weird. My grandma's always waiting outside for us. The windows should all be lit, and she should be up there sitting on the porch swing."

The swing in question is empty, swaying violently in the wind. What an interesting concept. Someone waiting for you on the porch swing. That'd be nice.

"Sorry," Hannah says. "I'm ready now."

I turn off the headlights so Thunderchicken's battery doesn't run down. "Go time," I say.

We explode into the night. The rain soaks us cold in seconds. We rip open the back doors and grab our stuff: guitar, backpack, painting, and then we're slamming the doors and pelting up the steps. Hannah scrabbles at the lock, then pushes the front door open, and we're tumbling into a shadowy living room.

Hannah clicks on a lamp. The soft light blooms over a pair of hideous floral couches, and everything smells like pine needles and lavender. There are framed photos on every wall and tissue boxes on every flat surface.

We're panting and wet, and I feel so out of place in the stillness of this grandma-cozy living room.

Hannah props her painting up against a wooly brown armchair. She's silent for a moment, standing forlornly in the middle of the room. Then she rubs her hands over her face and starts moving.

"I'll get us some towels," she says. "Do you want to borrow some clothes?"

"I've got some in here," I answer, patting the backpack I pulled from the back seat. I keep spare clothes in the car, because I never know when I'll be crashing at Asher's or some chick's house or who knows where. I think my Def Leppard shirt and a pair of jeans are in here. They may not be fresh-from-the-washer clean, but at least they're dry.

She shows me to the downstairs bathroom. I hang my head over the sink and rinse the rain out of my hair, then I dry off and change. I think my toes might be raisins forever.

When I come back out to the living room, Hannah's standing by the window, wearing fleece pajama pants and an oversized T-shirt. She hasn't even taken her hair down. Wait—I think she's actually redone it. Combed it and put it right back into that severe updo.

"Do you think we should have kept driving?" she asks, staring out into the rain. "Does it look like more's coming this way?"

I plonk down onto one of the couches, exhausted. "We probably won't be able to tell until the sun comes up."

"Maybe we haven't gone far enough," she says, chewing on her thumbnail.

"I don't think I can face getting back in the car tonight. Let's see what it's like in the morning. If it still looks bad, we'll keep going, okay?"

"I just don't want it to catch us. It must be a really serious hurricane if everyone left."

"We'll be fine for tonight. We need to sleep."

Hannah drops her head down and rubs at her temple. "I just can't stop thinking about what might happen, or what the storm might mean. It's such a mess in my head. All these scenes keep playing out, of ditches and drowning and trees flying around and smacking us."

"Hey. Don't think about that scary shit. Think about something nice. Leo's LifeHack, remember? Whenever you're upset, do something fun. Come here."

She mopes over and sits down next to me.

All I really want to do is find a pillow and pass out. Having to talk Hannah down off a ledge is not my idea of fun on a Friday night, but it has to be done. I can't just say *See ya* and go to bed.

I nod at the stolen painting. "What's this chick's backstory?"

"I don't know," she mumbles.

"You don't have to say it out loud. Just think about it for a minute."

While she stares, her arms start to relax. Her posture becomes merely straight, not ramrod.

"Better?" I ask after a while.

"Yeah. How do you always know the right thing to say?" she asks.

I bark out a laugh. "Trust me, I really don't."

"Well, you're doing great with me. I swear I'm not usually such a mess. I'm used to knowing exactly what to do. Before all this, I had routines and plans. This is all a little . . . improvisational for me."

"I think you're holding up pretty well, considering."

She pulls her legs up under her and hugs an embroidered pillow to her chest.

"You know what you need?" I ask.

"To get a grip?"

"Well, yes. But also a song."

I reach over and snag my guitar case, unzipping and lifting my acoustic out. My bare feet stretch out flat on the wood floors, and I curl my left hand around the neck. I strum a few times, testing chords.

I play her the same thing I played at the bookstore. The song is slow and in A minor. I worry that it's too creepy, too haunting, but she turns sideways on the couch and drops her cheek against the cushion.

Our eyes lock.

For the entire song, she holds my gaze. I can't bear to look away. My fingers press and glide on autopilot, because my brain is somewhere else, tumbling down into this stare, into the green of her eyes, into the electric soul-baring thing she does that comes out of nowhere and hypnotizes me.

When I finish the song with three long blue notes, we're still locked on each other.

A spell descends on the room. The patter of the rain, the glow of the lamp. The smooth lines of her neck, the freckles sprinkled across her nose. We're so close I can feel the heat rising from her, and my head is light, like I'm breathing through one of those tiny brown straws they give you to stir coffee.

My eyes drop to her mouth. I'm about to lose it. I don't have a shred of self-control on my best day, and this feels *good*. So, so good. The purest kind of high, an all-natural intoxication, and I want to feel good.

I reach out to touch her hair, and her breathing stutters. Her ear heats up under my palm as she leans in to me, and her hand comes up to mine, her fingertips fluttering on my wrist.

Our foreheads touch then, and I give in to the dizziness. There's no stopping this. There will be a kiss, I know that now, but I want to luxuriate in this hazy-drunk moment for a little longer.

We experiment with soft touches, our skin whispering together in a thousand small ways. It's a breathless dance. A brush of the tips of our noses. A nuzzle under her jaw. All the intoxicating teases leading up to a kiss. Then she smiles, and I smile too, and fuck it, enough teasing, I'm going to—

The pressure in the room changes. With the thwumping noise of a sonic boom, the house goes silent.

Hannah jerks back, eyes wild, panicked, and our hands drop like lead. For a second, I'm think I've gone deaf. I work my jaw and rub under my ear, but then I realize I'm not deaf—I just can't hear the constant white noise of the rain that followed us home.

"The rain stopped," she says, and I don't know if she sounds dazed because we were about to kiss, or because the silence is so absolute.

There aren't even any lingering drips from the gutters. It's like someone snipped the sound off with a big pair of scissors.

I look down and Hannah's hand is still on my wrist, her thumb looped under one of my braided leather bracelets. My stomach churns. I was about to do something bad.

I gently untangle Hannah's fingers and set her aside. The guarded look in her eyes comes back.

God, I wish I could tell her that I'm not doing any of this to hurt her. That it would hurt her more, in the end, if we were to act on whatever this is that makes me want to touch her. I can't lose her. I can't be alone again.

I stand up to put some distance between us. "We should try to get some sleep," I say, my voice sounding wooden and awkward.

"Right. Bedrooms." She gets up from the couch, swaying woozily. I'm still a little unsteady myself. I catch her elbow.

For a moment, we're an echo of a time when she caught *my* elbow, and then she's gently pulling away and leading the way upstairs.

At the top, there are two doors right across from each other.

"That's the guest bedroom," she says, pointing to the one on the left. "I'll sleep in here, in my grandparents' room."

We hear the *splat-splat-splat* at the same time. Hannah reaches into the dark room and switches on the light. There's a gray circle on the ceiling and the plasterboard is starting to buckle. Directly below the leak is an old-fashioned four-poster bed, its puffy comforter dark with water.

Her shoulders slump.

"No big deal," I say. "You take the guest room. I'll be fine down on the couch."

"You can't sleep on the couch," she says.

"Honestly, it's fine."

"No it's not. The couch is right under this bedroom. What if the ceiling falls through and kills you?" she asks.

Jeez. Who even thinks these things?

"Or what if the downstairs starts flooding, like at the museum?" she adds.

I suppress the urge to take her into my arms. "Shh. Stop imagining bad things. Imagine good things. I'll be fine downstairs."

She crosses her arms and looks down at her feet. "You know how you said when I'm in a different room you think I'm going to disappear?"

"Yeah . . ."

Her voice goes very small. "Can you please just stay up here?"

"What, in the guest bedroom?" I want to add *with you?* but it's already there, unspoken in the air between us.

She nods.

I try to smooth it into a joke. "Hannah Ashton, are you trying to get me in bed with you?"

She flushes scarlet. "That's not what I— I just don't want—"

"I'm teasing. It's fine. No big deal. I promise I won't try anything. We can even sleep with our heads at different ends of the bed. Top to tail."

Through her blush, the corner of her mouth quirks up. It feels like victory.

The guest room is rose pink and has more lace than I'm strictly comfortable with. I keep up a running commentary so she doesn't freak out, and so I don't think about what almost happened downstairs. I tell her about how my brother, Joe, lives like a gawky, stinky caveman, about how happy I was when Gemini moved out last year so I could finally stop sharing a room with him.

"Is Leo short for anything?" she asks.

"Nope."

"So your sister's name is Gemini, but your brother's name is Joe? How'd he escape the astrological theme?"

"I have no idea," I say. "My parents were either on more drugs when they had him, or a hell of a lot less, picking the world's most normal name like that. Or maybe Sagittarius was taking it a bit too far. Leo and Gem can just about pass for names."

I've barely thought about my family. First I was too busy trying to ignore being dead, and then I was too busy *not* ignoring Hannah.

Maybe I'll see them again after all. That rain felt so real that I'm starting to think Hannah's right, and that everyone did evacuate ahead of the hurricane.

While Hannah's busy getting things out of a closet, I wander over to a heavy oak bookshelf full of stuffed animals and fairy tales. On the top shelf, there's an open music box with a little dancer frozen in front of three tiny mirrors. I run my finger over the ballerina's tutu, then I spot a pink notebook with worn edges. There's a sticky note stuck to the cover, with scrawled old-lady handwriting: *Ask Hannah if she wants to keep her writing.*

Interesting.

"Do you want a foam pillow or a feather one?" Hannah calls from inside the closet.

I snatch my hand away from the bookshelf and clear my throat. "Uh, foam."

"Would you rather have a blanket instead of the quilt? Do you need a glass of water by the bed?"

"All right, cool it, Grandma," I say as she bustles out. "The quilt's fine. I'm good."

It's amusing, but it's kind of nice too. No one's ever asked me this kind of stuff before.

She moves a bunch of decorative pillows off the bed and pulls back the quilt. I toss my pillow down by the end and get in as casually as possible, jeans and all. In a second, she's going to be here too, under the covers, right next to me. *Do not think about it, do NOT even think about it.*

She climbs in gingerly and clicks off the light on her side. We're so close I can feel the warmth growing in the space between us. I'm flipping between *want*, which I'm familiar with, and something that scares the absolute shit out of me. Something steady and easy and peaceful.

I'm so confused.

"Hey, Leo?" Hannah whispers.

"Yeah?"

"Thanks again for driving. Are you okay? I should have asked."

"Better now," I say. "Thank you for checking."

"Okay. Good night," she whispers.

"Sweet dreams, Hannah."

I lie there, eyes wide open, staring at the ceiling. I thought I'd be the one snoring and she'd be awake and worrying. Five seconds ago,

I thought keeping my mitts off her was what would keep me awake, but instead I'm full of a warm glow, a sense that someone actually cares about how I feel. That I'm not here just to entertain her or charm her.

Hannah's breathing stretches out as she falls asleep. I match my own breathing to it, and everything that was aching just . . . stops aching.

I always thought Leo's LifeHacks had to be high-octane and loud enough to drown out the noise of my defects, but maybe the distractions can be soft and quiet. Maybe they can be cups of tea and a choice of pillows, holding hands and doing hard things to make someone else happy. Maybe this is why I let her talk me into going after that beam of light, why I drove all the way out here for her.

If Hannah had met me before all this, she would have gotten an entirely different Leo. No one's here to warn her, to tell her that I'm a flake, that I only think about myself, that I'm a loser who's going nowhere. I like that I'm getting a clean slate with her. It sounds weird, but it's like I'm getting a clean slate with myself too.

I shift under the quilt, not so afraid to get closer to her now. She still smells like pears, which is ridiculous because she's had about ten showers' worth of rain.

Tomorrow, when we wake up, I'll make her coffee, and now that the rain's stopped, we can go for a walk. We can hang her stolen painting up, and I can get back to work on coaxing that power chord smile out of her.

Hannah

Something wakes me before dawn.

My legs are numb with cold and sleep, and my eyes are swollen and hot. When I open them and blink out into the darkness, my eyelids feel sticky.

I dreamed of traffic lights again. Their glow, on my skin, glazing me acid green and sickly yellow and feral red.

I shake the image of the traffic lights from my mind, forcing my eyes to adjust to the night.

The room is still and blue around me, and it takes me a second to remember where I am.

I lift my head and look over my shoulder at the boy-shaped figure twisted up in the quilt behind me. That's why I was cold. Leo stole the covers.

His head is still at the wrong end of the bed, and his knee is touching my lower back. The touch is light, but I can feel the pressure of it through my shirt. Warmth multiplies between us.

Oh my god. I'm in bed with Leo Sterling.

The tips of my ears go red-hot. I scoot away, right to the edge of the bed, and the knee-sized circle of heat dissipates.

But it's too late. I'm suddenly hyperaware of every noise, every vibration in the air, every shift of shadow in the room. The candle-smoke smell of him is everywhere.

I try to go back to sleep, but being still makes me want to crawl out of my skin. I have to roll over.

It takes me five whole minutes to do it, but Leo doesn't stir. His shins are right in front of my face now, wrapped tight in the quilt. If I tilt my chin down, I can see the rise and fall of his chest.

The song he sang for me downstairs lingers in my head. While he played, he stared so deep into me I thought I would implode. And the music . . . I've danced in front of a forty-piece orchestra, felt the timpani shake the floor beneath my feet, but I don't think I've ever been that close to music.

Moonlight slants in through the blinds, cresting over the slope of his nose. His eyelashes lie on his cheeks like paintbrushes, and his skin glows in stripes of blue-gray light. Even though I know the light is coming from outside, it looks like he's creating it.

I think . . .

I think this is more than *like*.

I tried so hard not to, but I'm falling for Leo Sterling.

Everything slows. Even the ticks of the old-fashioned alarm clock on the bedside table. Leo is breathing and I'm trying not to breathe and I have to get out of this room before I give in to this tidal-wave urge to put my head at the other end of the bed and pull my half of the quilt back until we're under it together, face-to-face.

No. Do not even think about it, Hannah.

I slip out of bed and grab my phone before fleeing to the adjoining bathroom. Behind the closed door, I squinch my eyes shut against the hard light and press my palms against the cold white countertop. I drop my head and heave for breath.

When I look up, I barely recognize the girl in the mirror.

I'm not supposed to like guys like Leo. He doesn't fit into my plan.

The thing is, I know exactly who does. For the past three years, I've been autopiloting a crush on my pas de deux partner at the Academy, Jerome Fletcher. His family is just like mine: His mom's a ballerina, his dad works in a skyscraper, and he's their perfect, polished only child.

I suppress a groan as I slump onto the closed toilet seat. I've got to stop thinking about Leo curled up on the other side of that door, hair sticking out at all angles, warm and alive and imperfect. To distract me, I pull out my phone to look at Fletch's Instagram. In his profile picture, he's midturn. Perfect white smile, smooth brown skin, unbelievable quads. He's certainly not hard to look at.

I used to imagine some airbrushed future of us as ballet royalty, but my crush on Fletch feels like ancient history all of a sudden. A pale imitation of a crush. Because with Leo it's completely different.

When I look at Leo, everything in me says yes. Yes to his face, his clothes. His voice. His words. Even his shoes. How ridiculous is that?

Most of the time, when I meet someone, it's a tentative *okay*. Later I might think, *Hmm, sure. Maybe*. But eventually, they all do something that makes me think no. But with Leo, it's all yes. That handful of times that I saw him at school, and every moment we've spent together over the past few days, it's always an all-caps, fluorescent YES.

It's idiotic. I've known Leo for two days. #Instalove. I've seen it. I've judged it. Maybe it's some weird psychological phenomenon, like Stockholm syndrome or something—maybe I'm getting attached to him because he's the only other person here. If we weren't the last two people in Houston, I wouldn't know anything about him except his name.

I'm about to hyperventilate all over again. I crunch forward and put my head between my knees, grabbing on to the cool edge of the bathtub. My feelings come into hypersharp focus.

Leo's not who I'm supposed to like, but . . . I'm tired of fighting it.

Instead of doing what I'm supposed to do, I'm going to do what I *want* to do. I'm going to go back out there and be open to whatever. Be myself—whoever that is.

The decision makes me feel light-headed.

I get up and stand over the sink to wash my face, rinsing the hot color from my cheeks. Then I brush my teeth, because that's what people do first thing in the morning. I'm definitely not doing it for any other reason.

After, I stare myself down in the mirror. I want Leo to see more than just Ballet Chick. I reach up and start untangling the bobby pins from my bun. My hair is thick and coarse and springs out in a frizzy poof, stiff from the hairspray.

I close my eyes and take a breath, preparing to go back into the bedroom.

I open the door, tiptoeing through the room in the dark. I want to shake Leo awake and ask him for a hug like the one he gave me in my basement yesterday. Instead, I get an extra blanket from the trunk in the corner and sneak into bed. I click my phone on, and when I see the time, my whole body goes cold.

It's eleven a.m.

I blink, but the numbers don't change. They can't be right. I switch to the clock app and look at the world times. Houston, Central Time: 11:04 a.m.

But . . . the room is dark. The sky outside the window is dark.

During the windstorm, the sun went down too early, and now it's not coming up. This is bad. End-of-the-world bad.

I touch Leo's shoulder. Something shuddery runs through me when I realize there's only a thin layer of fabric between my hand and that tattoo that I'm aching to see, but it's not enough to derail me from my task. I start shaking him in earnest.

He blinks, groggy and confused. "What's happening? What's going on?"

"It's dark."

"Mm. Nights tend to be like that," he mumbles, then rolls back over and closes his eyes.

I shake him again. "Leo, the sun's supposed to be up already."

"What do you mean?" He finally pulls himself up to sitting. He rubs his eyes, blinking away the last bit of sleep.

"See? My phone says it's eleven." I press the home button and show it to him. The sun should be blazing high up in the sky.

"That can't be right," Leo says, still drowsy. "Maybe it's a glitch in the cell towers or something. Probably from the storm."

Oh. Of course. I should have thought of that. I was imagining the worst, nuclear fallout, apocalypse, end of days. But the simplest explanations are usually right.

"I feel stupid," I say.

His hand lands on my knee, patting in a way that seems like he's trying to comfort me, but there's a gracelessness to it that makes me think it's not something he's done many times before. It's a small thing, but it's *kind*, and I love it.

"Hey," he says suddenly. "Your hair."

He reaches over and twines his finger around a strand. His wrist brushes against my shoulder. "It's longer than I thought it'd be," he says. He tugs gently on the hair wound around his finger. The sensation shimmers through me, and everything in my head scatters except for this *feeling*.

That's when I notice—it's not night-dark anymore. The first tinge of golden-gray morning light is seeping into the room.

Leo gently unwinds his fingers from my hair, then gets up and goes to the window. "It stopped raining."

He turns to face me, half leaning against the windowsill, in his rumpled shirt and jeans.

"I did some thinking last night, and I've decided that we're going to have an awesome day today." He's bright and awake and more like himself again. "I want you to show me around this old farm."

"There's not really a lot to see," I say. "And besides—I think I'd rather stay here. Every time we go out something horrible happens."

"You left the house and found me. That was good, right? Then we got to ride on the swing carousel like you wanted—"

"And nearly got killed," I say.

"Meh. Small detail. Let's see what we can get up to out there. If we stay in here, I'll either shrivel up or have a breakdown."

I bite my lip. My instincts are telling me to stay inside, but I don't want him to think I'm totally unhinged. Something tells me Leo Sterling isn't the kind of guy who likes girls who lock themselves inside and never have any fun.

The morning light glows orange. Yesterday is over. The rain is gone, and it's only a matter of time before everyone comes back. They'll be in awe that we held our ground and survived the storm.

"Okay, fine," I say. "Let me get changed, then we can go outside. But only for a little bit, okay?"

Leo grins.

Hannah

Ten minutes later, I follow Leo onto the porch, crossing my arms as I scan the trees around the house. Thunderchicken sits patiently in the driveway, the raindrops on her hood sparkling in the morning light. Everything looks normal, but I have this weird sense that the sun is climbing too fast. And that's *not* a glitch that could be caused by faulty cell phone towers.

Leo trots down the steps, his guitar case slung over his back. "Where to?" He smiles like today is going to be the best day ever. "Is there a barn?" he asks.

"Yeah, a small one. But it's not red, and it's not full of hay."

I think he has the wrong idea about this place. There's a lot of land, but it's all woods. My great-grandparents called it a farm because they kept goats and pigs and chickens and sold dusty pecans in brown-paper bags at the farmers market. They were dirt-poor until the oil money started coming in. To our left, the rusted red metal top of the nodding donkey rises over the tree line. When I was little, I watched it pump up and down, sucking crude oil up out of the earth, but it's motionless now.

"The barn is over that way," I say, pointing. "Past the pecan grove. Or we can go down to the creek."

"What's your favorite?" he asks.

"The creek, I guess."

"Lead the way."

We crunch along a stick-covered path until we're deep in the woods. At one point, Leo trips over a root and stumbles, swearing about his crappy sense of balance. I have to smother down my smile.

All around us, the trees are spindly and hungry-looking, and the sunlight lances down in shades of green and gold.

The woods look exactly like I remember. That's strange—it's not wet out here. The leaves lining the forest floor should be a matted, soggy mess, but they're not. It's like the storm didn't touch this area.

I lag behind for a second to bend down and adjust my shoe. When I look up, I'm swamped with the urge to pull out my phone and take a picture, to save this image of Leo in the forest. The guitar strapped to his back rides at an angle, bobbing along with his casual stride, and his bedhead catches a few beams of light. For a moment, I feel totally inadequate. Kicked in the lungs. How can I like the way someone walks so much?

Leo notices that I've stopped just as I pull myself together enough to jog after him.

"Shoe malfunction," I explain when I catch up to him.

He nods, and then he presses his fingertips against the small of my back to guide me to go ahead of him. The touch makes me freeze in total sensory overload. Stupid, disobedient muscles. First they were moving without my permission, and now they're *not* moving.

Breathe. Keep walking, Hannah.

Somehow, I get my legs going again, and we pick our way through the trees until we get to the creek. It's nestled in the kind of dappled shade that reminds you why people used to live near water. There are fish, sometimes, darting under the surface, and the current moves fast enough to keep the mosquitos away.

My dad and my uncle Craig built a wooden dock out here when they were kids. It juts halfway out over the widest part of the creek. Leo takes off his shoes and socks and sits on the end of the dock. I do the same, sticking my bare feet into the creek before he can get a good look at them. Underwater, they almost look like normal feet. Pale instead of splotched red, smooth instead of bony. They're not as misshapen as my mom's yet, but in another year or two, they will be.

Leo wiggles his toes. "I'm not really an outdoorsy person, but this is gorgeous," he says.

He's right. All along the banks, leaves hang down like fingers, trailing lines in the water.

"I'm going to mess around with my guitar a little, but I brought you some stuff to read. Maybe it'll help keep your mind off things." He pulls three paperback books out of his case.

At first I can't speak. My chest aches a little, because it's so *thoughtful*.

"Thank you," I say. Then he hands me something else. A battered pink spiral notebook with a cartoon pointe shoe on the front.

I freeze. "Where did you find that?"

Leo's eyes are soft and encouraging. "It was on the shelf back at your grandma's. I swear I haven't read anything."

I take the book, and we're quiet for a long time.

"'Hannah's Writing,' huh?" he prompts.

"I used to write stories when I was younger. I had kind of a vivid imagination."

"You don't say," he says, throwing me a teasing grin. I give him a little smack on the knee.

I trace the outline of the pointe shoe on the cover of the notebook. After what happened with *Flower Magic*, I only ever wrote during the summer, out here at my grandparents' house, when I was far away from school and ballet. It feels like the words in this book were written by an entirely different Hannah.

"I brought it out here so you could write Starburst's story down," Leo says. "If you want to."

I nod, but I just got the lid back on my imagination. Why would I want to take it off again? Instead, I thumb through the paperbacks as Leo gets his guitar out.

He takes off his rings and starts to put them in his pocket, but then he stops. He holds his hand out, gesturing for me to take the rings instead. My hand meets his, and the rings drop into my palm. I close my fingers tight over them. For a second or two, the metal is warmer than my skin.

He tunes, then claps his hand on the hollow belly of the guitar and starts picking out a country beat.

I raise an eyebrow.

Leo keeps strumming. "What? We're out in the country; we gotta have country music."

I laugh. He grins, like he's accomplished some secret goal.

"I wish I had my viddle," he says as he thumps along in a twangy rhythm.

"What the heck's a viddle?"

He flashes me a smile. "You know Mrs. Jankowski, the band teacher? She tried to bribe me into joining concert band by giving me a secondhand violin, but I replaced the strings with steel so it would sound more like a fiddle."

"Right. Of course." I laugh again, shaking my head, and he looks so pleased that I go shy, ducking away from his sight.

"Tell me what else your dad played that you liked," he says, shifting out of the country beat and into something new.

I look up at the shifting leaves as I think. "What about that slow Guns N' Roses one, with all the whistling? I always liked that one."

"'Patience'?" He sings a verse.

"That's the one."

"You have *excellent* taste," he says. He tamps the strings, then starts the song from the beginning. This time he doesn't sing, but I can hear the words in my head.

Something between us feels fresher and easier. The constant stomach-cramp-inducing nervousness of being around him has melted into a buzzy happiness. I wonder if it's because of my decision last night. There's more at stake now, but since I'm not actively fighting my feelings for him anymore, I can just enjoy these moments. Enjoy being with him, looking at him.

The sun stabs down through the treetops, turning the creek to liquid silver. After he finishes "Patience," Leo slides into a soothing pattern of chords, the notes changing as slowly and smoothly as the currents in the stream.

I'm holding a book open in my lap, but I'm not reading. For now, I'm happy to just listen to the water and the guitar.

The past seven days fade into a hazy mist. Today is perfect, bright and fresh, not a single storm cloud in the sky.

If I was going to write something about Starburst, what would I write? I think about her wild swirls of hair, about her lost feet. What's her story?

I take my own feet out of the water and scoot around so I'm lying with my stomach on the dock. I spread the notebook open in front of me and stare out into the trees.

And then I start to write. Four clunky sentences appear on the page. I cross them out. Two more come. They're better, but they're still not right. Leo's music matches the scratching beat of my pen. Finally I grab something solid, pulling it out of his rhythm and onto the page.

We stay like that for a long time, him playing his guitar and me writing. The words come faster and faster, until my wrist aches.

I don't stop until six pages are full. I sit up as Leo gathers his music back to himself. His last chord resonates through the woods, then he claps his fingers down across the strings to silence them.

He tosses his hair out of his eyes. "You okay over there?"

I smile. "Mm. Really good. You?"

"I'm great. It was nice hearing you scribble away."

I think about what he said before, about how he feels when he shares new songs.

"Do you want to read it?" I ask, fighting down a wave of seasickness as I hold the notebook out.

"Absolutely. Only if you're sure you want me to, though."

I nod. He asked for a story about Starburst; the least I can do is share it with him.

As he reads, I try not to watch the way his eyes flick from side to side. When he finishes, he smooths his hand over the page.

"Wow. She's got a whole life. And you totally sucked me in again, just like with Lonely Girl in the museum. Made me feel. That's the point, right?"

Pride rises in me like an iridescent bubble. Usually people's reactions to the things I've written are . . . less encouraging. *Flower Magic* was only my first failure. Like in eighth-grade English, we had to write short stories and read them out loud. No one else took it seriously and spewed out junk that was designed to make one another laugh. When it was my turn, a bored silence fell over the classroom. After a minute, my classmates started exchanging glances—WTF glances.

But Leo is smiling, flicking through my notebook. He mentions a couple of sentences he really liked, and that gets me feeling even more stupid and giddy. I get so much praise for ballet, but it never makes me feel like this. When I dance, I'm just repeating steps that aren't mine. But these six pages about Starburst? They *are* mine.

"What kind of stuff would you write if you were a writer?" Leo asks.

"Umm . . . I don't know if it's really worth thinking about," I say. "Ballet Chick, remember?"

Leo narrows his eyes. "Hmm. Thought your name was Hannah."

I plop my feet back into the water and stare at them. I have no idea how you even start to become a writer. But it's pointless to think about now—ballet is my life. Everything I've done over the past twelve years was preparation for my career, and it's too late to turn back now.

I muster up a thin smile. "Anyway, I'll never be a writer. It'd be a big change, and I'm not brave enough."

"What? You're brave."

I scoff. "You of all people know that I'm not." Over the past couple of days, he's seen me at my worst.

He cocks his head. "What's that saying again? Bravery isn't the absence of fear; it's the ability to say, 'Hey, fuck off for a second, Fear. I got shit to do.' Or something like that."

"Ah yes, that old adage," I say.

I reach up to smooth my hair back and startle when I find it loose. I forgot I took it down in the bathroom this morning.

"Can I read some more?" Leo asks.

A fresh jolt of adrenaline fizzes through me. "Sure, but the other stuff is from before freshman year. It might be kind of ridiculous."

"I'm sure it's not."

As he flips through the notebook, I focus on our feet, pale and swaying in the water.

"I love this," he says, showing me a page that I dog-eared. I cringe—I should have known he'd find my messy attempts at poetry.

"These lines are so good," he says. "There aren't many words, but they're all important. You know . . . these could be lyrics. I wrote a song last year—well, just a tune—but I could never get words to stick."

He closes his eyes, thinking hard. "Yeah, these would definitely work as lyrics. May I?" He plucks the pen out of my hand and writes vertically in the margin, simmering my words down, letting the steam escape, leaving behind only the most flavorful verses. Then he picks up his guitar, and in some miracle of music and language, he turns my words into a song.

As he plays, I stop breathing. It's magic, and I can't tear my eyes away from him. When he gets to the end, he sings the whole thing over again.

My words, his notes.

My story, his voice.

We've created something together, and it's intoxicating.

When he finishes, he makes this noise that can only be described as a purr. "I like it, Hannah," he says, blue eyes blazing into me.

"I like it too," I say softly. "I feel like . . . you're me." I shake my head, wishing I could take it back. "I know that's ridiculous, because we're so different."

"We're not all that different, I don't think," he says.

He leans a little, and suddenly we're touching from shoulder to elbow. I'm hyperaware of every millimeter of contact. How can such an insignificant touch feel so good? Leaves rustle overhead. I could stay in this moment forever.

But before his warmth can spread all the way through me, he moves away. There's this strange pulling sensation when his arm disconnects from mine, like what happens when you pry two magnets apart.

Leo scrapes his guitar pick along a crack in the dock's old wooden boards, and I can tell he wants to say something. The words are right there in the air between us.

We're swinging our feet in the water and looking out through the trees when something rustles in the bushes a few yards away from us.

Everything in my body goes still.

"What was that?" I whisper.

Leo shrugs and speaks at normal volume. "Probably a squirrel or something."

But we haven't seen a squirrel since everyone disappeared. Or any other animal, for that matter. I stare hard at where the sound came from. What could be out there?

It's just your imagination. It's just your imagination.

But then I hear a growl.

I swear the air gets colder.

What do we do if it's something horrible? An enormous rabid boar or a cougar or a cannibal serial killer on the prowl for someone to eat? We're the only living breathing things in all of Texas, and if they're hungry . . .

I clutch at Leo's arm. How will we get away from it? We won't have time to put on our shoes, and the forest will rip our feet to shreds.

Stop it. It's just your imagination.

Wait. If it's just my imagination, then I can imagine that growl turning into a cute snuffle. I can imagine something sweet and harmless. A deer, maybe, rooting around for mushrooms. Yes—a gentle doe and a fawn with white speckles. I squeeze my eyes shut.

Imagine that. Imagine that. Something safe, normal, boring.

"Hannah," Leo whispers, nudging my elbow with his. "Look."

I open my eyes. In front of us, gingerly stepping out from behind the underbrush, are two deer. A mother and a baby.

Specifically a gentle doe and a fawn with white speckles.

Leo

Hannah is frozen beside me.

I lower my voice to a whisper so I don't scare the deer off. "See? Nothing to be afraid of."

The little one leans down to nibble something, and the bigger one—the mom?—stares straight at us, ready to bolt at any second.

"Leo? I think I imagined them," she says, in a voice so low I can barely hear her.

"No, you're not imagining things, I can see them too."

"No—I mean—I was worried that the rustling noise was a cannibal or something. I was about to panic, so I imagined two deer instead. A mom and a baby." Her eyes are wide and urgent. "I imagined *them* into existence."

Crap. I thought she was doing better.

The corners of her mouth wobble down like she's about to cry. "I'm serious, Leo." She looks even more freaked out than she did in the museum.

"There must be tons of deer here," I say, giving her an out. "It makes sense that you'd think about them."

"But we haven't seen anything else, right? No birds or squirrels or even mosquitos. But right when I focused on the idea of two deer and pictured them in my head, that's exactly what comes out of the bushes? That's more than a coincidence."

"It is kind of freaky, but probably still a coincidence."

Hannah shakes her head violently, eyes swimming with worry. "You have to believe me. I know I made them up. Okay, wait, what about this. Watch—they're going to leave now. They're going to run right toward us, leap over the creek, and disappear behind those trees over there," she says, pointing. Her eyebrows scrunch up as she stares at the deer, so intently I worry laser beams are going to shoot from her eyes.

Nothing happens. The deer continue to munch.

"Hannah, deer never run straight at people—"

I yelp as the two animals jerk their heads up and spring into action. They bolt toward us, and I nearly fall back in fear and surprise. Just like Hannah predicted, they turn at the last second and leap over the creek, disappearing behind the exact clump of trees she pointed at.

"Um . . . Hannah? How did you know they were going to do that?"

"I just—concentrated. Envisioned exactly what I wanted them to do and focused all my attention on them, and they did it. Now do you believe me?"

My heartbeat chugs faster, faster, faster. This is impossible. Awesome. Ridiculous. Electrifying. I'm trying to wrap my head around it, but my brain is hopping up and down and squealing.

She was right. She made them up.

Hannah stares unblinking at the spot where the deer disappeared. There's a meltdown only moments away. Her breathing gets louder and faster, and her hands fly to her forehead like she's trying to keep her mind from splitting open.

If I don't sidetrack this breakdown, I might not be able to scrape her back together later.

I put my hands over hers and draw them down. She shakes her head no, over and over, eyes filling with tears.

"This can't be happening," she says. "It's impossible, Leo."

"Don't overanalyze it. Breathe. Relax."

Great. Now she's starting to wring her hands. Who even does that?

"Try something else," I say. I've got to get her rolling with this. If we have some awesome superpower, I'm absolutely going to use it. "Come on, Hannah, I want to see what else you can imagine."

She shakes her head again and covers her face.

"Hannah," I say gently, peeling her hands away. "What would you change, if you could change anything in the whole world?"

Suddenly, underneath all the worry, I think I see a glowing spark of inspiration. It's small, but it's there. It's the same look she got in the museum when she was cooking up those backstories, and on the swing carousel before we got slammed by the wind. So often, she gets stuck thinking about bad shit, but when she gets carried away on something beautiful, it's magic. She just needs coaxing out.

"I can see you thinking about something," I say. "Go on, try it. Whatever it is. I want to see."

She chews her lip. Coming up with reasons why she shouldn't, probably.

"Well, if you're not feeling it, I guess I'll have to try something," I say. "But just to warn you, I'll do something boring like make a fully loaded recording studio, or a room full of every awesome vinyl record I've ever wanted."

That gets her stirring. "Okay, hold on, I'm thinking."

She reaches down and plucks a leaf off a plant, holding it in the palm of her hand. Under her stare, petals burst from the center. It's like watching a time-lapse video of a rosebud unfurling. It grows and grows until she's holding the most enormous, unreal flower I've ever seen, a lush riot of pinks and corals and lavenders. She sets it adrift on the water, and we watch as it floats downstream and out of sight.

When she turns to me, a whole world of wonder is blooming on her face, as fast and huge as the flower she just created.

It's magic. I have no idea what's happening, or how it's happening, but I don't care. This is mind-blowing. Shredtastic. I've had some wild moments in my life, but this takes the fuckin' cake. A mix of euphoria and WTF curdles in my stomach, but now that we've started, we can't stop.

"Is it hard to do? What does it feel like?" I ask.

"It took more concentrating before, with the deer. Now it's easier—like the gears are already in motion." She looks stricken. "Leo, do you think I've been changing things all along and haven't realized it?"

She catches me staring.

"What?" she asks, suddenly shy. The volume on her smile clicks down a notch.

"You're having fun. I like it when you jump in, instead of keeping everything up here." I reach over and tap my finger lightly on her temple. "You should do it more often."

A burning blush spreads over her collarbone.

I look up, and we're stuck. Eyes locked. She can be so skittish that it surprises me when she holds my stare like this.

A determined look settles over her face, like she's summoning up the bravery to do something—

And then she scoots closer and lays her head on my chest, and I freeze.

For a long time, we stay completely still, both of us pretending to look up at the sky.

The weight of her cheek against me feels new and fragile and forbidden.

I shouldn't be letting her do this. It's going to blow up in my face. But everything is running hot through my veins and I'm powerless to stop her. I wonder if she can feel my heart tripping over itself.

My arm, luckily, has a mind of its own, and has no intention of following along with *should*s and *should not*s. It wraps around her waist, squeezing her to my side. My thumb joins in, stroking the ridge of her hipbone through her pants.

Her hand drifts up to my chest. Her fingers rest gracefully right over my sternum, and it has everything inside me hitching and thrumming and reverberating.

We're lying in a meadow, and I'm *holding* her, and I can't stop thinking about our song, about how her words fit perfectly with the notes I wrote years ago, and all I want to do is roll over and kiss her.

And that's when the penny fucking *drops*.

That's when I finally figure out what's going on with me.

I don't want to be just friends with her. And I don't want to be friends with benefits either. It's more than that.

I want everything.

For the first time in the history of Leo Sterling, I actually give a shit about someone besides me. I give . . . kind of a lot of shits.

I'm such an idiot. How did I not put it together before now? I've listened to enough sappy romantic songs that it should have clicked right away.

For a second, it's exhilarating and earth-shattering and then—

Holy shit.

Fear hits me square in the chest.

Because I'm still Leo Sterling, and I still fuck up everything I touch. It's only a matter of time before I drive Hannah away. Before, I was holding myself back from the flirting and the touching and especially the kissing because I didn't want to lose a friend. If I lost *this*? If I had to be alone *now*?

Fuck.

On my chest, Hannah lets out this little happy sigh, and oh my god, everything is different now.

"What other skies can we make?" she asks, totally oblivious to the core-rocking realization that I just had. Her voice goes straight to my chest, vibrating so low and so deliciously intimate I want her to lie on me and talk for hours.

"How about night?" she asks, seemingly unbothered by my total inability to answer her question. The world plunges into darkness. The change is so abrupt it nearly makes me throw up, but playing our sky game is a good distraction from thinking about how I'm falling for my end-of-the-world buddy.

Above us, the stars sparkle too white and too large. It's freaky. Night when it's supposed to be day. Hannah must not like it either because it flashes back to daylight.

"You're getting faster," I observe.

She nods. "It's getting easier to change things. Do you want to try? Just think about what you want to see, and it'll happen. You have to be specific, though."

If I'm going to have to concentrate, I need her to not be touching me. She's too distracting. I roll her off my chest until she's lying flat on her back next to me again, then I narrow my eyes and *will* the sky to change.

The sky goes an angry red with acidic-yellow streaks.

"Bad ozone," I say. "Your turn."

Above us, the sky darkens. Hannah makes it look as easy as turning down the brightness on a phone. A cool breeze sweeps over the meadow. A faraway peal of thunder rumbles, and a fat drop of rain lands on the back of my hand.

"Hannah? Brighten it up before we get soaked."

"Sorry." Hannah wriggles her shoulders a little, and I have to slam my eyes closed against the pure FeelGood of her moving against my arm. Seriously? For fuck's sake, Leo, *shoulders* are not supposed to get people so worked up.

Flat gray clouds move toward us from the west, sliding in like a tray over the sky.

Wait—is this a real storm?

The sky glitches in panic. It strobes through colors, like it forgot what it was supposed to look like and is frantically guessing. Gravity presses me hard against the earth and grass, trapping me under this freak show.

"Hold on, whose turn is it? Are you doing this?" I ask.

"No, are you?" I can barely hear her over the roaring of the sky, but there's a frantic edge to her voice now.

"Slow it down," I yell.

"I can't!"

The sky flips faster and faster and faster, slapping image on top of image. We've lost control. It's like we've somehow tapped into the cells of our brain that are responsible for holding all our mental images of skies. All our memories.

And then they get really bizarre. A sky with clouds dripping red like blood. A sky made of jelly beans. A sky like cracked desert dirt. A kid's drawing of a sky, with a slice of lemon for a sun. A sky that looks like a virus under a microscope, organisms twitching in a putrid goo.

And then—the apocalyptic sky of an imagined end of days. Above us, there's an entire planet about to collide with ours. Darkness falls over the field as the meteor eclipses everything behind it. Hannah grabs my hand and screams.

It's going to crush us.

Then the first piece of rock slams into the field. A plume of dirt flies up as it lands, and the ground rattles under us like the world is breaking up. Chunks fall off the meteor as it swallows up more and more of the sky.

I scramble off the ground and pull her up with me. "Hannah? Run."

Leo

We bolt across the field, legs pumping, hands welded together. Another shard of rock slams into the ground ahead of us. The spray of dirt hits my bare arms, stinging like shrapnel.

I veer left and pull Hannah with me. *Bad. Bad. Bad.* This is really bad. It's like in video games where you have to dodge rocks raining down on you, but instead of losing a pixelated heart, we might actually *for real* die.

My lungs are full of jet fuel, propelling me toward the trees. I glance over my shoulder, quick, to see if any more rocks are headed for us. Big mistake.

Hannah turns too, and for a few seconds, we're both stumble-trotting backward, captivated by the sight above us.

"Holy shit," I say. It's weirdly beautiful. I thought the meteor would hit fast, a split second of terror and light, then darkness. Instead, it looms over us, suspended in the lurid orange sky, taking its sweet time to crush us.

Another meteor punches through the atmosphere and thumps down on the field. We snap out of it and sprint for the trees.

"Are you doing this?" I shout.

"I don't know," Hannah yells.

Another chunk hits off to our right, sending up a geyser of grass. Hannah screams.

Super. That one was on fire.

We're nearly at the edge of the meadow when Hannah slows down. Why is she stopping? Shouldn't she have more endurance than me? She bends over at the waist, a dead weight on my arm, nearly tugging me to the ground as she gasps, begging for a break.

"We have to keep moving!" I yell.

"Just—a sec," she says, panting. "Don't know—what's wrong with me."

I pull on her arm again, straining toward the woods. Everything in me wants to keep running. I know a few trees aren't going to stop a hailstorm of apocalyptic rocks, but it might be better than being out in the open.

Anxiety crawls up my legs. Hannah's still bent over, huffing and puffing. I look up at the meteor, and my lungs seize up in my chest. How stupid am I to think we can outrun this?

This can't be happening. This CANNOT be happening.

Hold on. Maybe it's not. We imagined this. It isn't real. We can un-imagine it.

Hannah needs to get this under control. It has to be her, her imagination's stronger, and now it's spilling right into the sky without her brain consciously filtering it. I yank on her arm, tugging her over to me. I put my hands on her shoulders and turn us to face the meteor.

"This isn't real!" I shout. "I think this is you. Make the sky blue again. Make this go away. Focus. Blue, blue, blue," I chant.

She whimpers, recoiling. I don't blame her—the sight of this thing looming in the sky like an oversized moon in some sci-fi movie is pants-shittingly scary.

"Breathe, Hannah. It's not real. Think happy thoughts." She smashes back against my chest, still trying to escape the sky.

Maybe I can help her out. I think blue. I will it blue.

Blue, blue,

      blue, BLUE.

But I can't change it. It's not coming from my imagination.

"Now, Hannah!" I shout. "Come on! Blue!" I wrap my arms around her, trying to be as calm as I can. "Breathe," I say.

She goes still in my arms. Closes her eyes. Takes a deep breath.

The meteor shudders in the sky.

Stops.

It vibrates for a millisecond. Oh shit. Is it going to explode into a billion pieces that will instantly obliterate us?

But then the meteor pauses on its fall to earth. The orange sky lightens.

"That's it—you're doing it!" I cheer.

The meteor shrinks. It's getting farther away.

And then, with a slap, it just . . . disappears.

The broad Texas sky is back, perfectly clear, stretching for miles in every direction.

Blue. Serene. Under control.

I let out a nervous laugh. Hannah peels my arms away and collapses to the ground, crumpling into a heap. I follow, landing hard on my butt.

"Well, that was bizarre," I say. I rake my hands through my hair. "I think I'm gonna hurl."

Hannah grabs two fistfuls of grass, like she's trying to hold on to the earth. I can't see her face through her frizzy curtains of hair, but I do hear her sharp, ragged sob.

I hesitate. I should go hug her or something. But I'm not good in situations like this. I never know what to do, what to say. Before, I could get away with not doing or saying anything at all. That was what everyone expected. Leo: helluva good time, selfish jerk when the going gets rough. But here, with her, I have to try. There's no one else.

I crawl over to her and reach out my hand, laying it tentatively on her shoulder. She melts into it and leans against me. I scoot closer and start rubbing her back.

"I'm sorry," she mumbles miserably. "I shouldn't have let myself get carried away."

"Hey, hey," I soothe. "That was scary. Undeniably. But a little fear never killed anyone, right? We're fine. We're okay. And how incredible were those clouds? Who else can say they've sculpted clouds?"

She relaxes a little. Am I actually saying the right things for once? I keep going, grasping for the upsides. The silver linings. "It was kind of like riding a roller coaster, right? Terrifying but fun once you've survived it."

I shake my hair out of my eyes, imagining all the awesome stuff we can do now. We painted *the sky*. How amazing was that shit? It's about to get a lot more interesting.

The glittery feeling of possibility I had before comes back, and I laugh. "I can't believe we can change things."

Hannah stiffens.

Uh-oh. That was not the right thing to say.

Hannah looks up, her face streaked with tears and dirt. We were so caught up with imagining, we didn't stop to think about what the fact that we can change things *means*. She's thinking about it now, though. I can see the moment she gets to the unavoidable conclusion, because her eyes fill up with tears and her mouth twists down.

The fact that we can change things is definitive proof:

This isn't an ordinary apocalypse.

It was never an evacuation. It was never a hurricane, or a miscommunication. There's no possibility left that means we'll ever be reunited with our families, or with the way things were. In real life you can't change the color of the sky like freaky magicians.

I was right. We're dead.

Hannah cracks into a million pieces in front of me.

"No, no, no," I plead. "Let's pretend none of that happened. Pretend I didn't say anything. Hannah, no."

"I have to go back," she croaks. "Please. Leo, we have to go."

"Go where?"

"To Houston. To my house. It wasn't a hurricane . . ." She claps her hand over her mouth, stifling another sob. "Was that storm at the museum . . . was that my imagination? Has everything just been my imagination? Are you— Oh no." She gives me a weird look then, like she thinks *I'm* not real.

This is a disaster. "Hannah—"

"We have to go. Please," she begs. She's shaking all over now. "I need to dance. I need my studio. My shoes. Please."

"Okay, okay, calm down. I'll take you home."

We'll have to stumble back through the woods to get my guitar and grab her painting from the house. At least it's not raining anymore— it won't take us three hours to get home.

I wrap an arm around her and help her stand.

"Come on. Let's go."

We ride home in silence. Hannah's stiff in the seat beside me, eyes closed to block out the world. My throat is tight with fear.

At some point, I take one hand off the wheel and grab hers, squeezing hard. I don't let go until we pull up outside her house a whole hour later.

When Thunderchicken rolls to a stop in the circular driveway, Hannah cranks her window down and clambers out through it. She runs up to her front door and disappears inside the house.

"Fuck," I say, shaking my head. Then I lurch into action, grabbing my stuff from the back seat in record time so I can go after her. I decide to take Hannah's painting too, lugging it into the house in awkward steps. Maybe it will help her.

After setting Starburst down in the living room, I hear Hannah rustling around in the kitchen. Her theory board cabinet is open, and she's ripping the sticky notes down and stuffing them in the trash can. She pushes the lid down so hard the plastic snaps.

"Hannah, wait—"

"I'm sorry—I know I'm freaking out, but—" Her lips tremble. "I just need—"

She shoves past me and bolts down the basement stairs, leaving me standing in the kitchen. Alone.

The silence is extreme.

I pace the kitchen, running frantic hands through my hair. I want to barf. Bright piano music starts up, muffled by the closed basement door. It's the wrong music for this moment. I fumble around in my pocket and pull out my phone. My thumb shakes as I scroll through my music to find something loud and angry. Ozzy, Nine Inch Nails, Metallica. I ram my earbuds in. There must be some alcohol in this house, right? I don't need to follow Hannah down her brand of rabbit hole. I've got my own coping strategies. I fling open the nearest cabinet and grab a jar of marshmallow creme and dig my fingers in, scooping glob after glob into my mouth as I open drawer after drawer. Finally—bingo—under the island, I find her parents' stash, six half-empty bottles of fancy whiskey. I grab one and head toward the living room, jar of marshmallow creme abandoned, wiping my sticky fingers on my shirt, bottle dangling from my hand.

The floor shakes, and I don't have to take my earbuds out to know that the rhythmic thudding is Hannah jumping. Doing her little switchy-feet ballet hops.

I look over at the couch. The nest of comfy pillows. I really want to shut this out. Before I start thinking about all the things I'm never going to see again. The things I'll never get to do.

But.

Hannah.

She can't go back to doing what she was doing before we met. She thinks she was doing okay, but what's less okay than living in your basement for the rest of your nonlife? She'll be miserable. She didn't see what I saw when we were lying there under the sky, shaping clouds. The power chord smile was so within reach.

And I . . . I care about her too much to leave her down there on her own. Even if it means plunging into something hard and messy. It's physically hurting me to think of what she's doing down there. I've never in my life felt like this about anyone.

Fuck, I'm so out of my element.

I take a deep breath. Set the bottle on the kitchen counter.

And open the door to go downstairs.

Hannah

The spotlights above the barre shoot down into sharp pools on the floor, but the rest of the studio is dark. I can see the outline of my body in the mirror, but my face—and my tears—are in shadow.

Everything in me is vibrating, clamoring to explode, like a pot of boiling water. I force myself to breathe. Inhale. Exhale.

Demi-pliés. Down, up. Gradual, controlled.

Repeat.

The sprinkling piano music makes me clench my teeth together, and my clammy hand sticks to the wooden barre.

Grand pliés, Hannah. Just keep dancing.

My legs are steady and strong as I bend with excruciating slowness.

I'm about to flow into the next part of my routine when my arm stops in midair, hanging awkwardly like a broken wing.

I can't remember what's next.

How is that possible? I know I haven't been practicing enough, so I might be a little rusty, but how can I not remember what's after PLIÉS?! I've known what's after pliés since I was in kindergarten.

All the blood drains out of my head. Have I forgotten how to dance?

222

I force myself to breathe. Slow. *One. Two. Three.*

Tendus. Of course. Tendus are next.

When I slide my foot forward, I lose my balance and have to grab the barre to keep from falling.

This isn't working. I can still see the searing orange of the sky as the meteor headed straight at us. This is why I stuck to ballet. See what happens when I let my imagination loose? Before everyone disappeared, it just made people laugh at me and think I was pathetic, but now it makes the sky fall.

I sink to the floor and crawl over to the sound system, ripping out wires to stop the incessant music.

When I was tearing down my theory board upstairs, I stuffed all the sticky notes in the trash—except one. I wedged it into my phone case, and now, with trembling fingers, I pull it out. I stare down at the single word written on it, tracing the lines of the neat capital letters.

DEAD.

My stomach lurches. Leo was right.

No, no, no.

It's not possible. I can't be dead.

Of all the swirling, toxic thoughts in my head, one stands out from the rest: I'm going to miss the audition if I'm dead.

It's finally sinking in. That audition won't be happening in *this* Houston. It'll be happening in the Houston that's still full of people. The Houston where my mom is sitting at the kitchen table with a cup of milky sweet English tea, her gray-streaked bun bent over her phone as she reviews my latest rehearsal video. The Houston where Astrid is leaning on the counter at Devil's Advocup, flirting with Jacob, the barista she has a crush on, her red Doc Martens swinging underneath her chair. The Houston where my dad is slouching on the couch in his rumpled work shirt, eating pizza and watching a rockumentary, arm slung around David Lee Sloth.

But if I'm not there—if I'm *dead*—what will they all be doing then? Will they be huddled together around some made-for-TV cemetery, all black umbrellas in the rain? Will they be blank with shock or crumbling in on themselves?

God, I *miss* them. I lie down on the floor and cry so hard for a second that I go silent, everything in my body seizing up tight.

I used to wake in the middle of the night, suddenly intensely aware of one single fact: that one day I'd be dead. Every time, the hugeness of that thought sucked out my breath and replaced it with dread. On those nights, the only thing that could comfort me was the thought that I wouldn't *know* I was dead. What am I supposed to do now? I don't know how to deal with *knowing*.

And then a hand lands on my shoulder, and I jump out of my skin.

"It's just me! Just me," Leo says.

I scramble up to my knees and rub my eyes, but there's no chance I can hide the fact that I've been crying from him.

"You didn't have to come down." I cover my face. I'm such a disaster. This whole situation is a disaster.

"I wanted to," he says. "I have no idea how to help, but I . . ."

The corners of my mouth turn down without my permission, but I keep it together and nod.

I can only stare as Leo weaves his fingers through mine. We're locked together now, and his candle-smoke smell envelops me. I feel better. Just a tiny bit. It could be worse—I could be alone.

"Sorry I'm such a mess," I mumble. "I swear I'm really not usually like this, falling apart every five seconds. It's just . . . it's not every day you find out that you've died." I wipe my nose. It would be really great if I could not look like a total sniveling wreck in front of the guy I *like*.

I bet the girls he likes would be putting their hands on their hips and jutting out their chins. They'd be giving this whole situation a huge middle-finger *fuck you*.

Leo peels the crushed yellow sticky note out of my hand. Unfolds it so he can read it. "Dead, huh?"

I give him a sad look. "You know it's the most likely explanation."

"Not little alien kids playing video games?"

"I don't think so."

Leo folds the sticky note in half. "So what if we're dead? No big deal."

My hiccup/laugh makes me sound unhinged. "No big deal?" Maybe for him. He doesn't seem to miss anyone. He hasn't said a single nice thing about his family to me. It occurs to me—have I said anything nice about mine to him?

We're quiet for a minute.

225

"In the car . . . I couldn't stop thinking about how it might have happened. How I . . . died . . ." I say, trailing off into a whisper.

His thumb flutters over my knuckles. "It doesn't matter how it happened. We're here now, okay? We can't think about why, or we'll fall apart."

Only one of us is falling apart, though.

"How are you not thinking about it?" I ask. "Aren't you sad about everything we can't go back to? About everyone we'll never see again?"

"Well, I'm pretty experienced with hard-core distraction tactics. Remember Leo's LifeHack? I was about to chug half a bottle of whiskey up there."

"You didn't have to come down."

"What, am I supposed to let you wither away down here like a hermit?"

"I guess you could," I say, sniffling.

"Hannah. Come up and have something to eat. I promise it'll get easier. My mom always says that if you stuff your face, have a little fun, sweep it under the rug, you'll wake up the next day and whatever's wrong won't seem so bad. It'll get easier and easier to sweep under the rug until there's nothing left to sweep."

I pick at the frayed end of my pointe shoe. "Is that really the best way to deal with things? Ignore them?"

He peeks around my bedraggled mess of hair and says gently, "Isn't that what you're trying to do? Just in a different way?"

When I don't answer, he sighs. "Come upstairs. We don't have to change anything. Just come up. You can't fall apart on me, Hannah."

I take a deep breath. He's right. If I stay down here, I'm going to dissolve into myself. These are the kind of terrible thoughts that don't end. They'll spiral, dragging me deeper and deeper down. I'll do anything to stop thinking about being dead. Anything.

If dancing isn't working, I might as well try it Leo's way.

"Okay," I say, wiping under my eyes and taking one last breath, straightening my back.

Leo beams and squeezes my hand. We pull ourselves up off the floor and head for the staircase. I look down at our fingers, still woven tight.

I might never let go of him again.

Hannah

Upstairs, I shiver and wrap my arms around myself as Leo turns on the lights. He fills the kettle and sets it to heat on the stove, then he knocks around in the cabinets for the chamomile tea.

"This is probably a better choice than whiskey," he says.

I spot an open jar of marshmallow creme, but I don't have the energy to ask him about it.

Leo shepherds me over to the couch. When we pass the french doors, the pitch-black expanse of night outside makes my steps falter.

"Nope, not allowed to worry," Leo says, nudging me onward. "Go. Sit."

I sink down on the couch and draw my knees up to my chin.

He comes back and hands me a mug, his fingers brushing up against mine, before he sits down next to me. There's an easy familiarity with this now, in the way we pass each other drinks.

"Is the tea helping?" he asks.

"Maybe a little," I lie.

He waits patiently until I've finished. I set my empty mug down on the coffee table, and suddenly his hand is reaching for mine and—*oh*—he's tugging me over to him.

228

My head lands right in the cozy spot between his chest and shoulder. For a fleeting moment, I wonder if my hand feels heavy to him where it rests on his rib cage. His arm wraps around me, his hand solid and warm just above my hip.

He sighs, eyes closing with bliss. "Let's do this all the time," he says.

I'm afraid to move, because the *want* in me is so big I'm afraid it will burst. I want everything. I want this bright, easy friendship. I want this closeness, this touching, this laughing.

If he thinks this is what friends do, and how friends touch . . . I can be okay with just being friends. Friends probably don't listen so intently to the heart beating under their ear, but whatever.

I match my in breaths and out breaths to Leo's and try to memorize this snapshot view: my hand on his chest, fingertips catching on the raw edge where he cut the collar off his shirt. His long, black-jeaned legs stretched out, his feet a little farther away than my own.

His thumb starts moving on my side, rumpling my shirt and then smoothing it. It's soothing: a slow, gentle arc, the way someone would pet a cat. It feels incredible, like a Fourth of July sparkler's been lit inside me.

God, I wish he liked me as much as I like him.

"I'm going to dream you up a desk next," he says. "A big serious one with a thousand pens."

I sniffle, mustering up the courage to play along.

"And I'll get you a harp," I say. "It'll be taller than us, and gold. With naked cherubs all over it."

Leo laughs. "And after I master this naked cherub harp," he says, "I'll start in on the kazoo. I'll imagine myself up a different instrument every few hours. Dulcimer, balalaika, Caribbean steel pan."

"Alphorn," I add.

He nods sagely. "Ooh, yes. And then bagpipes, and bongos. And—"

His voice falters. I tilt my head up to look at him. His mouth is drawn tight, and there's a look on his face I haven't seen before. There's nothing left of that Leo brightness in his eyes.

What happened? A moment ago, he was eager and bouncing, and now he's . . . not.

"Leo? Are you okay?"

"Yeah, fine," he says. He hitches his smile back into place, but something's definitely wrong. He starts listing more instruments. He's putting on a good show, but I can tell it's an act.

He hasn't played his guitar since we were out at the creek. Maybe he needs some music to help him cope, like I thought I needed to dance.

I've spent enough time dragging him down. I mean, what kind of person finds out she can have anything she wants and then decides to go hide in her basement and cry? So much for acting like a perfect, poised ballerina.

I don't want to be the girl who hides in the basement anymore—I want to be the girl who makes things beautiful and interesting. If I'm stuck with this overactive imagination of mine, I may as well use it to help him out.

I lever myself up on my elbow, looking down at his face.

"Close your eyes," I say. "I want to make you something."

He complies, and it takes everything I have not to touch him, to stroke my fingertips over his cheek, his eyelids, the bow shape of his top lip.

Instead I clench my hand and close my eyes too. I push it all aside, the *DEAD* note, the memories of my mom, the mourning for the life I used to have. I can be my own genie but with infinite wishes instead of three. I can do *magic*.

"Okay, you can open them," I say when I'm finished building the vision in my head, when I've fine-tuned the details so it looks just right.

The living room is gone. In front of us, carpet gives way to slippery lacquered wood. The same wood that Leo's acoustic guitar is made from.

We're in a long, smoky music hall with a raised stage at one end. The walls are grungy brick, like an old train station, and dozens of neon signs blink on the walls. Crisscrossing beams of light cut through the hazy air, in hot pinks and teals.

Instead of chairs and people, the audience is made up of two rows of instruments, each on their own stand. The alphorn and the Caribbean steel pan, the naked cherub harp. His viddle—or what I imagined his viddle looks like.

In the middle of the stage, in the brightest, whitest spotlight, is Galaxe.

"Oh wow," Leo says, breathless. He stands and offers me a hand, pulling me to my feet.

"Do you like it?" I ask. "I don't know much about rock and roll, but this is where I imagined you playing shows."

"I love it. It's shredtastic."

We walk toward the stage, swinging our clasped hands between us. Leo stops at the naked cherub harp, plucking a few strings and chuckling.

"Will you play something for me?" I ask, nodding at the stage.

"Sure." Leo lets go of my hand and leaps up.

I follow, running cables for him as he repositions amps and pedals and foldback speakers. I like the way he watches me work, still caught off guard that I know what to do with the equipment.

When he's done, I drop back down into the audience and lean on the lip of the stage, my chin resting on my folded arms.

In the corner, one of the neon lights flickers. Something dark slides by, just at the edge of my field of vision. My pulse jumps. It's okay. Things go a little glitchy when I'm imagining big new places, but I won't let it get out of control this time.

I focus on Leo as he tunes Galaxe, the notes thrumming through every bone in my body.

"What do you wear when you're playing a gig?" I call up to him.

"Remember we mostly do eighties covers, so . . . really tight pants and stupid hair. Why?"

"Can I see?"

He stops in his tracks and raises an eyebrow. "You sure you're ready for it?"

I nod.

"Okay, but I have to warn you, I will look freakin' ridiculous. Smokin' hot, of course, but ridiculous. Gotta keep the eighties luxe alive."

In the snap of a second, everything about him changes, like a magician disappearing behind a puff of smoke—except there was no smoke. I didn't even blink.

And the Leo standing on the stage now?

Wow. Just—wow.

He's wearing black eyeliner, and his rich mahogany hair is teased into a wild mane. His black short-sleeve button-down looks like silk, and the top three buttons are undone, revealing an enticing slice of the smooth skin over his sternum. His leather pants are even tighter than his jeans.

He's dripping with metal, bracelets and rings and three different studded belts hanging low on his hips. There's enough curve to him to keep the belts from falling to the floor. I imagine the strength in those thighs, those hips, and—

"Hannah? You there? What do you think?"

"Um."

"That bad, huh?"

"No . . . it's just . . . I can't tell you. It's not appropriate," I say, flushing.

His eyes lock on mine. For a moment, he looks desperately hungry. But then he lets out a ragged laugh, and the spell breaks.

"For a second there, you were looking at me like a Skilletina," he says.

"What's a Skilletina?"

"Die-hard Rat Skillet fan. They come to every show and stand right at the front. They run blogs about the band and giggle up to me in the parking lot after shows for selfies. 'Hashtag so fine.' 'Hashtag that ass.'"

"Well . . . if the shoe fits. Or rather, if the tight pants fit," I say, smirking.

He winks at me. I feel like I might float away.

"Right, let's do this." He slings Galaxe into position and taps the mic. It crackles in response and he murmurs, "Test, test," into it as he strums out some chords.

But when he looks out over the audience, he goes unnaturally still.

Panic squeezes at my lungs and I whip around, but there's nothing there. Just the empty music hall.

"Leo? Are you all right?"

"Huh? Oh, yeah, sorry. I just tried to imagine some people. It's not really performing if there's not a crowd. But it didn't work."

The thought of imagining other people had crossed my mind, but I didn't really want to get into that yet. We're still too new at this.

"Maybe people are too complicated," I say. They're always moving and have so many forces at play. "But it doesn't matter, right? Just play for me, okay?"

"Okay. Yes. Good plan."

But he looks less sure of himself than I've ever seen him.

His fingers start to press and glide, finding an easy, repetitive pattern of chords. Drums join in, coming from nowhere. Well, from his imagination, I guess. He steps up to the mic and wraps his hand around it like they've been partners for years. "What's up, Houston? We're Rat Skillet."

He tosses me a sheepish look. "That's usually when the audience goes wild. This is kind of weird."

He looks down at the guitar, but he's not loose and easy like he's been every other time he's played. He's struggling to get into the music.

When his eyes shift up from the frets to look out over the "crowd," his face goes blank. Something inside him shatters, and I can feel the crack mirrored in my own heart.

I bolt up onto the stage. I knew something was wrong.

Leo

The room tilts around me in a swirl of smoke and neon. My fingers are frozen. I can't play. I can't even breathe.

Looking up and seeing an empty room where a thrumming, sweating, jumping audience should be . . . it's finally sinking in. Talk about a fucking delayed reaction.

We're *dead*.

DEAD.

My lungs start to throb.

Chill the fuck out, Leo. Being dead isn't so bad. Think about the good things.

I scrape together the positives. The silver linings. We're together. Leo and Hannah, Hannah and Leo. We can still see and hear and feel and touch. We can have whatever we want. Guitars, food, clothes. I could stare down at my hand and conjure up a fully loaded taco like the one from the food truck at the edge of our school parking lot. And I won't have to wait in line behind fifty other seniors to get it, complaining about the Houston heat, surreptitiously maneuvering myself into Asher's mammoth shadow.

But . . . so what if I have a *taco*? Those minutes waiting in line with my best friend—they were what made my lunchtimes awesome, not the tacos.

And so what if Hannah and I can go to theme parks, to movies, to malls? They'll all be echoing and empty. There's no mosh-pit noise of a big city, no life thrumming around us.

I'll never cram myself into a sweaty rented van with Asher and Ro and Gage and Oz. I'll never have to argue with an in-house tech over how to mix our sound, I'll never test a mic, *check-one-two-check-check*, I'll never feel that flip-flopping rush of adrenaline when I step out onto the stage and see a bunch of Skilletinas screaming my name. I'll never again be in a room full of bodies that jump in time with one another like they're being tossed in a frying pan.

No one will get to hear all the music I wanted to write.

Somewhere inside me, a seal breaks. Every horrible, hopeless, pants-shitting thought I've ignored over the past seven days gathers into a swarm in my stomach. The thoughts buzz like the rumbliest, growliest bass guitar.

And then they start to rise.

No, no, NO, stay down there, do NOT COME UP—

It's not just the crowds I miss. It's Asher, my quiet and steady best friend. It's my little brother and my badass big sister, it's my hippie mom, who wakes up every day with a mischievous smirk and the unshakable certainty that she can conquer whatever the day's going to throw at her. She's so much like me, and now I'll never see her again. I'll never see any of them again.

Something touches my arm. I flinch, startled to find Hannah suddenly standing right next to me. I didn't see her climb up onto the stage.

"Leo, are you okay? What's wrong?"

I push some words out. "Nothing. I'm fine."

She's frowning. She doesn't believe me.

The way she's looking at me, all openness and concern—it's such a contrast from how everyone looked at me before. Everyone always saw me as the stumbling tornado of a kid I was at thirteen, hell-bent on imitating my rock-and-roll idols. They assumed I was selfish and out of control, unpredictable and unreliable. It became kind of a self-fulfilling prophecy, and I just got more and more wild and unreliable. After a while, that's not who I wanted to be. But I was too far down the path to do anything about it. I had my whole life mapped out already: a long downhill slide into the bleak future of Dumpsville.

Hannah has no idea who I really am.

She wouldn't be looking at me like this if she knew what I was like before. If she saw what my grades were, and if she knew that I had zero plans for after graduation other than hoping I can gig enough to eat. She wouldn't be looking at me like this if she knew that when the drug-sniffing dogs came to school after last month's Battle of the Bands, they headed straight for my locker. The smell of weed was baked into my backpack—if I'd had even a crumb in a baggie, it would have been a disaster.

And those are just the things that look bad on paper. There's worse stuff. Relationship stuff, family stuff.

Somehow, I'm still playing, but I'm caught in a loop. Strumming the same three chords over and over. The buzzing noise inside me is rising again. It's up to my chest now, banding around my lungs and squeezing the air out of me, getting louder.

I grit my teeth. *STOP THINKING.*

Hannah's peering at me, her frowny eyebrows even frownier now.

"Leo, seriously, something's wrong. What is it?"

I fumble around for a lie to throw her off. "I just . . . I feel a little sick. But don't worry about me, I'll be okay in a few minutes."

Prickly pressure builds up behind my eyes, making my vision go blurry. The buzzing noise flares into ear-piercing feedback.

Hannah's deer eyes could coax a confession out of the most hardened criminal. Everything about her is saying, *It's safe, you're okay, you can tell me.*

"Is it the guitar?" she asks. "The stage? Whatever's upsetting you, I can change it."

Oh my god, I wish she'd stop prying. If I stop to think about all the things I did wrong when I was alive, the stone-in-my-stomach, acid-washed guilt will destroy me.

I take a sharp step back, ripping myself out of her reach, and then I'm blurting out words I know I'll regret.

"Just leave it alone, would you?!"

My imaginary drums cut out, leaving behind a silence so loud it rings.

A sad, disappointed look passes over Hannah's face.

It sounds like a small thing. A look. A split-second expression. Something that shouldn't bother me. But I've seen that exact look before. A hundred times. On Asher's face. On my mom's and Gemini's and every girl I've ever hooked up with.

It's so familiar, the way the line of her mouth hardens from compassion into sheer there's-no-hope-for-him disappointment.

Because that's what I was to everyone before, and that's what I am now. A disappointment. Everyone else in my life gave up on me. And I let them, because it was easier than trying to prove them wrong.

I know exactly what that look means. Hannah's giving up on me too.

She starts to step back. I grab her arm, tripping over cables and nearly going down because my balance *sucks*. "Wait, Hannah—"

I jolt and look down. I can't feel her.

"Uh—I can't feel you," I say.

She looks up sharply. "What?"

I watch, disconnected, as my hand moves from her elbow to her wrist. "I can't feel anything," I say. I think I'm hyperventilating.

"That's weird. I couldn't feel a doorknob the other night. Maybe it's just a side effect of being dead? It went away." She looks at me, soft and kind and understanding. "Leo, I'm sorry I was pressuring you. Whatever was bothering you, we don't have to talk about it."

She takes my hands and squeezes them between hers. I nearly melt in relief. The pressure is lighter than it should be, but I can feel it.

I'm not used to having people do small, kind things for me the way Hannah does. If I tell her what I was like before, how many times I let people down, she'll stop doing stuff like this, and I don't want her to stop. She can't know what I used to be like.

"I'm sorry," I say. "I'm just feeling bad about some crappy stuff I did before, but you don't need to know the details. Just know that I was kind of a selfish jerk."

Her hand fades back into numbness. I suck in a ragged breath. Okay, maybe she does need to know the details. For this to work—for me to feel her again—apparently she does.

"Look—that wasn't the first time I've said I was sick to avoid hard shit. I used to do that kind of thing all the time. Whenever Gem was going through something rough, I'd get up and leave the room. I saw Joe start spiraling last year, getting so lost and angry, and I could have just knocked on his door and talked to him, or asked him if he was okay or something, and I just . . . didn't. When Asher was upset about his dad getting hurt at work, I dragged him to some party instead of just *listening*." I squeeze at my temples until it hurts. "Every girl I've ever been with has had a moment where they needed me to just be there, and that's always when I ran."

Except for you, I almost add.

The noise building inside me turns into a roar. This big auto-tuned wall of *oh fuck* is going to shatter me.

"There's so much I should have done differently," I say, my voice breaking.

But then Hannah's arms wrap tight around me, solid and warm. *She's here.* My legs crumple. She peels Galaxe's strap off over me and guides me to the floor like a helpless child. We end up slumped in an awkward puddle, my face pressed against her stomach, my arms flung around her waist.

"I don't want to be dead, Hannah."

Memories of my mistakes come thick and fast, each one ripping something else out of me.

"I want another try," I mumble into her shirt. "And I just want to stand in a really freaking long line with Asher to buy a freaking taco."

She holds me as I shake, as my tears spread in a damp patch on her shirt.

She holds me through it all.

In the end, I'm wrung out like a wet washcloth. My sniffles die down, and I loosen my hold on Hannah's waist, sagging down until my head is in her lap. She slides my bandanna off, smoothing my hair in a lulling rhythm.

When I open my eyes, I'm surprised to find we're still on the stage.

"It didn't go away," I say.

Hannah hums. "I stopped thinking about it, but it just stayed. Maybe if you imagine something and leave it alone, it stays."

I draw in a congested breath and let out a smooth, calm one. The feedback ringing in my head is gone.

"Feel better?" Hannah asks.

"Much. It felt good to get all that out. You know, it's weird. My whole life I tried so hard not to cry, or even let myself get sad. Not because I'm a boy and I was trying to be tough or some shit like that. I just genuinely thought Leo's LifeHack worked."

I thought all the big, bad thoughts I smothered with music and whiskey and marshmallow creme were gone, but they were really just incubating, growing bigger and bigger, waiting for their chance to pounce.

Hannah smooths my hair away from my face. "I have been kind of skeptical about your methods," she says. "But who am I to talk? I turned into a basement hermit."

"We all have our coping mechanisms, I guess."

"Where did the LifeHack come from?" she asks.

I lever myself up out of her lap so I can look at her while we talk. "It was my mom's to begin with. She always told me I can make hard things go away with FeelGood things. But it turns out she was wrong. They don't just go away."

One last memory surfaces. A few days before Christmas last year, I heard terrifying wails coming from downstairs. I thought there was a horror movie on TV, or one of those live childbirth shows, that's how intense the sobbing was. I went downstairs to turn it off, but it wasn't the TV. The wails were coming from the kitchen. I peeked around the corner. My mom was doing the dishes for the first time in months, banging bowls and cups around and bawling her eyes out.

It shook me. She always seemed like she didn't give a shit about anything, floating around high as a kite, all merry and blithe. She seemed impervious to the stress that other people felt, to life's struggles, and I wanted to be like that too.

I told myself that she'd had a bad date or something, and crept back upstairs and put my headphones on. I LifeHacked my way out of the situation, just like she taught me, because it would have been too hard to go in there and hug her. Talk to her. But maybe it wasn't a bad date, maybe a lot of small things built up and spilled over like it just did for me.

Hannah and I are sitting on the floor across from each other. I've got my hand on her knee, and when she reaches out to touch the soft skin on the underside of my arm, drawing patterns there with the edge of her fingernail, I shiver.

Just friends, Leo.

Her fingertips flick up to my bicep, where my one and only tattoo peeks out from under the edge of my sleeve.

"I've been wondering what this is," she says softly. "Can I?"

The raspy hum of her voice makes it hard for me to speak, so I just nod. She shifts my sleeve up, tracing the lines of ink. I shiver at the touch.

"A lion," she says, tracing the abstract lines of it.

I don't know what I'm going to do if she keeps touching me like that. I grasp for a change of subject. "I guess ballerinas don't have tattoos, huh?"

"Actually lots of them do. Most dancers are so fierce and so sure of themselves. Not like me."

I find her hand with mine, coaxing her away from my tattoo. I circle my thumb over the inside of Hannah's wrist, using my imagination to paint ink onto her skin.

It's a simple black outline of a heart, no bigger than a quarter. Around the edges, I add a watercolor splatter of paint in every color of the rainbow.

"There," I say. "That's to remind you not to keep all your ideas inside you all the time."

She takes my arm back. Under her fingers, colors spread like dye until I have a matching heart on my wrist. But instead of spilling out, all my colors are inside my heart.

"And that's to remind you not to ignore what you're feeling," she says. "To keep some of it inside for yourself."

We're quiet, just staring at the tattoos. They're a perfect set, like a lock and a key.

My feet start to go tingly and numb, and I suddenly remember that we're sitting on a hard wooden floor in a room that isn't really real.

We help each other up. My head's throbbing from all the crying, but everything else feels lighter. Once we're on our feet, I pull Hannah in for a hug.

"Thank you," I murmur into her hair. "For letting me cry all over your shirt."

"Anytime," she says quietly.

She's holding me as tight as I'm holding her. This is totally just a friend hug, right? But friend hugs are only supposed to last a second or two, and I'm finding it really hard to let go.

When she starts to pull away, I catch her, one arm still twined around her waist.

Hannah looks up. My stomach flips, and we're caught there, staring into each other's eyes, stuck in time.

It feels like one of us should laugh at how awkwardly long this moment is getting and peel away.

With Hannah looking at me like this, I know that someone's not going to be me.

Hannah

I'm suddenly intensely aware of all the places where Leo's body is touching mine.

My hands on his shoulders. His stomach warm against mine. His arms tight around my waist.

He swallows, and his Adam's apple bobs. The *I like him, I like him, I like him* rises up, refusing to be pushed aside.

For this one moment, I don't care that the world is falling apart. I don't care that we're dead.

He brings a hand up to cradle my face, and it's suddenly hard to breathe. The air between us is dizzy and thin. His thumb moves at the corner of my mouth, ever so slightly, and our faces are so, so close.

I'm going to kiss him.

It would just take one tiny move, just the slightest rise up onto my toes.

My eyes must give me away, because suddenly he's looking at me with such a serious intensity, like he's going to *let me* kiss him, or like he's going to *do* something about it if I don't. He leans down, and every inch of my skin feels like it's somehow both melting and sparking.

And then . . .

My phone chimes.

The bright noise turns me to stone. I haven't heard that chime in seven days. With a smashing wave of adrenaline, I'm twisting, grabbing, pulling my phone out of my pocket, fumbling with my passcode, and—

It's a calendar notification.

SOUTH TEXAS CITY BALLET

CORPS DE BALLET AUDITION

4 P.M. SALIX STUDIO

Oh god.

It's today.

It's right *now*.

Leo's staring at the screen too. He tries to tighten his arms around me, but I pry myself free and stumble to the wall. I slide down against it, a puddle of shock and numbness and cold.

He follows, tugging my phone from my hand and putting it face-down on the floor. "I'm so sorry," he says softly.

One stupid calendar notification, and now everything has changed. I'm missing the biggest audition of my life, because I have no *life*. And I never will again.

I feel like my whole self has been ripped out of me. No audition means no ballet, means no career, means no *me*.

But it's not just ballet. It's everything else too.

This emptiness is all it's ever going to be. Houston, Texas: population two.

I can barely breathe as it all finally hits, as the truths I've been protecting myself from come crashing down around me.

"Tell me what you're thinking. How can I help?" Leo asks, and it's so sweet, the way his concern is knitted between his eyebrows, and I can't help but think of that sleepover conversation with Astrid so long ago and how we thought we knew this boy.

"I don't think there's anything you can do. Just—be here?"

"Okay. I can do that."

A thick silence settles over us. Leo reaches for his guitar like it's a life jacket. He settles it on his lap, but he doesn't play, just fiddles with the knobs and stares at the same spot on the floor that I'm staring at.

There's something that needs to be said. Something we've both been working hard to pretend isn't true.

"Leo, I think this is . . ." My voice fails, cracking into nothing. I clear my throat and try again. "I think this is it. I don't think we're going to find anyone else."

The room goes still.

"We're really alone," I whisper. "And I don't think it's going to change."

There's a charged moment of processing. And then he says, in a voice as unsteady as mine, "I know."

A black hole starts gathering somewhere near my stomach.

I'll never see my beautiful ballerina mother again. Or my rock-and-roll dad in his corporate disguise, or zany bombshell Astrid or my sweet Southern grandma. Leo won't see his band or his friends or Asher or his family. We won't ever meet the thousands of other people we were supposed to meet in our lives.

The first tear is rolling down my cheek when Leo Sterling's fingers, glinting with all of Leo Sterling's rings, weave through mine.

"Hannah. Look at me."

He twists so we're almost fully facing each other, shifting his guitar on his lap between us. And then he brushes his fingertips under my chin, so gently, turning my face up to his. Our foreheads press together, and I stare into those blue-gray eyes.

"You want to know what I think?" he asks.

I nod, sniffling.

"I think we can do this. We've *been* doing this, for days. We've been surviving."

He's right. We'll just have to keep taking turns holding each other up. Sometimes it's easier to be strong if someone else is showing cracks.

He leans into me. Three days ago, he didn't even know my name, and now there's a tear-damp place on my shirt where he buried his cries. His shoulder is solid and real, and I'm suddenly just so grateful I have someone to be here with. And for it to be *him*, out of all the people it could have been—it's just the loveliest, most heartbreaking, most magnificent thing.

Acceptance washes over me, warm and calm, and the claws of all the lies I was telling myself retract—hurricane, evacuation, *they're coming back for us*. The claws leave wounds behind, but now at least they can start to heal.

I can finally accept that this is all it's ever going to be.

Leo

Hannah's fingers fit so neatly between mine. We've been sitting here like this for too long, but I can't drag up the willpower to let go of her hand. Not when we both need something to cling on to.

I should be relieved that her phone went off and stopped whatever almost just happened, because I would have screwed everything up with her eventually, but I'm not relieved at all.

She tips her head back against the brick wall and looks up at me with this exquisitely sad, resigned expression.

You know what? Fuck the consequences. I'm so *done* trying not to touch her.

Slowly, so slowly, so she doesn't spook, I untangle my fingers from hers and drift them over her wrist. Up her arm, light as a feather. She breathes out a little raggedly, eyes drifting closed until her lashes fan out on her cheeks.

Good lord, this girl. I don't care if the guitar I'm holding costs ten grand, I'd chuck it across the room to get it out of our way if I thought the noise wouldn't scare her off. I want this moment to last forever. It's better than food, than drugs, than whiskey, than music. This is what I've been looking for since I woke up alone: the ultimate distraction.

But after all that we've been through together, she's way more than a distraction, and I want this to be more than just hot, messy make-outs.

My fingers wander over her shoulder and onto her long, long neck, to the smooth skin there that's been tempting me for days. My whole body flashes hot.

A little jolt of surprise goes through her, but then she just . . . relaxes. Melts. And I knew the sharp lines of her shoulders would soften like this, and it is so, so delicious to see it happening.

Maybe I'll ruin everything later, but I can't stop now.

Hannah

Leo touching my neck makes everything in me *burn*.

He sweeps his thumb over my skin once, twice, then pulls back and looks at me with a tenderness that unlaces me, and all the kindness that no one thinks he has in him, and the joy is too big for my body. I'm smiling, and he's smiling, and we're both a little stupid and giddy to be on the edge of whatever's about to happen.

And suddenly I know: We'll be okay. As long as we're together, helping each other up when we stumble, we'll be okay.

Leo's hand feels big and warm as it cradles my head, as his fingers slide into my hair, tugging until my face tilts up to him. My eyes flutter closed, everything in me overwhelmed by all the sensations.

His mouth is almost on mine, and the moment spins out, golden and exquisite, and I want to be here for this, I want to see this, so I open my eyes and that's when—

—Leo flickers.

I snap back. Blink hard.

For a split second, he was just not *there*. Like he was a hologram and someone waved their hand over the projector.

And then he flickers again.

But this time he doesn't flicker back.

For a moment, his guitar hovers in empty space. I gape. *That's impossible.*

Then it drops to the ground with a splintering crack.

What.

The.

Hell.

"Leo?!"

I scramble onto my knees and shove his guitar out of the way. It skids over the floorboards, crashing into the wall with a twang.

"Leo? Where are you?!" I run frantic hands over the floor where he was sitting. Still warm. I don't understand. He was right here a second ago. I've got to do something before my mind—

Shit. Too late.

Because my imagination is already oh-so-helpfully supplying me with a video reel of what this city would look like without Leo. It shows me staggering through the shadows of my empty house, palms laid against obsidian-black windows, too afraid to leave. It shows me curled up around the pillow he slept on, my eyes empty and my cheek imprinted with guitar strings.

Oh god, I can't be alone again. I can't survive this city without anyone. Without *him.*

Stop. STOP IT.

I let out a roar. My scream ricochets around the empty room—and collides with something soft. Just as fast as he blinked out of existence,

Leo's back. I'm right in his face, my nose millimeters from his.

I nearly knock him over with a tackle-hug.

"Oh my god, you're back! What was that? Where did you go?" My hands can't get enough of the solid Leo-ness of his shoulders, the warmth under his black silk shirt, the candle-smoke smell of him. He clings to me, wound tight and shaking.

The air around us is thick with fear. Loud with the thump of our hearts. Maybe that was just a glitch. It's over, and we can get back to our lives. Afterlives. But now I can't imagine picking up where we left off, playing songs and staring at each other like we're not in the middle of one long nightmare, like he could be snatched away again at any second.

When I can finally bear to pull away, Leo crumples, clutching his head.

"What's wrong?" I ask. "Are you hurt?"

He nods. "Headache. Oh fuck." He gasps as pain twists his face.

I lean back to give him room, but he clamps a hand on my arm to keep me close. He's ashen, eyes squeezed shut.

"What's happening? What can I do?" I dart a glance around—for what? I don't know, first aid kit? Ice pack? Something to make this headache go away.

"Leo, tell me what to do. Please, tell me what's happening." My voice is shaking. *I'm* shaking. I don't understand. You can't have a medical crisis if you're already dead.

"My head feels like it's exploding," Leo grates out. "Everything's white."

We need a doctor. Some help—someone, anything.

He takes a ragged breath against my collarbone. "Hannah—this is bad. I think I'm going."

My insides go numb with dread. "What do you mean you're *going*?"

"I don't know," he says, voice cracking over the words.

"Stay," I plead. "We're dead already, Leo. There's nowhere to go."

But maybe I'm wrong. Maybe this has been an in-between place all along. The waiting room before whatever comes next. Maybe this has all been a weighing of the hearts, and this is the real end.

"Don't go back to the basement," he says. "Paint the sky. The city's yours, okay?"

I choke down another lung-clenching sob before it can escape. "The city's boring without you. You have to stay."

Leo presses his forehead to mine. "You'll be okay. You can do anything. Whatever you want. Write about me, okay? Write us a life."

"Stop it. You're not going anywhere."

"You know I wouldn't trade this for anything, right? Even if it has been a fuckin' trip." His words come in cracked whispers, in bursts and stops and starts. "You would have been Ballet Chick forever, just a girl I passed in the hallway."

"Stay with me. Please." I hiccup through a sob.

"Thank you for letting me be me," he says. "You know I—"

His words slice off into nothing. I lunge forward, but there's nothing there but air.

No, no, no, no, no.

I can barely breathe.

I try counting, but my mind is reeling, can't keep track, can't remember what order the numbers go in.

He'll come back. He has to.

I double over, pressing my hand over my mouth. Stagger down until I'm a heap on the floor, curling around the dark space growing from the middle of me.

The tattoo on my wrist begins to run, the colors dripping down my fingers.

This can't be it. This can't be real.

But it is.

He's not coming back.

"No," I gasp. It hurts so much. More than anything.

I'm the last person in the world.

Leo

The whiteness is blinding. There's a high-pitched beeping coming from somewhere, screeching through my skull. My head is splitting open, cracking wide, and the pain is so intense, so soul-shredding, I yell and scream and squeeze my eyes shut against it.

This has to be hell. I always knew that was where I was headed, but *fuck*.

And I can't feel Hannah anymore. Without her here to hold me, I'm spinning wild through the pain. If I can't figure out which way is up, I'm going to puke.

God, what *is* that noise? My eyes fly open, searching, but everything is searingly bright. One thing is clear, though: I'm not on Hannah's dimly lit stage anymore.

"Ah, Leo, glad to have you back with us."

I jolt up, my whole body going tense.

"Who's there?" I demand, blinking hard.

Through the bright blur, shapes come into focus. Finally my vision clears enough for me to see where the deep, masculine voice came from.

Two people are looming over me: a tall man with a shaved brown head and a white woman with a frizzy orange bun.

Who the fuck are these people? I've never seen them before in my life.

Panic pulses through me. Where's Hannah?

I squint and bring a hand up to my forehead. The light pulsing down from the ceiling is so fucking bright. If this is hell, why is everything so *white*?

"It's okay, Leo." The man reaches out, and my adrenaline spikes. I want to jerk back, scramble out of his reach, but my body is slow and sluggish.

"What do you mean it's *okay*? Where am I?!"

"Leo, you're in the intensive care unit at Memorial Hermann."

I stop breathing. That can't be right.

Memorial Hermann isn't hell.

It's a hospital.

Leo

I sit in shock as the man and woman talk over me.

"Blood pressure normal, other vitals stable," she says.

"Excellent. Family?"

"In the waiting room. Mom and sister, I think. Been here all night."

"He's a minor, right? Bring Mom in."

The woman—a nurse?—nods briskly and leaves.

"It's great to have you awake, Leo," the doctor says, smiling warmly. "I'm Dr. Olatunji. I'm one of the neurologists here."

I stare at him. I can't process his words, because my head is thumping out a steady backbeat of *where's Hannah, where's Hannah, where's Hannah?*

I don't understand.

We were alone.

We were *dead*.

And now here I am with some doctor in some hospital and it's not making any sense and I'm about to freak the FUCK OUT.

The ICU is obviously full of people, because now that I'm listening for it I can hear beeps and sniffles and low conversations. I open my mouth to ask him how everyone got back, why it was just me and Hannah alone, why Houston was *empty*, but the questions die on my tongue. They feel like the wrong thing to ask. Like they are *absurd*.

So instead I ask the only question that actually matters. "Where's Hannah?"

The doctor's expression doesn't change. "She's here too, and we're taking good care of her."

Okay. Okay, she's here. That calms the panicky ache in my stomach. So, what . . . we've been rescued? Was it really an evacuation after all? I don't understand. None of this is making any sense.

"Why are we in the hospital?" I ask.

"You and Hannah were in a car accident last night, and you lost consciousness on impact. You've been in a coma for the last eighteen hours."

A car accident? But I wasn't driving. I was sitting on a stage with Hannah. Like five minutes ago.

Wait, did he say *coma*?

"I'm— I don't—" I shake my head. "This isn't making any sense."

"Don't worry, confusion is completely normal," the doctor assures me. "And it's okay if you don't remember the accident; we call that post-traumatic amnesia. Aside from the head injury, there's some bruising on your ribs but no broken bones. And most importantly, there's no sign of cerebral hemorrhaging, but we'll keep a close eye on you in case of complications."

I'm trying to chew all that information down when there's a flurry of sound behind the curtains surrounding my bed. My mom bursts into view, frazzled and wide-eyed.

"Leo!" she cries.

She looks . . . different. Usually my mom wears billowy thrift-store dresses and no makeup, and she keeps her salt-and-pepper hair wavy and waist-length like a hippie. All that's the same, but she seems unraveled. It's in the dullness of her eyes where usually there's a spark of humor and the serious line of her mouth where it's usually curved in a smirk. Seeing her like this throws me off almost as much as the words *car accident* did.

She comes straight to my side and presses her hand to my cheek. I can't help it—my body flinches at the uncharacteristic display of emotion.

She casts a worried look at the doctor. "Is he okay? Oh hell, he can't talk, can he? You said he might not be—"

"I can talk, Mom," I croak.

Her eyes well up. If I wasn't already in total shock, her very un-Mom-like reaction to all this would be sending me over the edge.

Dr. Olatunji smiles serenely from the other side of my bed. "If you're feeling up for it, Leo, we need to do some checks. We'll take a look at your eyes first." That's all the warning I get before he pulls my eyelid open and shines a light directly into it. My pupils constrict and my eyes almost roll back in my head. I swallow down a yelp.

He tests my reflexes, my strength, my coordination. He asks me question after question: *No, I don't feel nauseous. No, I'm not dizzy anymore. No, my ribs don't hurt much.* He's impressed that I know my name and the year. I want to cut in and tell him, *No, I'm confused, I am so, SO fucking confused*, but everything is happening so fast and I can't keep up. He has me get out of the bed and walk around the room, trailing an IV stand on wheels. I'm a little fragile and unsteady, but it's not any worse than the morning after a hard night out on the town. He spews information at Mom while I sit stupefied in my bed, totally fucking bewildered.

I can't latch on to any of the millions of questions I should be asking. I get the weirdest feeling that whole hours are rushing past, but it's like I'm standing frozen while everything happens around me.

"Well, Leo, I think we can safely call you a bit of a medical mystery," Dr. Olatunji says at last, his voice rich with what might almost be a chuckle.

Mom frowns. "What do you mean?"

"Leo isn't showing any typical signs of concussion—you almost wouldn't know he'd been unconscious for eighteen hours. Then again, we were a little surprised that he was out so long in the first place, given the mildness of the head injury."

"So he's going to be okay?" my mom asks.

"We'll keep an eye on him, but I think he'll be just fine."

Mom slumps with relief. She looks so *tired*. This is definitely not the blithe, carefree Darlene Sterling I know.

A nurse leans in through the curtains. "Dr. Olatunji, we've got a trauma patient with a collapsed lung in the ER who needs a bed. When do you think we can move Leo up to Neuro?"

"I don't see why he can't go up now. Get the transfer started."

There's a flurry of activity. I sit there blinking as nurses swarm in, unplugging machines, making calls on the phone on the wall, piling folders and all sorts of other shit on the foot of my bed.

"Leo, I'll keep you on IV fluids and a mild painkiller for the bruising on your ribs," Dr. Olatunji booms over the noise, pointing at the sloshy bag that's been laid in my lap. I try not to think about how one end of the tube is stuck right into the back of my hand. Gross. "We'll do another round of scans in the morning," he continues, "to keep an eye out for any hemorrhaging. Mom, you'll be talking to the neurologists upstairs about what to look out for, in case symptoms start to appear. Sometimes head injuries can take longer to make themselves known, and the consequences can be serious and even fatal. Leo, it's important that you tell us about any dizziness, nausea, blurred vision, or headaches. Okay?"

I nod.

I'm about to ask about Hannah again, but a man in a different color of scrubs comes in and kicks the brakes on my bed, and suddenly I'm being wheeled through the ICU. We pass bed after bed, but I don't see Hannah in any of them.

Then I'm being pushed through two sets of big white doors and into an elevator. Mom bustles in just before the door closes, her long, gauzy dress brushing the floor. Her earthy patchouli smell fills up the elevator. I surprise even myself when I reach for her hand.

Upstairs, there's more chaos as my new nurses get me settled into my room. I get introduced to a whole stream of people, but the names go right over my head. It's just a blur of candy-colored scrubs. I keep trying to blink away the haze of disorientation, but no one gives me a chance to speak.

Every now and then, when there's a second between conversations, I feel something clenching in my chest. An awful, sick feeling of dread.

Accident. Coma. Eighteen hours lost.

Hannah, Hannah, Hannah.

Mom flags down a nurse. "Can my daughter come up now? She's been in the ICU waiting room all night."

The nurse agrees, and then it's only a minute before my big sister is swaggering into the room in her signature leather jacket and bedhead topknot.

"Hi, Gem," I croak.

"Good to see you awake, kiddo," she says, ruffling my hair a little more carefully than she usually does. There's a patch of gauze over the bump on my forehead, but it doesn't really hurt.

"Look who else is here," she says, stepping aside to reveal my brother—and Asher.

Joe comes over first, leaning down to give me an awkward side hug. For a split second, he looks like the kid he used to be. Just the little brother who idolized me, who followed me and Asher around the neighborhood on his scuffed-up Goodwill scooter. It's been a long time since I've seen anything but an angry fourteen-year-old boy.

And then Asher lumbers over, and I'm smiling my first genuine smile since I woke up. He must have run here, because there's a mottled blush under his freckles—Hannah's just got a sprinkling, but Asher has the kind of freckles that you only usually see on true redheads. You can tell when he's had PE or been embarrassed or emotional because his cheeks go so pink.

"I'm so sorry I wasn't here sooner, man," he says. "I only found out after Gem posted about it."

I don't get a chance to ask about that—she posted it on social before calling my best friend?—because *another* nurse comes in. I let Mom and Gem handle all the medical stuff, and time starts streaming past me again, not touching me.

Finally there's a moment where the room is nurse-free. The sky outside the windows is dark. I didn't even notice night falling.

I've had an intense afternoon, but now I can finally ask some of the questions that have been popcorning around in my head.

"Okay. Tell me what happened, guys."

For a second, no one says anything. The silence gets kind of *tight*, sending a lick of warning through me.

"Oh, we can talk about all of that later," Mom recovers, waving her wrist dismissively. She plops into a chair and pulls her huge, saggy purse onto her lap, digging through it until she holds up a stick of gum in a battered wrapper. She beams in triumph. This is the mom I know.

Gemini smooths the blanket over my feet. "Just relax, Leo, and work on getting better so you can get out of here."

"Don't you think I should know what happened?" I ask.

"All you need to know right now is that you're going to be okay," Gem says, infuriatingly calm. She pops to her feet. "Anyone want anything from the vending machine?"

I'm starting to get annoyed. "What about Hannah? Is she okay?" I demand.

Asher's slouching against the wall by the window, eyes flicking back and forth like it's a tennis match. He clears his throat, and in a very un-Asher-like moment of courage, he speaks up. "Uh, Gem, can't we just tell him—"

"Ash, babe, my mom's been awake for like two days straight and—"

"Well, I did have that twenty-minute nap on the floor in the waiting room," Mom supplies from her chair, smacking on her gum.

Gem rolls her eyes. "Leo's only been up for four hours. We can tell him all about it in the morning."

Asher shrinks, even though he's at least a foot taller than everyone in the room. He's always been a little afraid of my sister.

I know what she's doing. Classic Sterling avoidance tactics. Normally I'd be on board with this plan. I've had a rough afternoon and all I *should* want is to sleep, but instead a very un-Leo amount of pissed-off-ness is rising in me.

I'm about to unleash on Gemini when a nurse sails in with a fresh IV bag.

"Oh, for shit's sake," I mutter under my breath.

The nurse takes one look at all of us—my mom slumped in the chair, Gem with her hands on her hips, Joe and Asher cowering in the corners—and claps her hands briskly.

"Okay, family. I think your boy here needs some rest."

No, what I need are some fucking answers. I need to find out if this really is just Sterling FeelGood tactics or if there's something my family isn't telling me.

"I'm going to be bossy and send you all home to sleep," the nurse says.

"I've only been here since lunch," Asher protests.

The nurse fixes him with a firm stare. "Nope, everyone out, please."

My family shuffles past my bed in turns, giving me hugs and murmuring how happy they are I'm okay. I grumble my good nights. Why couldn't they just answer my questions? Fucking Sterling FeelGoods.

When it's Asher's turn, he hands me a page torn from his sketchbook. It's his usual style, simple lines of thick marker, but this time the quirky little monster he uses for me has Xs for eyes and is lying in a hospital bed. I swallow hard.

"Thought I was gonna have to find a new ride-or-die," he says, his voice rumbling as low as his bass guitar.

My throat swells up, but years of instinct have me changing the subject before I can even think. I feel a spike of guilt for it, but I can't deal with this right now.

"Go on, get outta here," I say. "No need to spend your Saturday night being bored in here with me."

"It's Sunday, but yeah. Lissa's having that party tonight, but I don't really feel up to going."

I scrub a hand over my face. That's right. It's Sunday. Tomorrow's a staff development day at school, so Lissa Montgomery is having a party. Lissa is Asher's ex-girlfriend, but they somehow came out of it friends. Mystifying, but that's the kind of guy Asher is.

"You should go, Asher. Have some fun."

He nods and gives me a hug, and then they're all gone.

The hallway outside goes quiet as the hospital winds down for the night. For the first time since I woke up, I'm alone.

The last few hours have been as flicker-fast and tipsy as a sketchy carnival ride. I'm so tired I might pass out, but I need to think.

I stare at the ceiling for a few minutes, sorting through my head. I'm still no closer to understanding what the *fuck* is going on. Where was everyone? Nobody's said a word about hurricane evacuations or floods or being gone. Everyone's acting completely normal. Which has to mean—

No.

No fucking way.

It was real. It had to have been real. They know what I'm talking about when I ask for Hannah.

Wait. I can prove it was real. I have that cut on my ribs—the one I got when I jumped off the swing carousel.

I pull my hospital gown up and press shaky fingers to my skin, searching. It wasn't deep, but it would have left a mark. The gory green bruise from the accident swathes my whole left side, but where the cut was . . .

There's nothing but smooth skin.

No scab, no scar.

Everything goes still.

No.

I have to find Hannah. She'll know. She'll help me confront everyone about where they all went, why they're pretending nothing happened, like they didn't just *leave* us. We'll tell them.

Because it wasn't just a dream.

It cannot have just been a dream.

Leo

Hannah's bay in the ICU is exactly like the one I woke up in.

After slipping through the curtains, I hold my breath and stay very still, listening to make sure no one saw me. My blood is pounding—I had to sneak out past the nurses station on my floor, then charm my way in here on the pretense of thanking the team who took care of me last night. On my way "out," I sidled into Hannah's bay instead of exiting through the double doors.

When I'm sure I'm safe, I turn. Everything is gray with shadows, and there are so many machines. A thousand blinking lights. Hannah is a long, sleeping lump under the bedding, surrounded by the electronic hum of the hospital.

I hurry to the side of the bed.

When I see her face, I clap a hand over my mouth to keep from laughing with joy. It's nearly impossible to keep all this bright, sudden happiness in.

She looks just like she did when we were last together. The smattering of freckles across the bridge of her little fox nose, the gorgeous neck, her hair loose and fanned out around her face.

She's here. She's real. The relief almost knocks me over.

I can't wait till she wakes up and sees me. She's going to flip out.

Her left hand is resting on the mattress outside of the covers. I twine her elegant ballerina fingers between mine.

"Hannah? Wake up," I say, keeping my voice low. If the nurses hear me, I'll get in a shit ton of trouble.

The ICU is humming with soft nighttime noises. As I was surreptitiously scanning for Hannah's bed, I saw patients with tubes taped into their mouths, patients wearing oxygen masks, patients hooked up to all kinds of machines. There's something familiar about the breathy patterns of the breathing machines, the bursts of compressed air separated by quieter moments of stillness. It sounds like the echo of a dream.

It's freezing in here, and Hannah's fingers are so cold. She's only got one thin blanket on; they really should crank up the heat. I press her hand between mine to warm it up.

"Hannah? I can't stay long," I whisper, more urgently this time, but she still doesn't stir.

And then her hand slides out of my grasp and flops limply onto the bed, and that's when it clicks.

Oh. She's not asleep—

She's *unconscious.*

It sends a twang of pure, liquefied fear right through me. My knees give out, and I crumple onto the chair by her bed.

I'm an idiot. She's hurt. Of course she's hurt. She's smashed and battered in places I can't see.

I don't understand. Last time I saw her, we were sitting on the stage she made for me, grinning at each other like idiots. This can't be happening. I can't have made that all up or dreamed it. It felt so real.

I drop my head to the mattress, pressing my cheek to her arm, heartsick and gulping for air.

Hannah's skin smells like the hospital, like rubber and blood and alcohol, but underneath there's the tiniest hint of almost-ripe pear. Like how she smelled in the empty city.

I wouldn't know how she smelled if I made it all up, right?

Or did I just get a tiny glimpse of her on Saturday before the accident? Did I see her face and smell fresh pear and create a whole dream-Hannah from just a snapshot of her?

No. I *know* it's real. Every memory I have of her, every moment I spent with her is a living, Technicolor burst. They feel just the same as any other memory. They're not even far-off and muted, like memories of my kindergarten classroom or the time I had my birthday party at a water park.

I think about the way our hands touched when Hannah handed me mugs of tea, the constellation of freckles on her arm, how she held me when I fell apart in her lap. How can I have all those memories if I don't even remember the car accident, or why we were even in a car together on Saturday night in the first place?

"Shit, Hannah, I'm freaking out here," I whisper.

I stare at our entwined fingers until my vision blurs and my nose starts dripping and I have to get up for a tissue.

And that's when I see it. On her bedside table, there's a to-go cup of coffee from Devil's Advocup with the name Astrid scrawled on it in red marker.

A memory slides back into place. More than that—a whole day full of memories.

I remember the car accident.

Fuck—I know why we were in a car together on Saturday night.

She was in Devil's Advocup.

I remember seeing her when I walked in. She was there with three of her dancer friends, but they were ignoring her to flirt with some baseball jocks. I was with a group of people I knew from Shoelace, recovering from a hangover and a little lost without Asher, who had such a bad one he wasn't even up for coming out.

I remember how I sat down next to her on the long bench that lines one whole wall of Devil's Advocup, because it was the only seat left in the house. I remember how my arm kept accidentally bumping against hers and how we both tried to ignore the awkwardness of it.

I remember how I couldn't keep my perpetually bouncing leg under control. It knocked into her table and spilled half her drink onto the floor.

I remember how I apologized and struck up a conversation, all charm and jokes. Any other day I don't think it would have worked, but something about that night had all the stars lining up, had all the sharp angles of her loosening. I remember being stunned by the crackling, campfire husk of her voice. More people squeezed onto the bench, and we had to scoot closer together. I kept my arm draped across the back, and I remember thinking how she fit just right tucked up against my side.

I remember how she actually *smiled*, just a little strum, and told me she was worried she was about to get ditched, that there weren't enough seats in her dancer friend's car if they decided to invite the baseball players out with them. How defeated she looked when she said she kinda just wanted to go home.

I told her I'd drive her. I blurted it out without thinking, because I didn't want to stop talking to her. I told her I owed her a ride for spilling her drink. She texted her mom to ask if it was okay. I remember thinking how weird that was.

I remember how we walked to Thunderchicken with the lights of Houston twinkling in the humid evening air. Her arms were crossed over her chest, but we'd bump together every few steps. Her eyes were bright, and she was trying so hard not to smile at my stupid antics.

I asked her if she wanted to go to an open-air concert I'd heard about instead of calling it a night.

I remember how fast she shut down. She told me the concert sounded fun, but she couldn't say yes. She told me she only dated dancers.

I remember how I quickly covered up my disappointment by saying, *Oh, I wasn't asking you out.* I remember how the shame had flamed on her cheeks at that.

I wanted to take my words back. But instead, I heard myself explaining how I don't really "date" at all.

I felt like we both knew it then. That there was no point even spending one evening together because we would just never *work*. I knew what kind of person she was, and she knew what kind of asshole I was, and it was obvious from first glance that we'd just clash.

I remember how the drive felt so awkward after that, all heavy and wrong. How she stared out the window, looking soft and sad in her pink-and-cream-striped cardigan, picking at the gum on my seat that had been there for years, blackened into the shape of Italy.

Up ahead, the traffic light at the corner of West Holcombe and Kirby blinked from green.

To yellow.

To red.

As we rolled to a stop, I remember how I felt like something important—*a chance*—was being thrown away.

The light turned green. As I let out the clutch and eased my foot down on the gas pedal, I remember thinking that the headlights approaching from the right seemed too bright.

I was weirdly detached from myself in the split second before it happened. All I could think was *Huh. That car must be running the light.*

And then the wall of noise slammed into us.

It dragged us sideways, smashed us, battered us, threw us forward.

And then everything was empty.

Leo

I press my face to the back of Hannah's motionless hand.

I'm so sorry.

I can barely breathe. My mind is whirring, going over all the details of the wreck that have just bloomed in my mind. Guilt grows sick and twisted in my stomach.

"Bloody hell! What are you doing in here?!"

I jerk up at the sound of the voice behind me. My IV stand topples, and my efforts to catch it while stopping myself from falling are honestly fucking farcical. Hannah would have risen from the chair as graceful as royalty.

So much of my focus was on Hannah that I didn't see the person slipping through the gap in the curtains. I finally get the IV stand to behave, then I lock eyes with them.

"Oh my god, *Leo*?"

I'm about to ask how she knows my name when I see the fire-engine-red strands of hair poking out of the Rosie the Riveter bandanna.

It's Astrid.

She's a lot shorter than I expected, but she looks ruthlessly capable in her enormous clompy boots, retro overalls, and black-and-white-striped shirt. I shrink a little inside.

"Everything okay in there?" someone calls from outside the curtains. *Shit.* One of the nurses has heard the scuffle. My heart feels electrocuted in my chest.

"Fine!" Astrid blurts. "Just stubbed my toe."

We wait for the nurse to ease out of alert mode, and then Astrid starts hopping up and down.

"Oh my god!" she whisper-squeaks. "I knew you were awake—I was in the waiting room when they came to get your mom. You actually look like you're in one piece!"

She grabs me, turning me this way and that to inspect me for signs of injuries, and then she flings her arms around me and *hugs* me. I stand there stupidly with my own arms glued to my sides, because she's . . . kind of a lot.

I clear my throat. "Uh, you're Astrid, right?"

She beams, eyes glinting with mischief. "So you spent enough time with Hannah that she told you about me, eh? My, how *juicy.*"

How much does Astrid actually know? And *how* does she know it? It's fucked up, because I still don't even know which parts of Hannah are real. If I misstep, I'll sound like a creepy stalker, and if I say anything about the empty Houston . . . I'll sound like I've lost my mind.

"So?" Astrid presses. "Did you put the moves on my girl in the coffee shop, then?"

I cough. "Did she text you before the accident and tell you that or something?"

"No. I was trying to piece everything together in the waiting room. Kept trying to talk to your sister, but fat lot of good she was. Just wanted to pretend it wasn't happening. Hannah's mom said you were giving her a ride home, and we got the specifics of the accident from the police. Believe me, Hannah and I will be having words about her not texting me about you right away, but I suspect she was just waiting until she got home to dish."

"Right," I say, mind whirring.

"Well, juicy or not, you are not supposed to be in here, mister," Astrid says.

"I know. I just— I had to see her." It comes out more broken than I'd intended.

"Ohhhh," she says. It's one long syllable, and on her face there's this dawning realization that there's a heart in front of her that's nearly as broken as hers.

"I'm sorry," I say, trying to sound less destroyed. I think about how Astrid must see me right now. Hair a disaster, face a crumpled mess, on the edge of a total breakdown in my mint-green hospital gown. "I know you've known her for way longer than me. We just kind of had—"

I go silent. I don't know how to put it.

"A moment?" Astrid supplies.

"Yeah. You could call it that."

She whistles. "You know, the nurses have been gossiping. It seems you were saying her name over and over before you finally came around."

"I was?"

No one told me that.

"Mmm-hmm. Leo Sterling, whatever will you do with your reputation when everyone finds out about this?"

I give her a weak smile. "I won't tell anyone if you don't," I say, but it feels hollow.

Astrid rolls her eyes. "Right. Well, you better get out of here before you get caught." She starts poking me toward the end of the bed, but I have to ask.

"Astrid, wait—how bad is it?"

She sighs. "It's not great, chuck. Coma aside, the broken arm isn't brilliant for the ballet stuff."

I startle. "What broken arm?"

"Er, it's in a bloody bright green cast, mate," she says. She pulls Hannah's blanket back gently, and there it is, a hard cast on her right arm.

"Shit," I murmur. I thought she'd just had that arm crossed over her chest like some sort of sleeping fairy-tale princess.

"Apparently they ran out of all the decent colors," Astrid says.

"Is anything else broken?"

"No. And there's nothing on her brain scans. The doctors keep saying, *All we can do is wait. There's still so much we don't know about brains,* blah, blah, blah." She pulls herself straighter and sets her jaw. "But you woke up. So she will too."

I wonder if she's thinking the same thing I am. That Hannah deserved to wake up instead of me.

My guilt is turning into panic now. A gray-green poison searing through my blood. I lean over, bracing myself on the cold rail at the foot of Hannah's bed.

I was driving. And it was my idea to offer her a ride home.

If I hadn't, she wouldn't be here.

"This is my fault," I mumble. The words are out before I can stop them, but they were so low and broken maybe Astrid didn't hear.

No such luck.

"It wasn't your fault, actually," Astrid says gently. When I don't respond, she pulls her phone out and starts tapping around. "Here, look."

On the screen there's a news article about the accident.

"See?" she says. "The police said it was an electrical fault. All the lights at that intersection turned green at the same time. It's no one's fault, Leo. It was just a freak accident."

I scan the article, but it doesn't take the edge off the guilt. My heart still feels achy and swollen in my chest.

"Listen," Astrid says, even softer now. "You really do need to get out of here before you get caught."

I nod, but I can't move.

She sighs and picks up her coffee cup. "Look, it's almost time for

Hannah's mom to take over sitting with her, so I'll walk you out. Unless you want to meet her?"

At the mention of Hannah's mom, my body pulses with fear. What are her parents thinking about all this? Fuck, what a disaster.

"I'm good," I squeak.

Astrid cocks her head. "Are you scared? Don't worry, they like you."

I snort a laugh. "Sure."

"No, seriously. Like I said, you kept saying Hannah's name before you were properly awake. You were so worried about her that they nearly had to sedate you. Trés romantic, mate."

She laughs at my terrified expression. "All right, another time, then."

As we sneak back out of the ICU, Astrid carries my IV stand for me. I'm starting to get why Hannah loves her so much. We push out into the fluorescent hospital hallway—

—and run smack into Hannah's parents.

I stumble. The universe has got to be kidding me right now. It's like it heard how scared I was and thought it'd have a laugh.

The urge to flee is *intense*, but Astrid grabs my arm and rises to the occasion.

"Look who I found," she says, all bright and cheery and English.

I give her parents the most apologetic, freaked-out, deer-in-the-headlights, please-don't-hate-me look. I'm glad I'm still wearing my hospital gown and have a patch of gauze on my forehead, because it seems awful to be up and about when their daughter isn't.

Hannah's mom's mouth opens, then closes. "Are you—"

It's no use. She can't get the rest of her question out.

"Yep, it's Leo!" Astrid crows. "Leo, these are Hannah's parents, Conrad and Eliza."

And then, absurdly, we're all shaking hands.

Astrid starts babbling something about how they've spent so much time with my mom and Gemini that they all feel like they know me. I'm grateful; she's like a yappy little British Chihuahua.

"Well, we're so happy to see you up and about, Leo," Hannah's dad finally says. "And we really have heard a lot about you. My wife and your mom bonded in the waiting room last night."

I can't think of two people who would be less likely to *bond* than Eliza Ashton and my mother, but okay. Mrs. Ashton gives me a little smile, and there's none of the icy ballerina tightness I expected to see there.

"Your sister showed us some videos of your gigs," Hannah's dad says. "They were awesome."

I dredge up some of my signature Leo Sterling charm, because it suddenly feels so important that Hannah's parents like me.

"Aw, thank you," I say. "I love doing them. Hannah told me you guys used to listen to some of the stuff I cover?"

Her dad brightens, just a little, and then we're having an actually awesome talk about Guns N' Roses and Whitesnake and the Scorpions. Guy knows his stuff, and I can tell he's impressed that I do too. Hannah's mom is looking at us with the tiniest strum of a smile.

Still, there's something churning under the surface of this whole weird-ass conversation. Not quite blame, maybe just sadness. They're trying so hard to keep it under control. It's a level of chill I wouldn't have expected from any parents, especially hers.

I'm suddenly so grateful that Hannah made sure her mom knew I was giving her a ride. At least they knew she wasn't with some rando.

"I should probably get back to my room," I say after a while. Hannah's parents nod, and Astrid rolls my IV stand back to me.

"Hey, um—can you keep me posted?" I ask her. "Maybe tell me when she wakes up? I'm on the ninth floor. Room 908."

"Of course," Astrid answers.

Hannah's parents smile at me as I go. I manage to keep up the impression that I'm in one whole piece until I've turned the corner.

Then I duck into an empty stairwell and sink onto the steps. I suck in air like I've got a collapsed lung.

They were so . . . *nice to me.*

I don't deserve to be the one awake and walking around. Sure, Astrid told me about the glitching light and flat-out said it wasn't my fault. But I was driving. And everything I touch turns into a disaster. I fuck *everything* up.

I bury my face in my hands. I still don't even know if all my memories of Hannah are even *real.* This is such a mindfuck.

And Hannah has a broken arm. What does that mean for her dancing?

My chest feels so, so tight. The guilt is acid in my veins. *I'm so sorry, I'm so sorry, I'm so sorry.* Have I ruined Hannah's life?

And if she doesn't wake up—does that mean I've *ended* her life?

How would that even look? I don't want to picture it, but I can't stop the images from coming. Someone telling me in soft, kind euphemisms that Hannah just couldn't hang on. Hearing her mom wail, seeing the smile slide off her dad's face and break all over the floor. Me, numb and floating outside my body, watching as everything collapses around me.

The fear of losing Hannah builds and builds and builds until it's a screeching crescendo that fills the stairwell. If something happened to her, it'd be the worst FeelBad in the world.

I have spent my whole life avoiding things that hurt. Feelings that suck. Pain, grief, hard shit.

When I was alone with Hannah, I finally had someone to hold me, and she made the emptiness bearable. If she doesn't wake up—

Fuck. I can't do this. I can't be here. I promised her I would feel my feelings, but this is too much. Seeing her like this is more than I can handle.

I stumble up the stairs to the next floor. I stagger out of the stairwell and tear down a dark hallway, my already-useless sense of balance so destroyed that my shoulder bangs into the wall. Something falls over and crashes to the ground, but I don't look to see what it was.

I just run.

Hannah

I can't breathe. I can't move.

Leo's gone.

I'm lying on the stage, curled up in a ball around the pain. I've been here for hours. I'm wrung out, my eyes swollen, head throbbing.

I've got to get up.

Dancing was what got me through those first five days without him, so I close my eyes and think of the "Danse des petits cygnes." I call up the music in my mind, the steady bassoon beat and the piping oboe melody.

I chant the words as I move my hands. "Entrechat passé, entrechat passé, pique passé."

When I open my eyes, I'm back in my living room. The world outside is slick and dark and terrifying. The room looks exactly the same, only Leo's not here with me anymore. It's like a punch in the stomach, how much I *miss* him.

Shaking, I pull myself to my feet.

I stumble through my dark house and down the stairs to the basement. I sink to my knees in front of my bag of dance gear, numbly sifting through my pile of pointe shoes. It feels like I'm moving underwater as I tie the ribbons, as I scrape my matted hair up into a bun, as I rise onto pointe.

There's a reason I kept all this stupid imagination stuff in. Why I planned my life around something steady and reliable. None of this would have happened if I hadn't gone to the bookstore that day. If I'd never left my house, I could have coped. The emptiness only feels this unbearable now because Leo's gone.

I grab the barre tight. Pull my spine up. Turn out. Neck long. Chin high.

Dance.

I have to dance.

I have to dance until I can't feel anything at all.

Leo

Everything is spinning. The lights, the night, me.

It's dark in the back seat of the taxi, and every time the driver turns a corner, I slingshot across the leather seats. I wasn't dizzy at the hospital, but now every change in direction sends me into orbit.

I'll just pretend I'm drunk. *This is fun, Leo!* Like a ride at an amusement park, like bumper cars or something. *Fun, fun, fun.*

Stripes of orange light strobe across my arms as we zoom down the highway. It reminds me of the night Hannah and I chased the beam of light across the city, desperate for it to be a rescue helicopter. I swallow down a wave of nausea. *Don't think about her, don't think about her, DON'T THROW UP.*

The dried blood on the back of my hand isn't helping with the whole not-throwing-up thing. After fleeing the ICU, I pulled my IV out like Wolverine. Okay, maybe not like Wolverine. It took me five minutes to work up the courage to do it, and when it finally slithered out, I almost fainted.

Nobody stopped me as I walked through the bright hospital atrium and out the door, even with blood on my hand and my hospital bracelet peeking out from under a leather cuff.

I smash the hem of my T-shirt over my hand so I don't have to look at the blood. I'm wearing clothes that I found in a gym bag in the corner of my hospital room, and I peeled the bandage off my forehead and arranged my hair over the bruise.

Right now, I need a LifeHack. A whole waterfall of FeelGoods. I want to drown in music and energy and happiness, and this taxi is speeding me straight to a place where I can get all those things: Lissa's party.

Asher doesn't know I'm on my way—he would have tried to talk me out of it. Breaking out of the hospital when you haven't been cleared by the doctors is not one of my more brilliant plans, but I couldn't take another second of being in that building.

Finally the driver pulls to the curb, and I stumble out of the car and into the humid Houston night.

The thump of shitty subwoofers rumbles through me right away. There are clusters of people in the front yard, talking and laughing and drinking from Solo cups. The porch is decorated with cheap strands of pineapple-shaped lights and the front door's gaping open. I plunge right into the fray and start weaving through the rooms. Sliding back into my old tricks feels so easy. Feels like where I belong.

The bruise over my left ribs is starting to ache, and my head isn't doing great either, but it's nothing I can't handle. I'd expect to have a headache after that taxi ride anyway.

I finally find Asher slouched on a couch in the corner of the game room, looking lost under his old skater beanie. When he sees me, his face goes slack with shock.

"Holy shit, Leo! What are you doing here?"

"Had to get out of the hospital. It was boring," I say, shouting over the pulse of the music. I wince—whoever's made this playlist has no idea what they're doing.

Asher stands up, frowning. "I'll drive you back. I haven't had anything to drink."

"No need. I am totally fine, my dude. Shred-fucking-tastic."

He looks unconvinced. "You just woke up from a coma. You have to go back."

I sigh and roll my eyes. He's being such a grandma about it. "Just give me an hour, okay? Come on, Ash, I need some distraction."

He shakes his head, but we both know he's no match for my stubbornness.

"Fine," he says. "One hour."

I clap my hands together in victory, my rings clacking. "First item on the agenda: What even *is* this music?"

"I know. I told Lissa not to let her brother do the sound, but—"

I don't wait for him to finish, I just plunge into the crowd. He follows, always my trusty sidekick. There's a twinge somewhere, some new awareness that there's something unequal about our friendship that I never noticed before. Thinking about it doesn't FeelGood, so I ignore it.

I find the laptop that's hooked up to the speakers and set it to shuffle eighties rock. No more of this shitty house music. These kids need some Leo Sterling Top 20 up in here.

The song changes, and the piercing screech of an electric guitar zaps me back to life. This is my *jam*.

I'm steady now, expertly weaving through the crowd. Some people I recognize come up to me, and a few Skilletinas are here too. I'm the center of attention, and finally, *finally*, the night blends into a kaleido-scope of awesome: the pulsing beat of the party, the rush of energy through my veins, the loud music all around me. It's fireworks and pyrotechnics and headbanging nirvana.

I can mainline this feeling forever. Live in it and ignore everything else. Everything feels good, and this is all I need.

This is all I need.

The house fills up and the party gets louder and louder, and my veins are thrumming and I'm full of so much FeelGood I could burst.

Asher and I are hanging out by the pool, surrounded by dozens of people, dozens of heads bobbing to the beat of the music, dozens of cheeks glowing blue from the lights under the water. We're laugh-ing about something stupid when the song changes into something slower.

All the blood drains out of me.

It's "Patience"—the power ballad Hannah asked me to play when we were sitting by the creek.

In that splinter of a second, the party blurs around me, and all I can see is one flashing, living, memory: the summer-bright snapshot of Hannah riding next to me in Thunderchicken, framed by the rolled-down window. Sun was streaming in between the skyscrapers, heart-shaped sunglasses were perched on her freckled nose, and my heart was beating hard because she was smiling and it was almost a power chord.

The real world—Lissa's party—tilts.

Suddenly the bright shine of this night feels like a flimsy disguise.

Asher's asking what's wrong, but I'm gone—clawing my way into the house until I'm in front of the sound system. I slam the next song button, once, twice, three times, going fucking BALLISTIC on it. A nearby gaggle of people who were belting out the lyrics to "Patience" groan, then start cussing at me.

In my head, my sun-bright Hannah closes her eyes and trails a hand through the rushing wind outside Thunderchicken's window.

I try to shove her out of my mind. *Don't think about her, don't think about her.*

It's no use. The night is already crashing down around me.

Highs like drinking, smoking, being at this party—they always end. They're fleeting and quick. Being with Hannah is a different kind of high. Before her, I didn't know that making someone else feel better was its own kind of FeelGood. Every time I coaxed a smile or a laugh out of Hannah, every time I made the empty city a better place for her . . . those moments made me feel like I was a worthwhile person, and that's the best high in the world.

It was stupid to think this would work. No amount of FeelGood could make me forget Hannah.

The black pit in my stomach expands until it reaches my ears, blocking out the sounds of the party.

I left her.

I should have stayed, but instead I decided to run to this party and act like I didn't learn a fucking thing from being alone with her in our empty Houston.

I have majorly, majorly fucked up.

Someone taps my shoulder and asks me if I'm okay, but I shrug them off. It's suddenly so clear.

I have to go back to the hospital.

I need to find Asher. I stagger back out to the pool, but he's nowhere to be seen. I suddenly don't recognize a single person out here, and it feels like a creepy fun-house joke. I work my way back through the house, knocking on bedroom doors, looking in fucking *closets*. I shove my way through the crowd and out the front door, scanning both sides of the street for Asher's car. Did he leave without me?

The comedown is intense. I didn't drink anything, or smoke anything—I'm not quite that stupid—but I still feel ill. The party looks totally different now, all fake laughs and shrill voices. I miss Hannah's voice. I'm panicking.

Where the fuck is Asher?

I lean against the porch railing. My heart feels funny. It's going haywire, my pulse skittery like jazz. I have no idea what kind of medicine I was on at the hospital. What if the IV was keeping me from feeling like this?

The whole night feels so close to falling apart, like I'm on one of those old wooden roller coasters where you can feel the bolts shaking loose as you clack around the track.

A wave of nausea rolls over me. I squeeze my eyes shut and breathe through my nose. *Don't puke, don't puke.*

My head spins, and I'm suddenly terrified that I'm going to pass out, right on the porch of this godforsaken party, and everyone will just leave me here to sleep off another drunken night because I'm Leo fuckin' Sterling.

I'm so sorry, Hannah.

It takes my last ounce of balance to make it down the porch steps. I duck behind a row of bushes and sink to the ground, shaking and sweating.

I can't breathe.

What are you supposed to do when the world is closing in and the edges of your vision are going black? Put your head between your knees or something? Is this a panic attack, or something worse?

I drop my head, sucking in air. I grab on to the grass to keep the world from spinning.

I'm going to pass out.

Fuck.

This suddenly feels like a familiar story.

All those rock documentaries I used to watch with Asher? They weren't always high-octane glamorous fun. Halfway through most of them, sad dirges would start playing, signaling tragedy. Band relations went sour, hotel rooms were trashed, drugs were taken and drinks were drunk and lives crumbled.

And sometimes guys died.

Overdoses. Fatal drug cocktails. Am I going to end this night choking on my own vomit?

Through my thudding, closing-in world, something suddenly makes sense that never made sense before.

This is why.

This is why I lied to Salina Sakurai about writing original songs, why I haven't asked Bruce for a job, why I didn't want to buckle down and do the hard work that might turn Rat Skillet into a real career. I didn't trust myself to be able to handle it.

If I ever got the resources rock stars get, I'm the kind of person who would OD on FeelGood. I'd end up strung out in a ditch, dead, cold and blue, because every time I can't handle something, I smother it with something loud and wild. This time I'm on whatever the hospital gave me, but it's not hard to imagine me on something else. Leo's LifeHack.

I swallow down a sob. I don't want to be dead at thirty, choking on my own vomit.

With Hannah, I was different. Maybe I could do the whole music career thing if she were with me. I liked the Leo I was when I was with her.

Here, behind the bushes of some unimportant party, I realize: I don't have to keep being the Leo I was before.

I can choose to stick to everyone's expectations, have them nod their heads and say, *I knew he'd turn out like this*. I can keep running from the hard shit, and everyone will think, *That's just what Leo's like. Entertaining, life of the party, but selfish when the going gets tough.*

I have to stop fucking up, stop skating by on this bad boy reputation. When Hannah wakes up, that isn't going to be enough for her. When you love somebody, you can't just take all the good stuff and weasel out of the hard stuff.

Suddenly Asher's here, trying to squeeze in behind the bushes to check on me.

"Shit, Leo—someone saw you crawl back here. What the hell are you—"

"You gotta take me back to the hospital," I grit out, trying not to puke, trying not to cry, trying not to fall apart.

"Oh my god, yeah—yeah, of course." His eyes are wide and panicked. "Should I call an ambulance?"

"No, I'm okay—just get me back."

I couldn't care less about my own health; that's not the real reason why everything in me is straining for the hospital. I need to get back to Hannah, no matter how hard it is for me.

Fear courses through my veins again, rancid and hot. *What if she's still not awake?*

It doesn't matter.

It's not about me anymore.

Hannah

I double over at the barre in my basement, sucking air into my heaving lungs. I just finished a grueling variation, and pain throbs through my feet. A layer of sweat suffocates my skin. For one oxygen-deprived moment, there's nothing in my head at all. No thoughts, no feelings, no memories.

It doesn't last long.

I press my fingers over my eyes as it all closes in on me again. The emptiness. The silence. The deep, ringing truth that I'm absolutely alone.

It's been so long since Leo left. It's always dark now, so I don't even know how much time has passed. Upstairs, the windows are cold black panes of glass, except when lightning flashes and illuminates the pelting sheets of rain. I'm in the center of a raging, never-ending storm, and my house feels like the last safe place in the world. Maybe it is.

I grit my jaw, draw up onto pointe, and start again.

This time I get halfway through the song before my vision blacks out at the edges. I trip and end up on the floor.

Pain. It's the only thing I can think about. So much pain. My feet are bleeding. My head is throbbing with sadness, hunger, exhaustion.

God, I need some water.

I drag myself to my feet, barely make it upstairs to the kitchen and to the sink to fill a cup. I stagger to the couch and sink into it. Earlier, I changed into my mom's *Swan Lake* Odette costume. The tutu crinkles around me, glass crystals glinting in the dark. The silk corset digs into the skin under my arms, rubbing me raw along every edge.

Just a little break, I think. Just a few minutes, and then I'll go back down.

I take a shuddering breath, and the smell of a just-blown-out candle fills my nose. Tears prickle at my eyes. My house still smells like Leo.

Outside the kitchen windows, the world is a dark and crumbling nightmare.

"What am I supposed to do?" I whisper into the dark. If the storm outside is just my imagination, why can't I make it stop? Maybe there was a limit to my power, and I used it all up painting skies.

As if in answer, a streak of lightning turns the room white. I go nearly blind when it reflects off something in the corner of the room.

It's the gilded edge of a picture frame.

Starburst.

I stumble across the room and sink to my knees in front of the painting. I run my fingers over the hard ridges of paint. I forgot Leo hauled it in after we got back from my grandparents—I was too much

299

of a mess to do anything. I trace a whorl of the woman's luminescent hair, and I swear I can feel something warm and living under my fingertips.

Starburst looks just like she did in the museum, floating in midair, bursting with life and momentum, back arched and hair flying out around her. *The Day She, the Starburst, Shook Loose.*

"I wish I were more like you," I say softly.

I flick a glance at my basement door. I can go back down. I can keep dancing. I can try to fight a little longer.

I look down at my pointe shoes, at my legs, at the stiff tulle skirt of my tutu.

I'm an imposter in a ballerina's body. I never asked the other girls at the Academy their reasons for dancing, but I knew they weren't the same as mine. Some were addicted to having a strong, healthy, capable body. Some were true performers, living for the applause and the accolades, or a jealous glint of admiration from another dancer. But for the majority, and for my mom, it was always a love of the artistry: the music, the grace, the beauty.

Me? I danced because it was all I knew.

I was always waiting to feel something—a passion for the physicality or the artistry or the performance, but it never happened. And it's never going to, because my heart's not in it. I'm not sure it ever was.

When Leo coaxed me out into the city, I had some of the best moments of my life. Speeding in Thunderchicken. Writing by the creek. Spinning out gorgeous, mind-blowing things. Painting the sky.

In between the fear and the panic, the real Hannah got to peek out. The Hannah I was meant to be.

If this is the end, I don't want to spend it dancing.

I press my hands to my chest and force myself to breathe slower. In front of me, the painting glows to life, lighting up the whole room with a vapor-wave glow.

It's gorgeous.

With trembling fingers, I pull my bobby pins from my hair. Slowly. One at a time. I tug my fingers through the crisp hairspray, breaking the bonds until my hair is soft. My scalp tingles from the released pressure.

And then, equally as carefully, I work my fingernails into the knots at my ankles. I untie my ribbons and peel my sweating, bleeding, aching feet out of my pointe shoes.

I take a deep breath and will myself to stop shaking. I want to spend my last few minutes being who I always wanted to be. A girl who pulls words out of the air. Who *imagines* things.

With one hand still on Starburst, I press the other palm against the living room's french doors.

I close my eyes and feel my power rally.

Maybe I won't be strong enough to turn the sky a different color. But who says darkness is bad? The same people who laughed when I wrote out my first stumbling stories, who made me feel like my imagination was embarrassing and stupid? Who made Leo feel like he was never going to amount to much?

There's nothing wrong with night. I can make night pretty too.

When I open my eyes, the rain has stopped. Beyond the raindrop-jeweled glass, there's a navy-blue night sky full of twinkling stars. More stars than I've ever seen before.

I wait to see if the vision holds. When it does, I raise up an iridescent moon. It's huge, looming, and it coats my backyard with a glowing, pearly light.

I ease the door open and step into the night.

Outside, it's silent. But instead of the terrifying quiet of the first few days I was alone, this silence is serene.

I take a step. Another. Until I'm in the middle of my backyard.

All around me, the world is muffled. At peace. The night smells like rain and growing grass. I'm sure I can even smell the moon, all cold rock and iron.

Steadiness returns to my legs. With each step, I feel magic swirling around me. The blades of grass lengthen, stretching out, waving softly at my ankles.

I think about *Flower Magic*, about how alive I felt when I was hunched over my little fifth-grader desk.

I can make my flowers real now. With each step toward the moon, buds bloom from the ground. They unfurl into pristine snowflakes, each as big as my hand, frozen in their own icy ecosystems. The snowflakes aren't white. They're magenta, searing turquoise, Prussian blue. More stems push up from the earth, and this time the buds burst into sparks, crackling at my ankles like fireworks.

The yard shifts around me as I walk, the very dimensions of the night opening up. The world breathes and steps aside for my imagination.

I tip my chin up and raise my eyes to the sky, just like Starburst.

I lift off the ground.

My bare feet dangle below me. They're gnarled and swollen and stained with bruises. My hair goes weightless as it fans out around me.

Floating here above my yard, I laugh at how absurd it is. I'm *flying*.

I rise and see nothing but darkness beyond the borders of my yard. I'm not in Houston anymore. The darkness starts to press in from every side, and the spot of color and light that is my yard shrinks as if I'm inside a deflating balloon.

Instead of fighting the darkness, I just concentrate on keeping the ever-shrinking orb I'm in as bright and colorful as I can.

I think about David Lee Sloth. My grandma. My dad. Astrid. My mom.

The darkness presses in closer, aching to blend me into its blackness. Into nothing.

A terrifying cold sweeps through my body. I tell my lungs to breathe, but they won't cooperate. I gasp for air, my head throbbing and my chest burning.

Is this what the end feels like?

My last thoughts are of Leo. How he looked when I let him in the bookstore, with his lopsided smile and all that excitement.

What would our days have been like if he could have stayed? If it was only the bright, lovely things and none of the darkness?

In my last seconds, I imagine it. Hours and hours of a life together, just me and him. I've got a million words to describe it all.

I hold it with me for a moment, and then I say goodbye. I have to let go of it. That life was just a daydream, not something I'll ever get to live.

I lean back and let my arms fall open

and everything ends.

Leo

It's one in the morning when I lurch to a halt outside the hospital entrance, swaying like a drunk in the yellow square of light in front of the automatic doors. My ribs are really hurting now, so much that my chest feels like one big achy bruise. Asher reaches out to steady me.

"What's up?" he asks, his voice slow and steady like it always is, even when he's not stoned.

"I just realized that I don't exactly have a plan."

"Since when do you ever have a plan, dude?"

"Eh . . . that's fair. Let me think."

We could use some help. If I get caught, they'll whisk me straight up to my room and I won't be able to find out if Hannah's condition has changed.

So I tell Asher where to find the family waiting room for the ICU, and then I wait in the shadows next to his car, trying not to puke.

It's only when I see Astrid charging out of the front doors of the hospital in her overalls and combat boots with steam coming out of her ears that I think maybe it wasn't the best plan.

Asher's trailing sheepishly behind her as she makes her way

through the dark parking lot. She plows up to me like a fiery little dragon.

"What the bloody *hell* were you thinking?" she hisses, eyes wild.

"I just—"

"You just woke up from a *coma*, you twit!" She whirls. "And you!" She pokes at Asher's chest.

I suppress a laugh at the way Asher's eyes go round at this tiny little British person giving him hell. He's gone furiously pink under his freckles. Their size difference is comical.

"How long was he at that party?" Astrid demands. "You should have thrown him over your big, brutish shoulder and hauled him right back here, you pillock!"

"Pillock?" Asher repeats, bewildered and glancing at me for help. I shrug. I don't know what that means either.

Before she can eat him alive, I step forward.

"I got freaked out, Astrid," I say. "I thought if I went to the party, I'd just—be able to not think about her for a few minutes. It didn't work."

I sound pathetic and broken and all kinds of in love. I sway on the spot, fighting another wave of wooziness.

Beside me, Asher is tense. He hates it when people argue. Ro and Gage argue all the time when our band is practicing—about lyrics, about tempos, about how Ro's guitar riffs fit with Gage's rhythms. If it gets really bad, I duck out on the pretense of getting a snack, but most of the time I wait and watch Asher. At first, he'll just sit down on an amp and pick at his baggy jeans and stare at the floor like he's not paying attention. But then he'll get up, shuffle over to Ro and Gage, and suggest something that perfectly combines both of their ideas.

People think he's just a dumb, quiet stoner, but he's brilliant.

In the shadowy hospital parking lot, Astrid blows out her breath, hands still on her hips.

"So . . . will you help me get back in?" I ask.

She pinches the bridge of her nose. "You two are bloody knackering." After another long silence, she exhales.

"Fine. Let's get you back to your room then, you muppet. Although I have no idea how we're going to manage that."

Asher clears his throat. "Uh, maybe you could go in and get a wheelchair, then take him in in that? And if you get stopped, you could say he couldn't sleep and you took him for a stroll?" He shrugs, looking a bit queasy, like he fully expects to get his head chomped off.

Astrid crosses her arms. Purses her lips. "It could work." She flicks an appraising glance over him, like she's reevaluating him. "Well, let's get it over with, then," she says at last, before turning on her heel and stalking back into the hospital.

We do get stopped coming out of the elevator on the ninth floor, but thanks to Astrid's smooth talking, we get me back to my room without incident.

Sneaking out of a hospital—and back in—might sound impossible, but adults are never as competent as they say they are.

"Before you go, Astrid—will you say something to her for me? I want her to know I'm here. I won't freak out again."

She huffs. "I can't decide if you're ridiculously romantic or just a stupid asshole."

"Stupid asshole," Asher helpfully supplies, and I punch his shoulder.

"Yes, fine, I'll tell her," Astrid says, stomping out the door.

Asher helps me onto my bed.

"Hey, Ash?" I have work to do, for Hannah, for my *future*, and it starts here. "I'm sorry I brushed you off before—when you said you missed me. I missed you too."

"It's okay, dude. I know it's not an easy thing to talk about. I just wanted to say it. Tell you how fucked up I would have been if you'd, like, died or something. In case you didn't know."

"I'd be really fucked up if you died too," I say. "In case you didn't know."

We hug, and I finally let myself collapse onto my hospital bed.

Asher glances nervously at the door. "I, uh, better take off. In case she comes back."

"Wait—are you scared of her?" I ask.

"Um, yes. So much yes."

I laugh and use the heel of my hand to scrub the tears off my cheeks. "Okay. Go get some sleep."

"I'll bring you lunch or something later. No school today."

"That sounds awesome."

Once I'm alone again, I stare up at the ceiling.

On the drive here, in Asher's car, I started reading about comas on my phone. Apparently the chances of waking up gets a lot slimmer after twenty-four hours.

Hannah's just passed that mark.

"Hannah, I'm here," I whisper into the darkness. "I came back. I got scared. But I'm here now, for as long as it takes."

I listen hard, with my ears and my heart, but I can't *feel* Hannah waking up. Astrid doesn't come bounding back with good news.

I'm such an idiot. Did I think she'd wake up as soon as I arrived on the scene, like I'm some kind of wholesome Prince Charming?

"I'm here," I whisper again, but it feels like it doesn't matter.

I feel so, so helpless.

Hannah

The first thing I hear is my mother's voice.

I feel my body moving—no, I'm *being* moved. Like a doll. Unfamiliar voices speak over me, but the words are muffled, like I'm hearing them through a pillow.

I moan and try to move. Someone says, "Yes, see that? She's definitely coming around."

There are more noises. Rustling clothes, people breathing. Why am I getting the sense that there's a whole audience watching me wake up?

My body aches. I try to roll over, but I can't. My right arm is weighing me down like an anchor.

"Hannah?"

It's my mom again. She's brushing her finger down my nose, over and over, like she used to do when I was a baby.

"You're okay," she says, her tone soothing. "It's okay, I'm here."

I drift off for a bit. I must go very still, because she's saying my name again, and the urgent panic in her voice has me trying to resurface. To reassure her I'm here.

"Hannah? Is she—"

I'm here. Just a second.

I fight up through the heavy urge to just *sleep*.

When I blink open my eyes, I'm surprised to find that I'm not in my own bed. I'm in a bright room with white ceiling tiles.

There are lots of people standing around me, staring down at me. My vision snags on the white lab coats first. The stethoscopes. Surgical masks hanging around necks. Okay . . . I'm in a hospital. That much is obvious.

My eyes wheel around, my body moving so much slower than my mind.

"Mama?" I croak.

"Yes, yes, Hannah, I'm here," she says, cupping her hand around my face and beaming love down at me.

I feel so floaty and disconnected.

"Hannah, oh, thank god," she whispers.

And then my dad is there too, leaning in to kiss my forehead.

"Daddy," I say, and the tenderness in his smile makes me melt.

It feels like a dream.

I close my eyes and drift off again. There's more conversation between all the people in the room, and the sounds of beeping and buttons being tapped. I feel lazy, too tired to think about what's going on and why they're all watching me.

"I can't move my arm, Mama," I mumble.

"It's broken, baby."

What?

That sends a sparking pulse of adrenaline through me. The sleepiness scatters. Before, Mom's voice was like an alarm you can hit snooze on. A broken arm is like hearing a doorbell ringing over and over: You have to scramble up because answering it is the only way to make it stop.

I crane my neck. Sure enough, there's a neon-green cast on my right arm, looming like a mountain over my chest.

When I try to move it, there's just a dull ache in my bones. No movement.

I have a broken arm.

Don't freak out, don't freak out—

Oh god, I have an audition coming up. It's been circled on my calendar for so long, the one day that I've been working toward for nearly my whole life, but I can't audition with this *thing* on my arm.

It takes months to recover from broken bones. Which means . . . I won't be able to audition for the corps de ballet until next year.

I almost throw up.

What does this mean for my *life*?

My mom is oblivious to my turmoil; she's just tear-streaked and grateful. "Conrad, go get Astrid. She'll be so happy." Mom brushes my hair back from my face carefully. "She sat with you all night. I couldn't get her to leave to get some sleep," she says.

A nurse raises the head end of my bed. They've just propped a pillow behind me when I hear squeaking, stomping noises. Astrid bounds into view, literally skipping in her Doc Marten boots.

"Hey, Astrid," I croak, with as much of a smile as I can muster.

I should feel comforted with the three of them here, but they all look as tired and shell-shocked as I feel. It's weird to see Astrid without her hair in one of her perfect 1940s updos—right now there are untamed tufts of frizzy red hair sticking out from under a bandanna. And my mom and dad look so . . . old.

Astrid keeps squealing my name, and then she thrusts something toward me—a Mylar balloon in the shape of Elmo's head. *Get Well Soon.*

"I would have got flowers, but they aren't allowed in the ICU, and I thought you needed something cheerful." She keeps talking, but the words don't go in. I'm far away, something rushing in my ears that makes it hard to hear.

Slow down. Slow down. This is an *ICU?*

"Guys," I rasp. "What am I doing in an ICU?"

"Hannah, you were in a car accident," Mom says. "Don't you remember?"

"No," I whisper. *A car accident? How?*

"Leo was driving you home from the coffee shop—remember you asked me if he could take you home?"

Astrid interrupts. "I cannot believe you talked to him, you sneaky minx. Did it turn into a little date or something? I cannot *wait* to hear all about it."

I'm so confused. "What do you mean Leo? Leo as in Leo Sterling?"

My mom's voice goes thin, hesitant. "Hannah? Do you not remember any of this?"

I shake my head.

It doesn't make any sense.

What on earth would I have been doing in a car with *Leo Sterling*?

Leo

I jolt straight up in my hospital bed to the sound of Astrid shouting my name.

She skids to a stop in the doorway of my room. I feel so rough and bleary that at first I can only blink at her, then at the clock on the wall that tells me it's seven a.m. I've only had four hours of sleep since she snuck me back in after Lissa's party.

Astrid's eyes are watery, like she's been crying.

My heart lurches into my throat.

But instead of saying the words that I've been so afraid of hearing, she says—

"She's awake."

It's been more than an hour since Astrid dropped her earth-shattering news and bounded off down the hallway.

I've been pacing around my hospital room ever since, completely destroying my hair. I can't believe she left without telling me *anything* else. It's still early, so my family's not here yet to help me do some reconnaissance. Every time a nurse passes my door, I ask them if they know anything about Hannah. They're sick of me. I'm sick of me.

At first, I was just purely, outrageously happy to hear the news, but I slid down into being *petrified* pretty quick.

I did the math. We got in the accident at ten on Saturday, and Hannah woke up at seven o'clock Monday morning. Thirty-three hours. That's how long she was unconscious. What will that mean? I sprang right up after my coma, but I read so many horror stories last night about all the people who don't, or have years of recovery to face. Some are just never the same.

Even if Hannah is the same, will she even *remember* me?

Or will she just remember Saturday, and not . . . everything else?

I know Saturday has to be real, because we have bruises and police reports and medical files to prove it, but the rest of it? Days of conversations and touches and almost kisses and the way she completely changed my life? I have no idea if those things are real.

Fuck, if she remembers the wreck, will she even want to see me? What if she hates me?

I stifle down a yell, tugging on my hair until it hurts.

I'm spiraling.

I can't take it anymore. If Astrid isn't going to come back and give me an update, I have to go see for myself. I'm losing my shit in here.

I smooth my hair down and attempt to look like a normal fucking person who's not exploding out of their skin. I stroll out of my room. I'm wearing normal clothes; aside from my medical bracelets and the fact that I'm not wearing shoes, I look more like a visitor than a patient. Thank fuck I don't have to drag that IV stand around with me anymore—I've graduated to huge pain pills presented to me in little paper cups.

The nurse on duty behind the ninth-floor desk looks up, peering at me over her glasses. "Everything okay, Leo?"

"Yeah, um—I just heard that Hannah—the girl I was in the car accident with—is awake? Do you think I could go down and see how she's doing?"

The nurse points down the hall. "They just brought her up here, Romeo. Room 932."

My arms and legs go fizzy with a sudden, swamping wave of nervousness. *She's here.*

Her room is on the other side of the floor, past the elevators. If she'd been on this side, I would have seen her being rolled into her room.

I count the doors as I go, my nerves vibrating. 932 is the last door on the left.

I'm almost there when my courage falters. I tip over and a smooth, calm blue wall catches me. I close my eyes. Deep breaths.

What if she doesn't remember me? What if she hates me, what if she's not okay?

And then, because her door is propped open, I hear her *voice.*

Relief hits me hard. It takes everything in me not to start crying on the spot.

Her voice is exactly how I remember it: low and warm and raspy, reminding me of jazz singers and curling wisps of smoke and the comfort of arms around me and whiskey on the rocks.

And someone's answering her. A cheery, bell-like voice, saying,

"I'll go ask one of your nurses for another one. Won't be a moment." My brain registers that it's an English accent, but I don't have time to move or hide or even straighten up before Astrid comes careening out of the room.

She squeaks to a stop two feet away from me.

I smile pathetically. "We've got to stop meeting like this," I say, going for a charming grin, but it falters. She's not fooled. "Okay, fine. I got impatient."

Something passes between us, some electric excitement—*she's really awake, yes I know, isn't it wonderful, I can't believe it*—and then Astrid's face sort of . . . twitches.

"What?" I ask, suddenly alert.

"What what?"

"What was that . . . twitchy look for?"

"What twitchy look?" she says, feigning ignorance.

"Astrid."

She slumps, leaning against the wall, mirroring my posture. "Um."

I squeeze my eyes shut. Bracing myself. "Astrid. Is she okay?"

"She's good, she's really good—it's not that. God, I'm so sorry, Leo. It's just—she doesn't remember the accident. She doesn't remember *you.*"

My chest caves in. The world is falling apart around me. My ears white out, all the sound sucked out of the world, and I'm glad I'm leaning against the wall, because it's the only thing keeping me upright.

"What?" I hear myself whispering it stupidly. How can she not remember?

"I'm so sorry," Astrid says. "God, something really amazing must have happened at that coffee shop."

I nod. Because that's not the truth, but it's close enough to it. Something amazing did happen, somewhere. Maybe.

No.

No, no, no.

It's devastation and discordant feedback and broken guitar strings and everything bad in the world. Because I'm in love with a girl who doesn't even know me.

I'm flooded with an overwhelming urge to just *see* her. I don't even know what I'll do. I just need to see her. I need to look her in the eye and make sure that she really doesn't remember.

"Can I see her?" I ask.

Astrid's eyes swim with pity. She glances at Hannah's open doorway, back to my face, over and over, thinking. "Um, ugh. You clearly like her so much. This sucks." She bites her lip.

"Please let me see her, Astrid. Are her parents here? Should I ask them?"

"They've gone to deal with some insurance issue." Astrid chews on her thumbnail. "Maybe if she sees you, it'll help?"

I nod again, afraid to get in the way of this girl's decision-making process, but my eyes are beaming, *Yes, let me see her, please, I have to see her.*

"Okay, chuck," she finally says, nodding. "But only because you're a ridiculously romantic asshole. Let's get this done before someone comes back to run more tests on her."

My stomach somersaults with the victory, but then I'm hit with a crashing, numbing, all-consuming *fear*.

I'm not ready for this.

Before I can wipe that look off my face, Astrid drags me into Hannah's room.

Hannah

Astrid's just gone to get me another pillow. The one propping up the stupid cast on my arm has already been smashed into a pancake.

Without her or my parents in the room, I start to freak out again. About the audition on Saturday that I'm going to have to miss. About my broken arm. About the uncertainty of everything.

I've only been awake for an hour, and I've been on the edge of tears for every minute of it. It's all too much to wrap my head around. It's unbelievable how one small thing—one slender bone breaking—has the power to tear my neat career plans to shreds. When I think about my future now, all I can see is uncertainty and emptiness. I know I should feel lucky that I'm not more seriously injured, but every time I look down and see the cast I start to hyperventilate.

I'm trying to figure out if I'm about to throw up or burst into tears when Astrid comes marching back into my room. I'm about to say, *That was fast*—but then I see the person she's dragging behind her.

It's Leo Sterling.

He's the very last person I expected to see in my hospital room one hour after waking up. I reflexively tug my sheet to make sure I'm covered. I don't want some random guy from school seeing me like this.

Has he come to apologize or something? I know he was driving, even though I don't actually *remember* being in a car with him. Besides, everyone keeps saying it was caused by a traffic light failure, so he doesn't have anything to apologize for.

But he doesn't say anything at all. He just stares down at the floor by my feet, his face stricken and panicked.

Well, this is awkward.

I'm about to ask Astrid why she brought him in here when he finally raises his head. Our eyes *lock* and then—

Oh—

In the space of one heartbeat, my entire world collapses, then rebuilds itself into something new.

Because it's *Leo.*

I clap my hand over my mouth to stifle a delirious laugh. Or maybe it's a sob, or a shout, or every emotion in the world rolled into one. All the moments we spent together come rushing back to me, in a kaleidoscope of images and feelings and *memories.*

Wait.

How do I have all these memories of us? My mind runs up against a huge wall of WTF. This is *impossible.* We were together in what . . . a dream? While I was here in the hospital? That's ridiculous.

The last thing I remember is finding Starburst in my living room and walking out into my backyard. I was so sure I was dying. But now I'm here. It makes no sense.

Leo shifts his weight onto one foot and sinks down onto his hip like he did so many times in the empty Houston. He gives me a small smile, and I don't care that it doesn't make sense, because I just *know* that it was all true. That it was all real, somehow.

"Hi, Hannah," Leo says, softly, almost *nervously*, shoving his hands into the pockets of his unfairly tight jeans. He's wearing the same gray shirt that he was wearing when we met in the bookstore.

"Hi," I whisper.

"Bloody hell," Astrid says, breathy and mystified. "Did it actually work? Do you really remember him now?"

I nod, too blissed out to speak. I remember *everything*, and I can't take my eyes off him.

Astrid squeals in delight. "Well, get over there, then," she says, nudging Leo toward my bed.

He comes to sit on the edge of my mattress. We stare at each other for a moment, and then—then I just *throw* myself at him, and he crushes forward too, and we're colliding with an impact that's almost painful, but I don't care. I'm half in his lap and his chest is solid and huge and he's all I can see. We're pressing and wrapping and squeezing, so tight I can't imagine ever being able to peel ourselves apart.

I thought I'd never see him again.

I bury my face in his neck, throat thick and close to tears. *God, he smells the same.*

I'm glowing with one single, ultra-clear thought: I never want to let go of him. I never want to be without him again. When he left me on that stage—

323

My grip on him gets even tighter. My cast is probably hurting him, scratching against his neck, but I don't care.

We stay like that for a long time, and then we're rocking back and forth with the relief of it, and then we're finally loosening our grip on each other. The heat of it gets uncomfortable, but I still don't let go until I remember that Astrid's here.

We draw apart at last, but Leo doesn't go far. He presses his forehead to mine, and I breathe him in.

"Thank fuck," Leo says softly. "I was so worried you wouldn't remember."

But I do. Because of him, I have a whole handful of sea-glass-beautiful moments from the empty city. Speeding downtown to get to SpandexFest. Leo strumming his guitar on the dock. Lying next to him under a painted sky. Pressing napkins to his stomach and struggling to keep my eyes off his happy trail.

I flush hot with embarrassment. Out of all the memories of our days together, did my brain really have to snag on that one?

Leo raises an eyebrow at the color rising on my cheeks. He chuckles. "Mmm. You really do remember."

From somewhere outside our little bubble, Astrid cheers. "Ooh, girl! As soon as we are alone, you are telling me this whole steamy story."

I turn even redder, dropping my head to Leo's chest to hide my face.

He flinches. I know him well enough to know it's not him flinching from me. It's a . . . pain flinch?

Oh no. He was driving—he must have been hurt too. My lungs constrict as my eyes rove over him, checking for injuries.

"I'm okay," he says, like he can read my mind. "Just some bruising on my ribs and a bump on the head. Knocked me out for eighteen hours, though."

We have a whole conversation with our eyes. I have so many questions for him. Where were we? *When* were we? He shakes his head and gives a little shrug. He doesn't have the answers, and we can't talk about this in front of Astrid anyway. She must think we met the night of the wreck and spent like an hour together. We'll have to get our stories straight later, about how we know so much about each other, how it feels like we've been to the end of the world and back again together.

Leo finds my hand, weaving his fingers through mine. Everywhere he touches, I light up with heat. That reminds me: We haven't even kissed yet. I almost laugh at the absurdity of it.

"Crap," I blurt suddenly. "I have to go for a CT scan."

Something flashes over Leo's face—he's reining something in, and whatever it was is replaced with worry. I'm worried too.

"That's okay," he says. "I should probably get back to my room anyway."

I grab his hand. *Don't leave me*, I want to plead.

He must understand, because he squeezes my hand, says, "Hey, my room's right down the hall, okay?"

I swallow.

He leans in, mouth close to my ear, and it feels like he presses the tiniest of kisses to my hair.

"I'm not going anywhere," he murmurs, and the vibrations of his voice skitter down my spine even as the words soothe me.

Of course, that's the moment my nurse chooses to bustle in with a wheelchair, chirpily asking if I'm all ready to go down to diagnostic imaging.

Leo's lips are still hovering near my temple, and he mumbles crankily against my skin, "You know, all these interruptions are making that empty city look pretty attractive."

The nurse helps me into the wheelchair, even though I don't really need it to walk. It must just be procedure. Leo stands and moves away from the bed, and it's almost physically painful when the distance between us grows. I want him with me. All the time.

"Can I tag along?" Leo asks suddenly.

"Sorry, sweetie, only family." She adjusts the pancake pillow supporting my cast. "Hannah, your parents should be finishing up with that paperwork soon, so your mom will be with us for the scan, okay?"

Sure enough, my parents appear in the doorway a few seconds later. I watch, dumbfounded, as their eyes light up when they see Leo.

He crosses the room to say hi, and I look at Astrid with wide, disbelieving eyes, like *What sorcery is this?* She just laughs.

"Okay, Mom, Hannah, everyone ready?" the nurse asks, pointing my wheelchair toward the door.

I want to say no. My eyes stay glued on Leo. I want him to come with me and hold my hand the whole time.

I'm so afraid he'll disappear.

"Come back later?" I say, sounding small and silly. It's only a fraction of what I want to say. That if I had to choose between having all this with no Leo and having just him in an empty city, I know what I'd choose. I can't say that, of course—my *parents* are here. He understands me, though, all the words behind my words.

He levels his gaze.

"Wouldn't miss it for the world, Hannah."

Hannah

I end up falling asleep right after the CT scan. I wake to find the Houston sun slanting orange through the windows, pouring over my sheets like fire.

I feel weirdly refreshed.

Leo's right down the hall, I think, smiling. I'm high on the knowledge that we're both here. We're with our families again, and Houston's back to normal. We weren't dead after all. We never were.

The way he hugged me, and smiled at me, and told me he'd come back later to check on me . . . it's just *everything*.

Not long after I wake up, a nurse comes in to take my IV out. My mom helps me shower, holding my cast outside the shower curtain.

Back in my room, I can't seem to wipe away the smile tucked in the corner of my mouth. I get to see Leo again. Today, and tomorrow, and the day after that, and the day after that.

My mom starts combing through my wet hair, and I tumble into a daydream about writing, about being loose and free and creative. This morning, I could only see a blank page where my life was supposed to be, just the tattered remains of a ballet career, and now it's all hope and plans and possibility. I'm not the cardboard-cutout ballerina I was when I found Leo in the music store.

My dad is in the corner, tapping on his work phone. Astrid had to go home to get some homework done for school tomorrow, but before she left, she kissed my temple and told me how much she loved my face. She keeps texting me, trying to pry out juicy details about my Saturday night with Leo, and nearly every one has me dissolving into giggles.

I won't even need to be in the hospital for much longer. They're keeping me here to make sure I don't have a latent brain bleed, but I feel fine. The nurses are still buzzing about it, how they had two coma recoveries in a row after years of passing patients to long-term care homes to sleep their lives away.

"Hey, I have some good news," my mom says, deftly braiding my hair. "I called Madame Menard while you were napping."

A little jolt of alarm skitters through me. Madame Menard is the head of my ballet academy.

"She was happy to hear that you're awake and doing so well."

"Oh. Okay. Good," I say woodenly. Where is this going? I suddenly feel like something very, very bad is about to happen.

"So, I asked her what our options were," Mom continues, excitement building in her voice. "About the audition on Saturday. You've been working so hard for it, Hannah. So . . . she's going to pull some strings and see if we can send performance tapes and recommendation letters in as your audition material, instead of being there in person! Isn't that fantastic?"

"Wait . . . so, like, there's a chance I could still join the corps de ballet?" I ask cautiously.

"If they're impressed with your videos, which of course they will be."

"But my arm . . ." I trail off. A video might be fine for the audition, but what about when I show up to a rehearsal and can't move my freakin' arm? It's hardly the way to start a career.

Mom's voice takes on a reassuring hum. "You're really doing so well, Hannah. All the doctors keep saying so. Your arm should heal just fine."

There's so much bright hope on her face, but my stomach is sinking, sinking, sinking.

"The doctor said to rest for a couple of weeks, but after that you can start doing lower-body work, and we'll get you back up and running before you know it. It's a good thing it wasn't your leg."

My eyes start to sting.

This feels wrong.

If she'd said all this yesterday when I woke up, when I was freaking out about my future as a dancer, I would have been grateful. I would have been so happy to hear it. Soothed, reassured.

But I don't feel that way anymore.

Now it feels like all my possibilities are being yanked away.

I stare down at my hospital blanket, tugging on the threads until there's a hole. I think about the way I feel when I write, when the words are filtering through my fingers like sand. I think about painting skies and writing songs with Leo and inventing whole daydreams for us. I think about the way I felt when I came up with a backstory for Lonely Girl in the museum—JoyPuke.

I never felt like that with dance.

I realize I don't want to retrain. I don't want to do weeks and weeks of rehab to get back to where I was. I don't want to show up on the first day as a member of a huge ballet company with a neon-green cast on my arm.

I don't want to dance anymore.

I said that in the empty Houston too, albeit for slightly different reasons. There, it was because dance wasn't *working*. It wasn't helping me forget Leo. It wasn't helping me forget that I was alone.

Here in the real world, I don't have to lean on dancing as a crutch or a coping mechanism.

But it's still the choice I made when I thought it was the end, when I was floating in my moonlit backyard as the darkness closed in on me. It's bone-deep.

I can be whatever I want to be now. And I don't want to be Ballet Chick anymore.

I don't want to be a dancer.

Mom smooths my hair back away from my face. "Hannah? Are you all right? You've gone so pale. You know I'm going to be beside you every step of the way, right? We can do this, okay? I know—let's think about what videos we can use."

I open my mouth—almost entertaining the idea of answering her question, of tonelessly listing my best performances.

I could go on pretending ballet is something I want to do. I could keep pretending that I'm still the Hannah I was before the accident.

But I'm not.

And it's time I started taking steps toward becoming the Hannah I caught glimpses of in the empty city.

My mom looks at me, her elegant neck craning, her eyes sparkling. I have to tell her *now*. The longer I wait, the worse it will get. She'll send a video off to the Academy, and there will be no turning back. I can just see myself trying to please everyone, going with the flow, hoping that the passion will come eventually.

Too bad the very idea of saying those words to her is giving me severe stomach cramps. I'm starting to sweat, and everything in my body is thudding with nervousness.

Waiting won't make it easier. I have to tell her.

I have no idea how she'll react. This is our life. This is everything we've been working for. She might totally flip out. My whole body feels wound tight and hypersensitive.

"Hannah? Are you all right, sweetie?" Mom lays her hand over my forehead like she's checking my temperature. "Should I get a doctor?" she says, suddenly alert.

"No—I—"

I'm shaking. My tongue is suddenly as dry as cardboard.

I take a deep breath. Brace myself.

"Mom? I don't want to dance anymore."

As soon as the words are out, my stomach drops.

My mom goes very still.

Oh my god. Did I really just do that? I can't believe I just did that. The old Hannah would have *never.* I hold my breath. It's out there now.

"I don't understand," Mom says, voice thin, stunned. "What do you mean?"

In the corner, my dad stops typing on his phone, suddenly tuning in to this looming disaster between his two girls.

I swallow hard. "I don't want to send in an audition tape, Mama."

Her face is ashen. I think I can hear her heart thumping. Aching.

My nerves are going haywire, and I've got full-body tremors. I feel ill, like something's wrong with my body, but it might just be the thrill, like a dive on a roller coaster. Even though I'm thoroughly freaking out, there's a beaming part of myself that's *proud.* I said what I wanted. I stood up for myself.

Mom plasters a weird little smile on her face and shakes her head. "I'm sorry. I don't understand. Conrad?" she says, looking at my dad.

Dad stands up and tucks his phone in his pocket. He comes to stand next to Mom.

"Where is this coming from, Han?"

I suck in a breath. I can't tell them anything about the time I spent alone, or with Leo, or about the empty Houston I lived in. But I can tell her the reason itself. It's so simple. I can't believe I didn't see it before.

"My heart's not in it," I whisper. "It hasn't been for a long time."

Mom's face goes slack.

She stumbles over to the window, the limp from that long-ago injury more pronounced than ever. With her back to me, she looks out over Houston. She makes one single sniffling sound, and my whole body feels rotten.

"Mama?" I say. My ears are starting to ring. Tears well up in my eyes.

This is why I stuck to this stupid plan for twelve years. I was so scared of disappointing her, and now I've done more than that. I've wrecked her.

My whole life, I've been her sidekick, her mini me. Eliza Ashton and her perfect little daughter, hand in hand. Like those photos in catalogs of gorgeous mother-daughter pairs wearing matching outfits, romping in a field of sunflowers.

My heart is breaking. Have I ruined something here?

I'm terrified I've ruined something here.

"Come back, Eliza," my dad says, soft and cautious, holding his hand out.

She walks to him in a daze and leans against him. I feel so small down here on the bed.

"Hannah . . . what will you *do*?"

She looks genuinely anguished. I know what she means, because I've thought the exact same thing. *Who will you be without ballet?*

Fear flares in me. It's what always stopped me from quitting before.

"Hannah's only seventeen," my dad says gently. "Not many people know what their whole career is going to look like at that age. I didn't go to college right away, and look at me now. I am a Very Important Businessman." He smiles, trying to lighten the mood. "It's okay to not have everything mapped out yet. We were both so happy you took to ballet—weren't we, Eliza? But if it's not what you want anymore, you shouldn't keep doing it."

I sniffle, nodding in agreement.

"If anything, maybe this injury means you can figure out what you're interested in. Try a few new things. And if you miss it, you can always audition for the corps next year."

My mom and I glance at each other, because he doesn't really understand. That sounds like a nice, simple solution, but we both know that if I spend a year not dancing I'll never be able to get back to where I was.

"You're such a hard worker," Dad continues. "And if ballet isn't what you want to do, I know you'll apply yourself to finding whatever it is that you want to do."

I don't know if I'm any good at writing, but I think I deserve to see what it's like to do something that doesn't make me feel exhausted and empty. If that's stupid and entitled, then okay, but I tried it the other way. I really did. For thirty hours a week, I tried it her way. I bled and ached and molded myself into the shape of a perfect music box ballerina. I gave it my best shot, but I just couldn't find the passion. For a lot of other careers, you can get by without passion and drive, but not ballet.

My mom finally loosens, sighing as she sits back down in the chair next to my bed.

"I'm sorry, Hannah. You just caught me off guard."

And then she looks up and really looks at me for the first time today, and I see it: the same warm love she's given me forever. Relief floods me. Maybe I haven't lost her.

But how could we possibly be the same? Be as close as we were before?

I feel awful. I thought this would feel cleaner, more triumphant. I'm not going to take it back, but it doesn't change the fact that I feel horrible for doing this to my mother.

"I'm sorry I'm disappointing you," I say, my voice thick.

"Oh, sweetie," she says, and then she's taking my hand. "Whether or not someone wants to dance professionally—that has to be their decision. And I'm sorry you've been feeling this way. You should have said something."

"I didn't know any different. I didn't even know I wasn't doing it for the right reasons."

She shakes her head sadly. "I should have seen it. I knew you weren't approaching the work the same way I used to, but I thought it was just your way. I've seen the signs of burnout on so many other dancers, but when I saw them on you, I made up excuses. I didn't want to believe it."

The guilt of it washes over me again. "I wish I didn't feel this way. I'm sorry," I whisper.

"Hey. You almost died," she says, her voice breaking. "After seeing you being rolled out of that ambulance with an oxygen mask on your face, I can handle having a daughter who's not a dancer. It's a million times better than no daughter at all."

And then we're all hugging.

She reaches out and finger-combs my hair. "I never really dealt with losing my career, and you've kept me bound to ballet, like Peter Pan looking through the window at what it was like to have a family. I don't know who I am without rehearsals to attend and classes to watch. It's going to be hard letting go of it all. It was my whole life," she says.

"Then you shouldn't let go of it. You can still stay connected to ballet without me. You should teach, Mom. You were amazing with me. I would have been a pathetic dancer without you."

"Teach?" She laughs a little, like it's a silly thought.

My dad smiles. "I like that idea."

"You could open up your own studio," I say. "Maybe I can even take one of your easy classes every now and then."

I might still need a little bit of structure in my life. As a way to get out of my own head.

"It might be worth thinking about," Mom murmurs. She presses her fingers to her eyes, inhaling deeply.

"I might look into some writing programs," I say shyly.

Dad squeezes my ankle through the sheets. "You and your books. It always used to amaze us, how you gobbled them up. We didn't even have to teach you how to read, you just suddenly started."

"I remember that book you made when you were in elementary school," Mom adds. "What was it called? Something about flowers?"

"*Flower Magic*," I say. She remembered.

Mom straightens up and pats her hair back in place. "Okay. I'll call Madame Menard back tomorrow," she says.

"Thanks, Mom."

I can't believe it. I made it through, and it didn't destroy us.

Part of me is still freaking out: If I don't send in an audition video, there'll be no turning back. That thought is, quite frankly, terrifying.

But the idea of finishing up my senior year and concentrating on grades, letting my broken arm heal, looking at colleges, having time to *read*—it sounds blissful.

And now there's Leo.

All thoughts of schools and books and grades flee. I'm lost in the thought of a whole summer full of Leo.

Leo

The late afternoon sun streams through my hospital room like a song. In this golden light, even my dysfunctional family looks postcard-perfect.

The world is shock-bright and full of purpose, and I feel like I'm about to explode out of my skin.

I'm not alone anymore.

In a little while, I'll be with the person who makes me feel like my feet are firmly on the ground, and I'll feel that bone-deep calm you get when you're with someone who really loves you, but right now, I'm just going to bask in the chaos. It'll make the moment I see her again that much sweeter.

I went back to her room after lunch, but she was sleeping. It's probably for the best; I don't think I could sit on the bed next to her again and keep my hands to myself. Hannah's parents like me so far but probably not *that* much.

I'm fresh from the shower, and I'm wearing my lucky Scorpions shirt. Mom brought me my acoustic guitar to while away the time, and I'm noodling around on it, and ping-ponging texts with Bruce.

I've been perfecting that song I used to keep all to myself. My slowest, saddest song, the one that Hannah heard me playing in the music store.

I'm going to record it. Then I'm going to dig through my box of spare cables and find that card from Salina Sakurai so I can send her my demo. I'm going to go to SpandexFest this weekend and ask Bruce if I can hang around at a few of his shows, learn the ropes. Sound systems don't make sense to me yet, but I've never really tried to understand them, and Hannah was probably right when she said that being a successful musician is just as much about hard work as it is about luck. Maybe she can give me some pointers about hooking cables up so that the speakers actually work. I need to figure out some way to make a career out of music, even if I'm not the one performing onstage.

Real life has flooded back in, mostly in the form of emails from my teachers with makeup work. Hannah and I are graduating in a month, and I have some epic decisions to make. All day, I've been typing a million stupid questions into my phone, looking up dance companies and writing programs and record labels and sound engineering stuff. I need to talk to her and figure out what she's thinking, but I know one thing: I want to be wherever she's going to be.

There are so many paths laid out before us, when before all I could see was one. For the first time, I'm actually excited about where my life might go.

My mom is sitting on the window seat in her work outfit, sucking down coffee to wake herself up before her night shift at the diner.

I understand her better now. Maybe the whole laid-back approach to parenting was always just fear. Just like me, she knew that trying could lead to failing, so sometimes she just didn't try at all. Hard work doesn't always pay off, but sometimes it does. I'll always like the FeelGood things more, because who doesn't, but now I'm here for the whole ride. Good and bad, easy and hard.

As I pass the window, I lean down and give Mom a big smacking kiss on the cheek.

She smiles, but I can tell she's surprised.

"What's going on with you?"

"Nothing. You're a good mom, you know that?"

She gives me a where's-all-this-coming-from side-eye, but I can tell it's made her happy.

"I bet he's acting weird because of that girl," Joe mutters, without looking up from his video game.

"She's not just *that girl*, she's my girlfriend." Well, maybe. I have to ask her first, but I think she might say yes.

"Lord have mercy," Mom says, clutching her hand to her chest dramatically. "I don't think I've ever heard you say that word before."

"Ha. Like you're one to talk," I retort.

She blinks.

And then she cracks the widest smile and laughs so long and so loud, and I'm laughing too.

"Love is gross," Joe mumbles from his chair.

"I disagree," I say cheerily.

I pull out my phone and text him *love you little bro!* He looks at it but doesn't respond, just blushes bright pink and grunts. I think I'm making progress.

I'm about to put my phone back in my pocket when I see that it's flooded with notifications. Astrid posted about Hannah waking up, and our whole school is going nuts. I snort at some of the new hashtags—Hannah's not going to believe them.

The sun is sinking down into twilight when Mom and Joe leave for the night. Outside my windows, the city is alive. Headlights and taillights blend into ribbons of white and red as cars stream past on the darkening highways. I know there's sound everywhere even though I can't hear it through the thick hospital windows.

I wait until nine, and then I sneak past my nurses station again. I can't stop smiling on my way down the hallway.

I'm on my way to the beginning of everything.

Hannah

At nine o'clock, I turn off all the lights in my room so the nurses will think I'm asleep, then I settle onto the window seat to wait for Leo.

I'm a mess of scattered thoughts and fidgety anticipation and a sort of crystal-clear *happiness* that's totally new to me.

As I look out over the twinkling lights of downtown Houston, I experiment with picturing different futures for myself. Imagining what each one would mean for Leo and me.

I think I want to apply to a creative writing program somewhere. I have so, so much catching up to do. I don't even know what kind of stuff I want to write, so I'll have to figure that out, but I'm trying not to put too much pressure on myself. Now I know that it's okay to not have a specific goal that you go after with intense, structured precision.

The moon is a high silver crescent when the door to my room snicks open.

I look up and there he is.

Leo.

He slips inside and closes the door behind him, leaning against it.

I'm sure I can hear the thud of his heart from across the room.

"Hey," he says, the corner of his mouth tipping up in a roguish smile.

"Hey," I say back, trying to tamp down the idiotic grin blooming on my face.

And then we're both moving in the dark.

I launch myself at him, and he wraps me up into a tight hug. My cast clunks awkwardly on his back, but I don't care. He's warm and solid, and so real it almost makes me cry. Everything about him is familiar, from the rings on his fingers to the stupid way he sinks all his weight into that one hip.

He pulls back so he can look at me, arms linked around my waist.

"Missed you," he says roughly.

"I missed you too," I whisper.

He threads his fingers through my hair, tilting my face up to his. My gaze flicks down to his mouth, back up to those blue-gray eyes.

My breath catches, hitching on air that's suddenly too thin, my head spinning and dizzy.

Oh—I didn't know desire could stop you breathing.

He hears the footsteps in the hallway before I do. He stiffens and steps away from me.

I feel like screaming.

Seriously? SERIOUSLY?

A head pops in through the doorway. It's Neve, the nurse with the

coppery-orange hair. She's not as nice as my favorite nurse, Glynnis—
even Astrid can't get Neve to crack.

"Visiting hours are over," she says brusquely.

"I was just on my way out," Leo says, charming as ever. "Mind if I
say good night?"

Neve grunts. "I'll be back in two minutes," she says, and then she
plods down the hall to check on the patient in the next room.

My heart cracks. I can't bear for this visit to only last two minutes.
I've been waiting for Leo all day.

I grab both of his hands in mine. "Let's sneak out," I whisper.

He laughs. "Hmm. Didn't I say you were going to be trouble?"

I roll my eyes and drag him to the door with my good arm. I peek
around the corner. Neve's in the next room, and there's a droning
exchange of pleasantries and the *pump pump pump* of a blood pressure cuff.

Leo and I make a dash for the elevator, and my heart lurches with
the thrill.

Once we're inside, I lean against the wall. I close my eyes and tip
my head back, trying to catch my breath. I'm nearly giggling. I never
do things like this. Static electricity makes my hair cling to the mirror, and I feel it spreading out around me.

It takes me a while to notice that the elevator's not moving.

I open my eyes to find Leo grinning at me.

"Were you going to push a button?" he asks.

Oh. Right. I look at the panel, but I don't know where to go. "Um,
this is kind of where my escape plan runs out," I admit.

Leo laughs, then reaches out and jabs a button. "I think I know a good place."

During the ride down, he laces his fingers through mine. I can't stop beaming.

When the doors slide open on the second floor, Leo leads me down a long, empty hallway—this must be where people come for business hour appointments with their doctors.

I'm starting to think there's nothing but closed doors, but then he pulls me to the side, toward a cutout in the wall, and suddenly we're looking into a huge glass atrium.

"Oh wow," I whisper, taking a step inside.

"It's a café," Leo says softly, hands shoved into his pockets as he looks up through the high glass ceiling to the starry night sky.

That makes sense. There's a coffee counter at one end, and dozens of Parisian-looking bistro tables are arranged around the large space.

And there are plants *everywhere*. In one corner, there's a whole copse of tropical trees with little paths winding between them, obviously designed so patients and their families can feel like they're not in a hospital for a few precious minutes.

I move like I'm under a spell, entranced by the inky sky I can see through the glass. It's like we're inside a diamond ring. Leo trails behind me as I weave between the bistro tables until I'm standing right at the window.

We're surrounded by sleek, metallic skyscrapers. Through the glass, the lights of downtown Houston seem magnified, multiplied.

"This is gorgeous," I say, marveling at the after-hours magic of the place. I couldn't have imagined anything better myself, even with the things we could do in the empty Houston.

Leo comes up behind me. I can feel him, warm and real and so close.

His fingers catch at the curve of my hip. The touch is so hesitant, so light, but it sparks through every inch of me.

Slowly he pulls me away from the window.

"I have something for you," he says, guiding me to the corner of trees.

He's as jumpy as usual, all energy and frayed edges, and he's not paying attention to the ground. His shoe catches on the uneven edge of one of the stones on the path. He trips, starts to stumble, but before I can even think about it, my arm shoots out to steady him. It feels like a reflex, like something I'll do again and again.

Leo flips his hair out of his eyes with a sparkling smile, not a trace of embarrassment to be seen.

"Thanks. Lucky one of us has good balance, huh?"

He leads me to a bench tucked between two sago palms. We sit, turned into each other. I'm exquisitely aware of the foot of space that's still between us.

"Close your eyes," he says.

I do, but I flinch when he puts something cold in my hands.

"Okay, open," he says.

I look down. It's a can of Dr Pepper.

I laugh, flashing back to that day outside the bookstore, when I was a basket case after the eclipse.

"Is this our thing, then?" I ask.

"Sure. I like us having a thing," he says, smiling.

I'm touched. For us, getting the other person a drink is a small way to say *I care*. It always has been, from that first Dr Pepper he handed me to keep me from falling apart.

I take a sip. It's sweet and fizzy and goes to my head. I pass it to him, and in taking it, he leans closer, just enough so that our shoulders are brushing. I nearly shiver at the touch.

He smells just like he did in the empty city. Candle smoke and heat. How could I know what he'd *smell* like? The weirdness of our whole situation bubbles to the surface.

"Leo, where the hell were we?" I whisper.

He lets out a long breath. "I have no fucking idea."

"But it was real, right?" I ask softly. "When it was just you and me?"

Our eyes meet, and just like on that first day, a buzzy hum crackles to life in my veins.

"It was more real than anything else in my life, Hannah."

I shift a little closer, tracing my finger at the edge of his shirtsleeve.

"You know, I was thinking—I didn't see your tattoo in the coffee shop. But it's a lion, right?"

He swallows, never taking his eyes off my hand. I push his sleeve up. The tattoo looks exactly like I remember, when I first saw it on a made-up stage in an impossible place.

And then Leo's fingers are on *my* shoulder, seeking out *my* skin.

"I remembered what your freckles looked like too," he says, and I'm sure his voice is more hoarse than usual. "I thought they looked like a constellation." He draws a line between them like stars. "You know, before you woke up—I was so scared that I'd made it all up. That I'd made up a whole *person*. I was terrified that you'd wake up and not know me at all." He huffs out a laugh. "And then you actually didn't, and that about killed me, Hannah."

I catch his hand, stilling him. "You didn't make me up," I say softly.

I feel almost hypnotized, and I'm so, so aware of every vanishing millimeter between us.

"Do you think anyone will ever believe it except us?" I ask.

"Nope, not a chance."

He shifts closer, his arm draping across the bench behind my shoulders. In a desperate bid to get closer, I pull my knees up onto the bench so I can face him fully.

His knee presses against my leg, and where we're touching it's all melted warmth, comfort with a fizzing edge.

"You know the best part about everyone being gone?" he asks softly. "I got to start over with you. I could try to be me, whoever that is, and not just play the part that had been cut out for me."

"Same," I whisper.

He's so close now; it's making it hard to breathe. His blue-gray gaze is so intense. I couldn't look away if I tried.

"Hannah . . ." He clears his throat. "You know I've never had a girlfriend, right? I mean, I liked people, but it never went any deeper than that. I tried very hard to be just friends with you. It was impossible." His fingers drift up, feather-light across my jaw, brushing under my chin. "Everything I felt for you in there—it's real out here too. I don't want to be just friends. I want everything, Hannah."

It's almost too much to take. I have to look down at my lap, and that's where I'm still looking when I whisper, "I want everything too."

I can feel his eyes on me. His stare is searing and intense, and I'm heating up from the middle out.

"Hannah."

I look up.

The air around us shifts into something blazing and urgent.

His eyes flash, and heat drops through me.

And then he surges forward, and I'm clashing to meet him, and—*oh god, finally*—his mouth is on mine and *we're kissing, we're kissing, we're kissing.*

Leo's mouth is *everything*, hot and slick and delicious, and I'm lost in these feverishly deep kisses that feel like my heart might burst right out of my body. A second later, he catches my bottom lip between his teeth, and *oh*, I had no idea kisses could be like this.

His hands move over me, fingers digging into my thigh, pulling me closer, and all the anticipation that's been thrumming through us since we shook hands in the bookstore finally catches and flares across me. Everywhere he touches turns to liquid, melting heat.

"Fuck, you're amazing," Leo whispers against my mouth. He sounds like he's *breaking*.

My own hands are out of control, tangling frantic and wild through his hair, and I've wanted to do this for so long, and god, it's so soft. I twist into it and tug him closer in a way that has him gasping sharply against my mouth.

He pulls back, looking a little stunned. His eyes are so dark it makes me shiver.

He recovers, presses kisses along my jaw, up under my ear.

"Oh my god," I say. He's going to melt me, in every single place he's touching me. My voice isn't clear or high-pitched at the best of times, but I sound destroyed.

Leo notices. "God, have I ever mentioned that your voice makes me *insane*?" he asks. "I want to record you. Just talking."

We kiss and kiss and kiss, burning through days and days of holding back.

When we finally stop, I'm limp, utterly swamped with glittery, fizzy amazement.

I drop my forehead to his chest. His heart is beating hard and fast, and he clings to me like he's as wrecked as I am.

"Shit. You . . . are very good at that," Leo whispers, breathless.

You're not so bad yourself, I want to say, but I can't speak yet.

I wonder if there will be a Hannah-shaped mark on the bench

when we get up. *This is where Hannah Ashton spontaneously combusted*, it will read, on a little plaque next to a black soot outline of my body.

We hold on tight until we've come down from the high, until our breathing gets less ragged and the heat melts into something softer.

I finally find my voice. "Can we please do that all the time?" I say, dazed.

"Absolutely," Leo murmurs, rubbing soothing circles on my back.

Slowly, the outside world filters back in. The bench, the atrium, the *hospital*.

Oh. We *can't* just do that all the time.

"Fuck," I say, and Leo jolts a little at the sound of me swearing. "What do we do now?"

"What do you mean?" He's distracted, pulling his hand through his hair in a failed attempt to look like we didn't just make out like weasels.

I groan and drop my head back against the bench. "This is going to suck."

"Excuse me?"

"I mean, it's so stupid. In there, we could do whatever we wanted to, and now it's like, *Rewind!* I'm a teenager with parents and a bedtime and homework and school again." I shudder at the thought.

"It is a little messed up," he agrees, mouth quirking at one side in amusement.

"We're going to have to do stuff like make out in the back seat of your car," I say miserably.

He laughs and tips my pouty chin up. "I think you'll still enjoy it. But if we have to get a little creative, it's no big deal. You'll just have to throw rocks at my window and sneak into my bedroom every now and then," he says, his eyes dancing.

I sigh, dropping my head to his shoulder dramatically.

"Do you think we'll be able to figure all this out? Now that it's not just us?"

"Hannah. We survived a meteor, and a demon bouncy castle, and a flood. I think we'll be able to handle *dating*."

He presses the Dr Pepper into my hand. I have no idea where he put it while we were kissing, or how it didn't spill. I take a swig.

For a few moments, it's just companionable silence as we pass it back and forth. It's so easy to be with him.

"What do you think would have happened after that night at the coffee shop?" I ask. "If we hadn't got in the wreck?"

"I don't know. I guess I would have dropped you off at home, and . . . that might have been that."

I don't say anything. My heart is in my throat.

"To be very clear, I'm glad that it wasn't just that," Leo adds.

"We're so lucky our injuries weren't worse. Other than this hideous cast, we're fine." I turn and brush Leo's hair out of the way, examining the purpling bump on his forehead.

"Not so bad, right? My doctor said he was surprised I was out for so long."

"Mine said the same thing to me."

"Maybe the universe thought we needed an intervention, Ballet Chick," Leo jokes.

I frown. What if he's right?

God, and speaking of Ballet Chick . . .

"I told my mom I wanted to quit ballet," I say.

Leo's eyes go wide. "You didn't."

"I did."

His face transforms, lighting with surprise and pride and joy. "Hannah, that's fucking *huge*! Oh my god, I'm so impressed, that must have been so hard. How did she take it?"

"Not well, at first. But I think it's going to be okay. My dad was really awesome about it. Oh, and hey, I think they actually *like* you," I add. "How the hell did you manage that?"

Leo breaks into a crooked grin. "Do you really have to ask? I'm so charming."

I laugh. He snags a hand under my knee and lifts my legs, draping them sideways over his lap. He props up my cast, trying to make sure I'm comfortable. Being with him feels so *right* that I can barely believe this is my life.

"So. No more Ballet Chick, huh?"

"Nope."

"I've got news for you too, actually. You know that song I was singing when you found me in the music store?" he asks.

"Yeah?"

"I'm going to record a demo of it and send it to Bruce's producer.

I'm going to see him at SpandexFest this weekend—with you, if you're up for it?—and talk to him some more about it. Maybe I can shadow him on some of his gigs, learn the ropes, that kind of thing. There's got to be a job for me that has something to do with music."

"Oh, Leo, that's amazing. It sounds perfect."

Something hopeful and beautiful rises in my chest.

"And, um, where exactly is Bruce based again?" I ask.

"LA. There's a lot of music stuff out there, but I'll only go out there for shows, if you want—"

It's those little words—*if you want*—that have me pulling my phone out of my pocket. I open my web browser and pass my phone to him.

It's the application requirements for the creative writing program at a university in California.

In Los Angeles, to be precise.

Leo doesn't say anything.

"There's still time to apply," I explain, suddenly nervous. It's one of a few colleges that has a later May deadline. "I think I have something I can use for this first requirement, but I'll need to write something for the other two prompts."

"Is this really where you want to go?" Leo asks. He looks so sweet and stupefied I want to grab his hair and kiss him silly.

I nod. "It's an amazing program. I've been looking at a lot of schools, trying to think about what I'd choose if you weren't in the equation. That really is one of the best ones. And besides," I say, shrugging, "you *are* in the equation."

"What a coincidence. You're in my equation too," Leo says.

He trails his hand over my collarbone, sweeping soft touches over my neck.

Then he's dipping his head and touching his lips there too, and it's the best feeling in the world. He presses once, twice, and then he raises his head and we're kissing again in earnest.

This time it's slow. Soft and lovely and delicate, like inhaling the fumes of every daydream I've ever had.

We savor each other, like we've got all the time in the world, and his hands cradle my face like I'm made of glass.

Inside me, flowers are blooming. Spinning snowflakes of every color, buds bursting out of the ground, white-hot sparklers in the dark. I'm floating, just like I was in my backyard, but this isn't an end—it's a beginning.

My heart is a lushly unfurling rose, and the feel of his mouth on mine is so perfect. Kissing him feels like the only thing in the world that make sense.

It tapers off sweetly, with us there on the bench with our eyes closed and our foreheads pressed together.

I feel like an entirely new Hannah. I think about us, striking out in LA, writing music and stories in the sunshine, and it actually seems like we could do it. It's going to take a huge leap of faith, one I would have never even considered if I'd never met Leo. It's an enormous life change from ballet, and I'm still freaking out, but it's also so, so freeing.

Leo clears his throat. "LA, huh? Let's do it, Writer Chick. You and me."

Before I have a chance to respond, a beam of light flashes through the leaves behind us.

"Oh shit," Leo whispers, ducking down and peering through the trees. "I think it's a security guard."

"Anyone in there?" a voice calls out.

Leo and I commando-roll off the bench and slide behind the trees. The security guard is by the café counter, shining his flashlight over gleaming coffee machines and juice glasses. I stifle a nervous giggle, and then Leo's pulling me through the plants until we're finally back in the bright hospital hallways.

We break into a run, laughing like loons.

"Hey!" the guard shouts, but we've got a head start. We make it into an elevator just as the doors are closing.

We spill out onto the ninth floor, breathless and flushed and lit up so happy.

Leo drops me at my door, stealing a glance at the nurses station. It's empty—for now.

"I should go," he says.

But the adrenaline's still surging through me, and I grab his shirt and haul him to me for another kiss.

When I pull away, I'm smiling so much it hurts my face.

Leo sucks in a breath beside me. "Oh wow," he says. "There it is."

"There what is?"

"When we were in the empty Houston, I was trying to get you to smile like this. Power chord smile."

Before I can ask him what a power chord smile is, he presses another fervent kiss to my mouth, one that has me seeing starbursts.

"One more thing before I go," he says.

His eyes sparkle.

"Hannah Ashton, can I have your number?"

ACKNOWLEDGMENTS

The fact that you are holding this book is a quiet but awesome form of modern-day magic, and I am so grateful to all the people who had a hand in getting this story out of my mind and into the world.

Thank you first to my razor-sharp, totally lovely editor at Scholastic, the extraordinary Jody Corbett. You took one look at this story and knew exactly how to make it shine. I'm so in awe of your skill and insight, and I've loved every second of working on this book with you.

Massive thanks also to everyone at Scholastic who helped turn this story into something you can hold. Josh Berlowitz, Jael Fogle, and Janell Harris made sure it became an actual book, and Maeve Norton created the absolutely dreamy cover art—it might always be my phone lock screen. To David Levithan, Ellie Berger, Erin Berger, Rachel Feld, Shannon Pender, Alex Kelleher-Nagorski, and the entire sales team: Thank you for all your hard work and for loving this book from the very first acquisitions meeting.

Huge gratitude to the awe-inspiring team at Madeleine Milburn— not only my fiercely smart agents, Alice Sutherland-Hawes and Chloe Seager, but also Liane-Louise Smith, Sophie Pélissier, Hayley Steed, Georgina Simmonds, Georgia McVeigh, and Giles and Madeleine Milburn. Thank you all for taking such wonderful care of author-me.

To the teams at my international publishers, Carlsen Verlag in

Germany, Rizzoli in Italy, and AST in Russia: Thank you for believing in this story. I am starstruck that you wanted to translate my words into your beautiful languages.

I am immensely lucky to have found the most fabulous group of writing friends and critique partners in "Storymill." Liz Flanagan, Sally Ashworth, Tara Guha, and Kate Sims: You are such kind, intelligent women—not to mention outrageously talented!

To K. C. Karr: There is not enough gratitude in the world. Thank you for choosing my story, for asking the hard questions, and for pushing me to my limits. Huge thanks also to Stuart White for creating the incredible WriteMentor community that led me to Sharon M. Johnston and K. C.

To all the best friends I've had along the way: You are all way more interesting than me and I'm honored to have spent time fluttering at the edges of your lives. Extra thanks to the two who aren't with us anymore, Jared Neff and Hannah Henson. And to the one nearest to me as I wrote this book, Elizabeth Aggett: Thank you for reading this book so many times and pretending to be my agent before I had a real one.

I owe so much to all the theater technicians and dancers I've worked with. You are the most passionate, badass people I have ever met. Thank you to the ethereal ballerina Antoinette Brooks-Daw for checking over a few ballet facts for me—any inaccuracies regarding dance are entirely my fault.

To the city of Houston: Thank you for being so lively, diverse, and tough as nails. The Houston in these pages is a slightly altered, fictional version of the city, but imagining a girl walking barefoot down the real I-10, not a car in sight, was the image that inspired this story.

Endless thanks to Richard and Terry Bourne. You are the absolute best parents-in-law a girl could ask for. I'm so grateful for all the ways you support us and this writing dream of mine.

To my parents, Dara and Dennis, and my darling grandparents Jo and Elton: Thank you for giving me an extraordinary childhood and for always making me feel so loved. Mom, thank you for taking me to the library so often, for letting me read under the table at Red Lobster, and for not locking up your romance novels. (Although perhaps you should have!)

To my daughters, Lila and Mina: You are such gorgeous, amazing people. If not for you, this book would have only ever lived in my head.

To my very own once-in-a-lifetime love story, Henry Bourne: It would take me a thousand words to write all the things I need to thank you for. You are the most incredible person. Thank you for loving me.

And lastly: Thank *you*, reader. For picking up this book and coming on this surreal trip with Hannah and Leo. I hope you've had a blast.

ABOUT THE AUTHOR

Brianna Bourne works as a stage manager for ballet companies around the world when she's not writing. Originally from Texas, she grew up in Indonesia and Egypt and now lives in England with her rock musician husband and their two daughters. You can find out more about her at briannabournebooks.com.